SPLITSVILLE. COM

An Olivia Davis Paranormal Mystery
Book One

Tonya Kappes

Splitsville.com
2012 Double Finalist
Next Generation Indie Book
Awards
Mystery Category
And
Humor Category

Dedication and Acknowledgements
This book is dedicated to my boys, Eddy, Jack, Austin, Brady,
Charlie and Scooter.

To my dear friend, Joni White. Thank you for always celebrating
my milestones and being more excited than me. You are a true
friend

To all my readers on my STREET TEAM, you keep me going
with all your reader mail, Twittering, and Facebook Messages.
Without you, my dreams would've never come true. Thank you!

Edition: April 2012

ISBN #13: 978-1463720889
ISBN-10: 1463720882

What others are saying about Author Tonya Kappes

"Full of wit, humor and colorful characters, Tonya Kappes delivers a fun, fast-paced story that will leave you hooked!" Bestselling Author, Jane Porter

"Fun, fresh, and flirty, Carpe Bead 'Em is the perfect read on a hot summer day. Tonya Kappes' voice shines in her debut novel." Author Heather Webber

"Tonya Kappes strings together the perfect blend of family, friends, and fun." Author Misa Ramirez

"I loved how Tonya Kappes was able to bring her characters to life." Coffee Table Reviews

"I love, love, love this book. I enjoyed reading about Hallie's friendships and her trials and tribulations. Her Aunt Grace was a hoot, especially the pink poodle. Too darn funny. As you already know I was crying and I had to put the book down. That, makes a truly awesome read for me, because I became a part of the story and loved Aunt Grace as much as Hallie.

Again, this was worth the wait and I can't wait to read your next story." Reader, Dru Ann

"I don't write many reviews but some books are so outstanding I just have to. This is one of them. Tonya Kappes is one of the freshest new voices in women's fiction, and I can't wait to read more from her." Reader, Melissa Lapierre

"This book was fun, entertaining and good to the last page. Who knew reading auras could get Olivia in so much trouble? Sit back, smile and cozy up to Splitsville.com, where Olivia does the dumping for you. There's heap loads of humor, a dose of magical realism, sprinkles of romance, and mystery when someone ends up dead!" Author Lisa Lim

"This book was funny and clever with a unique premise. I truly couldn't put it down." Author Diane Majeske

"Tonya Kappes has written a fast paced cozy mystery that kept me guessing till the end. Full of likeable characters, Splitsville.com is humerous and I was caught up in the story right from the beginning. I'm definitely looking forward to more books in this series!" Author Sheila Seabrook

"Unique, imaginative, funny, with a tantalizing mystery to boot. What more could one ask. But there was more ... compassion and passion ... Olivia is an animal lover with the good sense not to become jaded by her "day job" of helping people break up. She gets the guy, solves the puzzle and rises above all of life's messy situations. Aunt Matilda was the icing on the cake ... as I said ... PURE MAGIC." Reader PJ Schott

"I loved this book. Grandberry Falls is my kind of town and I for one would love to live there and get to know all the local folks. I enjoyed reading this book and can't wait to read the next book about Grandberry Falls by Tonya

Kappes. I have added Tonya Kappes as one of my new favorite authors." Jean Segal

"I love it when I pick up a book because of its cover and the story to follow is just as great or better. That's what happened here." Stephanie Overton

"I read this in a day and loved it! You felt that you were part of Grandberry Falls. The small town folks who know everyone and know everything about someone in a matter of hours." Avid Reader

"I was looking for something different and easy to read...meaning nothing too involved, something that if I put down could come back to and remember all the characters and where I left off at...well I didn't put it down I finished it in a day... what a great read !!" Cimarron

Also by Tonya Kappes

Carpe Bead 'em
Something Spooky This Way Comes
Believe Christmas Anthology

An Olivia Davis Paranormal Mystery Series
Splitsville.com
Color Me Love (Mini-Mystery Prequel to the second novel)

Grandberry Falls Series
The Ladybug Jinx
Happy New Life
A Superstitious Christmas (Prequel Short Story to Never Tell
Your Dreams)
Never Tell Your Dreams

A Divorced Diva Beading Mystery Series
A Bead of Doubt

A Magical Cures Mystery
A Charming Crime

Non-Fiction
The Tricked-Out Toolbox~Promotional and Marketing Tools
Every Writer Needs

SPLITSVILLE. COM

An Olivia Davis Paranormal Mystery
Book One

Tonya Kappes

One

"Is Brittany there?" I question the quiet voice who answers my call. The quiet voice whose heart is about to get run over by a Mac truck. A Mac truck driven by me.

"Yes, this is she." Brittany confirms while I'm uploading her picture sent to me by Terry, her soon to be ex-boyfriend.

"I'm Jenn from Splitsville.com," I say going into my spiel, "and I'm calling on behalf of Terry who wants to break-up with you."

Brittany's picture pops up on the screen. My heart bleeds for the smiling twenty-something-year- old gal staring back at me. Her straight red hair is cut in a blunt bob, not a strand out of place. Glistening white teeth come off whiter up against her perfectly belted black cardigan.

Let me backtrack a minute. Splitsville.com started a couple of years ago when a friend wanted to dump her boyfriend. She was a big chicken, so I did it for her. Called his ass up, broke the news and Splitsville.com was born.

Here's how it works. Clients contact me through the online form where they give their name, email address, working phone number, reason for dumping, a few details of their relationship, and a picture of the victim and, this is the most important part, payment in full. The reason for the cashola up front is in case the dump is a joke. In that case, they deserve to lose their money for being an ass and I deserve to keep it for having to deal with them.

I offer three "Break-up" packages. The cheapest and most popular is "the general break-up" for a low price of fifty dollars. "The engagement break-up" is a little steeper at one hundred dollars. It totally should be more because I can't imagine being in the fiancé's shoes on this one. And the worst and most expensive break-up of all is "the divorce break-up" setting the big jerk back a mere two hundred dollars.

I know, it sounds heartless, but really, I'm helping people who are in loveless relationships be free. Like the girl on my computer who's staring back at me. Sometimes, no matter how badly a person wants out, they just can't pull the trigger. Splitsville.com (which means me) does it instead. Sometimes it's not easy, but it's my job so I don't let my emotions into the equation.

Right on cue, she says, "Terry hired you?" Brittany is starting the first stage in "The Process."

And the panic button is being pushed.

"The Process" is a list I've carefully crafted over the course of breaking up for people. No
 matter what the circumstances of the dump, the process is still the same.

The Process

1.   Panic (This is the first emotion when they hear the words break-up.)

2.   Disbelief (They think I'm playing a joke on them.)

3.   Defensive (After they realize I'm not joking, they want to explain their side.)

4.   Explanation (They want me to explain the situation all over.)

5.   Denial (This is where they take it out on me and deny my existence.)

6.   Anger (Awww…where my ear drum becomes busted.)

7.   Acceptance (Finally! They have to acknowledge the break-up and I can end the call.)

"Yes Terry hired me to break-up with you. Your obsessive habits drive him crazy." I only state the facts in the beginning because I know she's only taking in one word at a time. And if I get soft, the whole call will go to hell. I show my weakness and it's over.

"How do you know Terry?" Her voice is beginning to escalate. "Is he cheating on me with you?"

Ahh…here goes number two in "the process." She wants to cross-examine me on how I know Terry.

I take a deep breath and keep going. One thing's for sure, this job is not easy. "No, Brit. Can I call you Brit?" I don't wait for her answer. "He hired me to dump you because your OCD is getting in the way of your relationship." I look at the sweet picture of Brittany that Terry sent me. I can image the fear in her eyes, especially if she's OCD.

"I'm sorry?" She questions me like she doesn't understand English.

"Terry emailed my online break-up service, Spitsville.com. He hired me to break-up with you for him because your OCD is getting in the way of the relationship." I practically repeat myself, but it's usually necessary. Breakup services, after all, aren't common like matchmaking websites. I'm one of a kind.

"Okay. Let me get this straight, Terry wants to dump me because I'm OCD?" She starts to laugh. "This is a joke right?" Brittany is trying to play nice, but the quiver in her voice cues me in on the beginning of step three in "the process."

I lean back in my chair and roll my eyes. This is definitely going to be one of those calls. Anytime there is a medical reason involved, it takes so much more explaining. It's not like Brittany can help her OCD.

I peel the already chipped paint off my desk to let out my energy. When I started Splitsville.com I wanted my office to be homey since I would be spending a lot of time in here. I found the coolest farm table that someone had painted white, along with these white bookshelves on the side of a country road just north of town. I took my Aunt Matilda's truck and hauled it off. It fit perfectly in the room. I cleaned it all up and added baskets to the shelves to make it cozy. I even added a pink rug and pink curtains.

I felt like I hit the jackpot when I went back to the same house a couple weeks later to find a wicker chaise lounge and crystal chandelier. That time I called my aunt to come get it because I wasn't in her truck and I didn't want someone coming by to pick up *my* treasure.

I did have to purchase the cushion for the chaise, but the room is entirely perfect and goes with the rest of my cottage style home.

"No Brittany, this is not a joke." I use my flat break-up voice. The harshness in my voice always takes me off guard. It isn't the same as my everyday voice. It's uncaring and monotone. Even though I sympathize with the break-up victim, I can't show any emotions when I work. "Terry hired me because he is tired of spending his entire paycheck on hand sanitizers, watching you freak out in public places, not using public restrooms and not having sex unless there is a clean towel under you." It has to be done this way. It's like ripping off a Band-Aid. The quicker you do it, the less pain in the end.

She moves right into stage four of "the process." Her side of the story.

"First, the clean towel is because I don't want to get anything on my bed and secondly haven't you ever heard of Swine Flu?" She begins to talk so fast I can hardly keep up.

"I don't care why he is breaking up with you. I just have to tell you the reasons he's listed." She does have a point about the towel and the bed. *I'm just saying.*

She doesn't say anything.

"Do you understand why I am calling? A "yes" is all I need.

Give me the "yes" Brittany, I silently beg, still looking at her picture staring back at me.

"Wait." She pauses for a second to gather her thoughts. Which, at this point, are swirling around her little brain. "He *paid* you to break-up with me?"

Damn! She's not caving easy. "Yes he did," I confirm. From her picture I thought I'd be able to skip part of "The Process" because she looks like the type that'll break down in tears and be accepting of the fact she's getting dumped.

"Seriously?" I can hear water running in the background. "The Swine Flu can kill you." She says, "Don't you know that?"

Stage Five. She's in denial and wants me to side with her.

"I don't know about the Swine Flu. I am not a doctor. Are you washing your hands?" I know she is.

"How do you know?" She's getting angrier by the minute.

"I can hear water running and this is the exact reason Terry is breaking up with you. He's tired of your scaly, dried up hands touching his penis." I only state the obvious.

"Yeah, well he doesn't seem to mind it when we are, you know..." Brittany's high-class demeanor is diminishing quickly.

"I am a person who is hired to break-up with people for people and Terry has broken up with you. Do you understand?"

"So he paid you to do this?" She says it again, this time with venom in her voice.

 Full-blown stage six of "the process."

"With what? He has no money," she says.

I click on my PayPal to make sure the dump was paid for. "Yep, he paid." I confirm.

Soon I know this call is going to be over. At this point, the dumpee usually rants about what they don't like about the client. They usually say a few colorful words about me and my job. I have touched on some hot buttons and she doesn't like Terry right about now. Or me for that matter.

Unfortunately, this particular client is paying me extra to record the call and I have to get stage seven on the recording.

"You can tell him to kiss my ass!" she shouts through the phone.

"Such bad language coming from a pristine young woman." I love how I can draw the best out of someone. "Brittany, I can't tell Terry to kiss your, well anyways, I won't be talking to him." I never talk to clients on the phone in fear they may know me. Strictly email, that's my motto. "Do you understand that you and Terry are broken up?" I say slowly.

"Yes." The quiet Brittany is back and is holding her heart in tiny pieces. She's resigned to the fact her relationship has ended.

Stage seven of "the process." And happy to be here. "Thank you for using Splitsville.com." I quickly hang up the phone before Brittany can ask any more questions. I take a few seconds to breathe and let Jenn from Splitsville.com morph back into Olivia, and then I attach the recording to Terry's email, and hit send. It's crucial that

I get to him before Brittany does. And believe you me, she will contact him – immediately.

I often wonder what happens to these people after I hang up. In this case, I can picture the perfect Brittany losing it on Terry and still not getting a hair out of place. Sort of like Bree Van deCamp from Desperate Housewives. The epitome of anal retentiveness.

"Poor Terry." I shake my head and type a note in his file: *Dumped*. I'm actually worried for him. Usually it's the other way around, but I sense there's another layer to Brittany.

I'm exhausted and already need another cup of coffee. I didn't sleep well last night. I do this every once in awhile. I wake up after I dream something and usually jot it down. I'm fascinated by dreams and what they can mean. And in my world, when I have a dream, that usually means there's a storm coming. Well, a storm in my life that will uproot all that has been neatly planted.

My butcher block counter is my favorite part of the kitchen. It ties in so well with my black distressed cabinets. It feels like home in my kitchen.

"Hmm." Even more exhausting is trying to find a clean mug. My house is really cute when it's clean, but unfortunately, it's not high on my to-do list these days.

Carefully I sit my filled-to-the-rim mug on my desk and pull up the file of my next victim. It's from a girl who's sick of watching her two-bit loser boyfriend play video games. He is constantly neglecting her, inviting his friends over to play, and spending all their money on games when he should be out working.

I make the call. "Hi, is James there?"

"This is him."

I can tell by James' deep voice (and by the picture that's now on my computer screen) that he's a big man and definitely not someone I want to cross in a dark alley. This is the very reason I never tell anyone what I do. When people ask, my standard reply is, "dot com nerd." There are so many dot com jobs, usually people accept my answer and move on. I'll say it again. I just can't take a chance on someone I know recognizing me by my voice or by the website. Anonymity is crucial. I mean, if a dumpee found out that I am the person behind the dumping, well, my life could get a little dangerous. I've pissed off a lot of people in the name of ending love.

"My name is Jenn from Splitsville.com," I say, and James, the Neanderthal, actually grunts at me. "I'm calling because Candy is breaking up with you."

"Who…who are you?" James demands.

I tap my fingers on "the process" list and begin all over, *again.*

"I'm Jenn and Candy has paid me to give you the boot." I have to use a blunt tone with James. "She says you're a bum who plays video games all day when you need to get off your ass and get a job to help her pay for the bills."

James laughs.

Ah James, I rub my finger over his big ego picture, let's see who gets the last laugh. I grin knowing I always win in this particular game. I'm on Candy's side in this break-up.

He's obviously a body builder that could snap me in two or maybe a few more pieces. I can see he's going to make our little cat and mouse game fun. Breaking up is never easy, don't get me wrong, but it's a good thing when the dumpee is a jerk.

"Who're the victims today?" Aunt Matilda whispers as she creeps around the corner of my office. I smile admiring her new headscarf with dangling bells.

I tap on the computer screen at James's picture and she moves like she has a pee shiver-you know when a kid shivers from head to toe when they have to pee.

James is ranting. I cover up the microphone and snort. The bells dance around the scarf as she shakes.

My Aunt Matilda raised me, and living with her was nothing short of fun. She's a retired palm reader who was never closed for business. I've seen it all. From 2 A.M. drunks, which were usually flighty sorority girls, to people trying to connect with their loved ones that have moved on to the other side. Our home was a revolving door.

My home is still a revolving door since she has a key and she comes and goes as she pleases.

"Is this Sabrina?" James questions if I'm one of Candy's friends. My attention snaps back to my job. "I know Candy put you up to this." James's voice is as confident as his mind and ego.

I wave bye to Aunt Matilda as she slinks back to the family room to catch reruns of our favorite shows, *Snapped and Murder She Wrote*.

"No, I'm Jenn from Splitsville.com. Did you take the grocery money and buy the latest video game?"

I always have my clients list a few details about the relationship that only the two of them know about. This way the dumpee begins to realize I'm for real.

"Who the hell is this?" James's panic is beginning to set in. "How do you know my Candyland?"

Ahhh, the funny pet names lovers give each other makes me down right SICK!

"*Your* Candyland?" I laugh out loud. "She isn't your playground anymore. Do you understand she's dumped you?"

I can hear scuffling in the background.

"Hold on, let me turn off my TV."

Typical. When they hear from someone else that their significant other is dumping them, they tend to take notice. Too little, too late.

"Oh, you mean the sixty-inch plasma you spent Candy's tax money on?"

I know *that* got his attention. Candy said in her file that this is a big fight with them. He illegally signed her name on her tax return check while she was at work and went to Best Buy where he bought the biggest television he could find.

"You're a bitch and this is a joke." All the background noise from his video games is gone. I can hear him fiddling around and I picture him loading bullets into his illegal handgun.

"Yes, I am, and this is *far* from a joke," I assure him. "I never joke about money or my job. James I need you to understand that Candy is dumping you using Splitsville.com."

"There's no such thing." The clicking in the background sounds like James is typing on his computer.

"I know you're looking it up." I don't want him to think he's pulling a fast one over on me. "As you can read, Splitsville.com is a real website where people hire me to dump people like you. Jerks who never spend any time with their significant others."

"This ain't funny, man." James is becoming increasingly desperate.

"Mmm, yeah, I know this isn't funny." I'm glad to know he is finally getting it. Plus it's time for lunch and my stomach is growling. It's been a rough morning.

"Hold up, she paid you to break-up with me? Is this for real?" James is starting to throw me for a loop. He's not really following the stages and that's never happened before. It's there in plain computer text. Splitville.com, "The place where you can split and not feel guilty." Really James, I want to say, you don't *look* stupid.

Ay, ay, ay, I hit my forehead with my palm. "Yes, James, this is for real. It's a real website."

"No, no, no!" The boisterous voice is turning whiney and pleading with me. "No."

"James, James!" I yell in the phone to get his attention, "I'm Jenn from Splitsville.com. Do you understand that you are being dumped by Candy? It's time to get your things and get out James."

This man is now a babbling, bumbling idiot with sentences that are inaudible.

Time for the kill…

"James do you acknowledge Candy is using Splitsville.com to dump you?" I'm not sure if he hears me. I scream louder, "JAMES, do you understand?"

"Yeah." James's manly voice is much weaker than it was seven minutes ago.

"Thank you." Exhausted, I hang up the phone and send the dump file to Candy. I suspect that James won't be leaving quietly and I feel worse for Candy. But my job is done. I close my eyes and imagine both of my victims today. Slowly, I can feel the hole in my heart deepen as I imagine their auras turning a light shade of grey.

Reading auras is my gift as some people call it. I call it—chains. I'm locked into my life of suffering.

I see auras. People's auras, animal auras, you name it.

I didn't really know what it was as a child. I quickly learned not to talk about it. My dad left when I was eight and the only memory I have of him was yelling at my mother. "Damn it Dawn," he'd say, "You've got Olivia believing in that crap." And he'd grab me and scream, "Don't you dare go around telling the town folk about your crazy colors. They'll lock you up in juvie."

I didn't know what juvie was, but I knew it didn't sound good. Momma and I'd keep our mouths shut, that is until Aunt Matilda found out daddy left us and she came to stay. "Be proud of who you are!" she'd say, and she'd give me scarves to match the auras I'd describe to her, and make me skirts with all the colors of the rainbow in them. That's when I wished Aunt Matilda was my momma instead of Dawn. Then one day momma went to the market and never came back. For the longest time I thought I'd actually wished her away.

In fact, I rode my bike to the south end of town where a bunch of abandoned buildings stood, because I thought that might be juvie and my dad sent Dawn there. But it wasn't. There were only a bunch of broken buildings that are now restored and becoming a very attractive place to live.

As a child I was able to ignore most of the aura colors swirling around me. I'd just play and pretend they were part of the sky. But as I got older and understood about emotions, feelings and the truth of what I was seeing, being anyplace but alone become impossible.

People arguing and fussing, their aura colors colliding, gave me migraine headaches on a daily basis. Then one day it all changed. "Help me, Liv. Please!" Erin my best friend, begged me to break-up with her boyfriend. "I just can't face him. He'll talk me into staying and I can't stay!"

She'd been dating a guy named Kyle who was nothing more than a gigolo. He was using Erin for her money, but poor thing, she had a hard time admitting that to herself.

"You can do it," I'd told her. "You're better than he is."

"But I love him."

"Then why break-up with him?" I played devil's advocate, hoping it wouldn't backfire. She totally needed to break-up with Kyle.

"He keeps asking for things. At first it was cute. A briefcase. A beer making kit." She twisted her hands together. "But now it's fiberglass bicycles and state-of-the-art stereos. You were right," she added. "He just wants my money."

I'd balked when she'd first asked me to drop the bomb, but I couldn't let her throw her money away on a guy who didn't appreciate her. I called him up, explained the situation, and...viola!

Splitsville.com was born. It's the perfect job.

Aunt Matilda breaks my trip down memory lane. "You seem a little tired this afternoon." She cautiously looks me over. She always could read me better than anyone else. She has the gift, too, but hers is fine-tuned after years of practice. I could hide my headaches and my exhaustion from almost anybody...except Aunt Matilda.

Some days the dumps take more out of me than others and this is definitely one of those days.

"I'm fine. I didn't sleep well last night." The letters "DS" rolled in my dream all night long but I had no idea why.

This is how I know there is a calm before the storm. When I start seeing vision in my sleep, somewhere, somehow those will appear in my life. But DS?

She puts down her coffee and comes closer to inspect my eyes.

"Maybe I should stay the night tonight." Her bells jingle in my ears like gonging bells. She knows me better than anyone.

Park City, Ohio isn't big, but when Aunt Matilda isn't here, it feels like she lives on another planet. There are five stop lights through town with several side streets. Aunt Matilda lives in a small brick house smack dab in the middle of Main Street, next to the retirement community.

Over the years people have moved to Park City due to less taxes and wanting the small town life.

Just the mention of having her in my house calms me down.

"Did you have a dream?" She questions me like I'm still a ten year old little girl, but I don't mind.

When I was younger and had my dreams or what she called pictures, I would wake up with her standing over me taking notes on what I would say in my sleep. Since she thought it was important to take notes on what I said, when she would leave my room, I'd write down everything I could remember about my dream.

I have scads of journal entries on ramblings I don't even understand.

"No," I assure her. Total bald face lie, but I don't want to worry her. "I'm fine." I sit down to catch the end of Snapped.

I can see Aunt Matilda weighing her options. Should she press me for details, or keep quiet? She murmurs to herself, keeping a cautious eye on me as I thumb through my BlackBerry to retrieve my Splitsville.com dumps that seem to be piling up on top of each other.

Finally she settles back onto the sofa and turns back to the TV. I must be getting better at hiding my anxiety, which is a relief. Aunt Matilda spent her life caring for me when she'd never asked for or wanted a child. She didn't need to keep worrying.

I click on the dump file that doesn't have a name, only a comment. "How do you live with yourself?"

I read it several times and try not to make any faces or eye gestures to clue Aunt Matilda in on the unpleasant email. She wouldn't let me out of the house if she knew dumpees were getting disgruntled.

I read it again. First, there is no way someone would know me, and second, the threat doesn't seem…well…really like a threat.

Great! I look up at the commercial on the TV. Not only are the dumpee freak flags flying, I didn't get to see the end of *Snapped*!

I pick up the paper on the table. The headline grabs me: Young Business Executive Found Dead. Foul play. Strangled.

"Dabi Stone?" I gasp, seeing that name.

Two

How could forget a name like Dabi? She's a rich gal whose dad is some bigwig in a local company. She was a few years behind me in school. There were only three times I came in contact with Dabi Stone. The first time was on the playground at Pleasant Ridge Park when I was ten years old and she came up asking all sorts of questions about Aunt Matilda. I can see her now in her pigtails, fancy dress and play shoes. "Who's the crazy lady with you?" she'd ask me, a nasty tone in her voice. "My daddy said she's crazy and swindles people out of their money. She tells lies and pretends to see the future."

I snarled and punched her square in her jaw. Her nanny came running over yelling, "Get away from her!" She yanked Dabi away from me, their auras mixing until they were all different shades of green and said, "That's what happens when you don't have a momma."

"You shouldn't be on this side of town anyways!" I yelled back knowing this park was where the poor kids came to play. Her dad put his money behind rehabbing those old buildings and she played there while he worked.

The second time I saw Dabi Stone was that same night when her momma brought over brownies to Aunt Matilda and apologized for what her daughter and the nanny had said. Dabi hid around her momma's skirt with her tongue sticking out at me the entire time.

And I just stared, hating Dabi Stone.

The third and final time I saw her was right after she used Splitsville.com to break-up with her boyfriend, one Michael Schultz. He didn't fit her father's mold, but she was too chicken to call it quits with him. I stopped by White Castle to pick up a cup of coffee and there she was still dressing in fancy clothes, but without the silver spoon attitude to go with her Gucci bag. She nodded and said, "Hello Olivia."

I smiled feeling a little sorry for her (only a little) that she didn't know it was me she was spilling her guts to on the internet about her love life.

The distaste for her comes back into my mouth. I hadn't liked her, but she didn't deserve to die. I shudder and put the file back in the drawer. I shake the murder from my head. I can't. The letter DS are rolling around inside my mind like they did all night.

I can't take it. My sixth sense is pulling me in, kicking and screaming. I *know* something about Dabi's death. Only I have no idea what it is that I know.

One thing keeps rattling around my brain. What if she got knocked off all because of my break-up service? Could hers have been a breakup gone badly? Was Mr. Nice Guy not so nice after all? It made sense. Scott Peterson. OJ Simpson. They all looked like innocent good guys, but deep down they were cold-blooded killers. Was Michael Schultz like this?

I open the computer file on Dabi's breakup with Michael and carefully read through her email to dump him.

Holy Crap. I nearly fall out of my chair. There it is in black print.

Name: Dabi Stone

Dumpee: Michael Schultz

Reason for dump: First if I don't break-up with him, my dad will kill me and if I *do* break-up with him I will not be disinherited, my family will be happy, but Michael will kill me. Well not *really.* I mean Michael does love me, but I have to do this for my family.

Excited I jump up to get my backup discs and run my finger along the alphabetical names. I stop when I reach Dabi and Michael.

"Ah ha!" I take the disc out and slip it in the CD drive. The audio recordings I routinely do of the breakups have never come in handy. Until now. God, maybe I'm psychic, too, and knew I'd need one of them one day. I push that thought away. Can't deal with that idea right now.

I listen to the break-up, listening for anything unusual, but the usual dump is taking place. At first Michael doesn't believe it; he claims their relationship is great, except for her overprotective family. But then something changes. "Guess she doesn't have a choice," he says. But it's not what he says that has me spooked. A chill flits over my skin. It's the eerie tone in his voice.

I close the file and put it back. A million different things run through my head. Did Michael do it? Was it her family? And most importantly, is this something I need to take to the police?

***

I'm still a little freaked by my phone call with James, the email threat, and the discovery of Dabi Stone's body by the time I head downtown to meet Erin, my best friend and the only friend who knows about my "gift". I don't know how I let her talk me into this. Again.

My heart palpitates faster and faster as I approach the volunteer sign in. Being in public always makes me nervous. Even though the dumpees don't know my name, they do know my voice. And trust me, I guarantee they hear my voice in their sleep. Add to that the colliding auras and the headaches I end up with every time I'm in a crowd, and the last thing I want to do on a Saturday is volunteer.

My pace slows as I cross the grass at Pleasant Ridge Park and look at all the spring flowers in full bloom, dotted all over the park, just waiting to become the bathroom for many of the male dogs sniffing around. The SPCA is putting on its annual adoption drive and Erin's hospitality company, Plan It, is in charge of the festivities every year. Once again, she's called on me to help.

"Olivia!"

I turn toward the lake and see Erin flailing her arms in the air like a mad woman. "Over here." She yells and waves me over like I'm an airplane ready to land on the runway.

Embarrassed, I duck my head around, but no one seems to notice. Every other person is walking their dogs or chatting with another dog owner. The once peaceful lake is full of the four-legged creatures chasing the ultimate frisbee that's probably sunk to the bottom by now.

Erin doesn't care who's around. She's still yelling my name over the barks and voices around us.

We've been friends a long time. Our story is sort of the same but different, meaning her parents are dead, which mine might be but I don't know, and they left her a fortune, while mine left me nada. That's how she had the money to start her business. She invested most of her money in the company and made sure she did it right. She has. Her business is flourishing.

I can't say the same for her love life. After Kyle, she used my service to dump another freeloader. She had a horrible habit of picking the wrong guys. Considering how smart and beautiful she is, I couldn't understand it.

My job this year had better be better than last, I think as I make my way across the grass to Erin. How humiliating is walking around in an orange vest holding a pooper scooper picking up dog poop all afternoon? Plus, last year at this time was a record-breaking weather day. Instead of the usual sixty-four degree temperature it was eighty-five degrees. There's generally a breeze coming off the lake, but not that day.

Really I can't complain because looking for the little flags did help me keep my eyes on the ground and not queasy from colliding auras. Even dogs have a tendency to emit their auras in my direction.

"Ready for poop duty." I salute Erin like a good soldier, lying through my teeth.

I can handle scooping out cat poop from the litter boxes, but not the hot steamy piles of dog poop. Give me a guy like James to break-up with any day of the week.

"Shut up," she says with a laugh. "I don't have you picking up poop this year." She points to a young man walking around in my orange vest with my scooper. "He needed community-service hours for school." Her aura changes from a sparkle to yellow and shimmers like a halo around her entire body.

Erin's aura is crystal. She is a chameleon of sorts. She reacts to other people's auras, another sign of her insecurities. My parents left me and I had more confidence than she did. But parents dying can feel like abandonment, too, and Erin never had an Aunt Matilda.

Aunt Matilda always told me, "Tell me who you run with and I will tell you who you are." Only she can read auras too, so she used that talent to her advantage to tell me who I could play with and who I couldn't. Erin and I've been best friends since the third grade, and Matilda warned me from the beginning. "She's unsure of herself. You'll have to help her."

The crystal aura is rare; it changes to match the people around her. Erin generally has a great aura, but lately, since she met her new beau, it's been a little off. I'd gone into protection mode. I don't want Erin to get hurt yet again.

She's also always had that contagious laugh. You know, the one you wish you could sound like. It's flirty, fun and fits her personality. She's the outgoing, petite part of our duo while I'm the girl next door, down to earth recluse. But hers is all an act. The bubbly personality hides the scared girl inside.

We're total opposites, Erin and me. Her black hair to my blonde. Her side banged bob to my side part with long hair below the shoulder. She has the deepest blue eyes and mine are green. Worst of all, I'll never be able to stuff my size eight body into any of her size four clothes. Today she's wearing her white a-line skirt that hits perfectly above her knee, paired with a light blue t-shirt which compliments her aura, creating an angelic looking Erin.

"So what will I be doing?"

"Over there." She points in the directions of a hundred or so pink, red and white balloons all floating above a booth.

Finally! Those balloons have to mark the adoption process area. I feel like I've been promoted.

"Great." I smile knowing I'm going to get to place sweet animals with their rightful owners. For once I'll be bringing people together with a loved one instead of tearing them apart like I do at Splitsville.com.

"Good." Erin sighs with relief. "I thought you might freak out."

"Freak out?" It's not like I'm afraid of animals, plus I can tell people if I don't think their choice is a good match for them or their environment. It's in my *real* job description. "It's for a good cause," I reassure her.

"You're right." She leads me to the booth. "It *is* a good cause. Have fun."

I stop dead in my tracks. I shake my head and close my eyes. Open them. Squint them. Rub them to make sure I'm reading the words above my booth correctly. "Kissing Booth? Kissing Booth!" I scream and try to grab Erin, but she's already too far away. Now I understand her reaction.

"You *said* it's for a good cause."

"No!" I yell back, "I'm not doing it." I can't believe she wants me to be the kisser in the kissing booth.

"There's lip gloss and Chap-Stick inside," she yells back. Her evil grin tells me I'm stuck. "You'll do great! Besides *you* don't have a boyfriend who'll be jealous."

"Only peck kisses. Nothing with saliva!" I touch my lips thinking about all the nasty diseases out there.

Plus, it's nice of her to remind me that I'm lonely and single. Besides my little problem with auras and headaches, my job has made me a little cynical. It's not like Erin's new boyfriend will care if she mans the kissing booth. I've never met him, but from what she says, he sounds like a creep. It's a mystery how she doesn't see it. Every time we all go out for drinks, he never shows up. He always has some kind of excuse. Or he's standing her up. Plus his name is Kent. What kind of name is Kent? "He's like Ken, you know, from Ken and Barbie," she told me after she first met him.

I just didn't get it. Ken isn't even her type. And Erin's Kent is certainly no Clark Kent. He doesn't sound at all like Superman.

I glare at her, wanting to run and tackle her, but unfortunately there's a line of about twenty guys warming up their lips, a cloud of red aura's surrounding them.

I look over my soon-to-be kissing partners and take note of the first hungry beast. The AC/DC shirt he's wearing isn't throwing me off, it's the ripped up jeans-and I don't mean the cool ripped up jeans look, and studded belt that's not doing it for me.

Totally grossing me out, he licks his lips like I'm some piece of red meat. He does look like one of those predatory types; his eagerness leads me to believe he isn't very good at the hunt.

"Let's get this over with," I mutter as I take my place under the "KISS ME FOR $5.00" sign. I make a tight pucker for the meat eater to come attack his prey.

He moves in, locks lips with me, and it seems to go on forever. Finally it's over and the predator backs away and stares at me while licking his lips again.

Nasty! I take a tissue from the box and wipe away what I've dubbed The Hard Kiss. I'm no kissing expert, I'm a break-up expert. When you're hired to break people hearts, they tell you all sorts of things about their sex lives, including their kissing patterns.

A list I've come up with is the Art of Kissing. There are definitely nine different types of kisses I've compiled.

"The Romantic Kiss" is the best one of all, in my opinion. This is also a fun one that takes a while to develop in the relationship. It's where he bends you back, with one hand placed on the small of your back and the other resting against your face. Hold onto your hat! This kiss means "I am going to take care of you and love you always."

"The Peck," also called "The Quickie". It's the beginning of all kisses. The "why waste my time kiss," in my opinion. Generally the first in a relationship where the lips are fully closed and sometimes puckered. It's where you are feeling out the waters to see if there is a spark and if you might be able to move onto bigger and better (longer) kisses.

"The Pehhhck." The one that generally comes after the first version of The Peck. It lingers a little longer with the closed mouth. Your man might say, "mmm" during this kiss or your toes may tingle.

"The Hard Kiss" is the "I want you and I want you now" kiss. Usually hard in the beginning to state his desire or "I'm going to teach you." Depending on what your comfort level with him is, you may stop at this point and be grossed out, or keep going, blending into a different kissing type.

"The Rapid Fire" with playful puckers one after the other, is "the Machine Gun." These are acceptable in public for all the public display of affection out there. Trust me, *no one* wants to see you swallowing your man's face in public.

"The Nibble" is when you get to take a little bite on the lip letting your man know you are in a playful mood. Don't draw blood, because there is *nothing* romantic about blood—unless you're a vampire.

When you are so mad at your man that you can't decide whether you want to kiss him or you don't want to kiss him and it usually leads to great make-up sex is what I've dubbed "the I love you, no wait, I hate you." This can be a very stratifying experience.

Meat eater is definitely a Hard Kiss. I don't know what he thinks he's teaching me by his nastiness, but I find he's totally not my type. Still, he paid his money and it's all for the dogs, right?

"Don't waste your money, man," the meat eater says to the next guy in line.

His words sting a little. I try to get a better attitude, and look at my next victim. He's pretty cute and I decide I can chalk this up to research and really test out my kissing list first hand. It'll be great if I can say to a dumpee, "He's dumping you because your kisses are slobbery. I know. I've researched it."

Yum! I smile, thinking my next victim will taste as rich and dreamy as Dove chocolate. The closer he gets, the tastier he looks. His gaze lingers for a moment too long, making me look away. I can't stare for fear of drowning in his deep dark eyes or seeing an aura that can ruin it for me.

"What exactly do I get for my money?" The tall, handsome man with perfect cheekbones puts his hand on mine, the five dollar bill attached to his palm.

I jerk my hand at the lightning bolt that zips through my body and his aura jumps out completely surrounding him.

His mouth flinches up in the corners to a full smile, like he's well aware of the emotion he's giving me.

"Duh," I sputter, doing anything to get my mind out of the gutter because he's completely blue. "Can't you read?" I point my finger up to the sign among the balloons.

I close my eyes to see if, when I reopen them his aura will change.

Damn! Still blue.

He steps back and tilts his head up. "Kissing booth, five dollars." I hear his words cross those lips and suddenly *I'm* willing to pay to kiss *him*.

"Okay," he states blankly, replacing the five with a ten spot.

I close my eyes. I hold my hands up to my chest in fear he'll be able to feel my powerfully pounding heart. I want this to be over. Secretly I wonder what he thinks of a girl who'd offer herself up in this capacity.

All my coherent thinking flies out the window as I lean in with a not-so-much pucker lips and kiss him. I freeze, unsure what to do next. My lips linger against his and he kisses me back.

The tip of my nose tingles as I smell his scent. It falls over me and leaves a trail as he pulls away.

For my research, I decide that he definitely used The Pehhhck method. I rock back on my heels with my lips rubbing together as though I'm trying to absorb every fiber of his kiss into my soul.

"Come on, buddy," the next guy in line yells. "Move it or get a room!"

Oh crap! My eyes open and I find him staring at me. This is not a normal kiss, for a kissing booth, that is.

"Thanks," I say, but I really want him to say something. "The animals appreciate it." I blush realizing how stupid I sound.

He holds up his fingers. "I paid for two."

I blush. I look beyond him. "He paid for two," I confirm to the waiting line behind him and we lean in toward each other again.

Three

There has to be a relationship between pheromones and kissing. Time has passed and my mood from this morning is drastically different from what it is now.

I admit, I didn't want to work in the kissing booth, but it's been fun. I've mainly only had a peck here and a hand shake there. More importantly everyone wants to give money for the animals. Even the girlfriends of the guys kissing me don't seem to don't mind since it's all going to a good cause.

Don't misunderstand me; I do get some nasty stares.

"It's for a good cause," I holler at the lady who tips her nose up at my booth.

"Ah, the good ole' kissing booth." The suave, neatly coiffed blonde-haired hunk, is walking next to the booth with his mutt and another guy whose baseball cap is pulled down over his eyes.

I walk around the booth, and since it's five minutes until quitting time and no one's in line, I figure it's time to shut down the lip business. "Hey, buddy." I point to the fluffy dog. "What's his name?"

I look back and forth at the two, and notice the one with the cap doesn't look my way.

"Tramp." The blonde guy bends down next to me as we stroke his dog. "Or at least that's what his papers say." He pulls the adoption papers out of his pocket.

"Oh good." I'm a little uncomfortable being close to this guy. I don't know what the vibe is, but I know it's not good. He stares at me in a creepy way. I stand up and take a step back, every break-up I've done racing through my mind. Do I recognize his guy? Is that what the vibe is? Is he a disgruntled dumpee? Has he tracked me down?

"How's business?" He refers to the booth behind me.

I take a couple steps back to put some distance between us. "It was fine."

The light radiating between the two men is not good. I've only sensed this type of aura once before. No, no please. I steady myself against the booth and close my eyes.

When I was a teenager, a little boy went missing. I dreamed of him in a scary basement. When I woke, Aunt Matilda wrote down all the details and took it to the police. Afterward the police found him in that same basement. From then on the police called upon Aunt Matilda to help them with crimes their department had problems solving. Only, *I* was the one helping them, they just didn't know it.

When they put the boy's kidnapper in a line-up, Aunt Matilda had to go in and tell them if he was in the vision— totally unusable in a court of law, but helpful anyway. Even though the police objected, she took me. She didn't want them to know I was the one who had the vision. But she was determined that all the bad guys got put behind bars since the love of her life turned out to be a thief who got away with it. She was a big believer in paying it forward even if it meant bringing me to the police station. I'll never forget the moment I laid eyes on that man. His aura popped up –*magenta*.

"Was?" The perfect blonde specimen looks at his watch, and then peers at me. "You have a few minutes left." He puts his hand in his pocket and pulls out a five. I blink, hoping the auras will go back to their normal colors. But when I open my eyes, they're still the same. These guys' auras aren't pure magenta, but a combination of yellow and violet. I'm having a hard time reading them, but I know they're not good.

I gather my belongings. "I'm sorry. The booth is closed." I turn around relieved to see Erin walking toward me. I point at her. "See. She's coming to collect the money."

He steps back and hands me the money. "Keep it. It's for charity."

"Uh, hi." Erin's eyes dart nervously between me and the guy. "Uh, I've been looking all over for you." She continues with a faint grin. Oh no. I've seen that look before. Is this another loser in her notched up bedpost? Her smile fades slightly.

My head is pounding, the auras of all the men at the kissing both colliding like bumper cars in my mind. I need my house, where there are no kaleidoscopic auras. Or maybe dinner.

"I've been right here all day." I hurry to grab my purse. Definitely dinner, I decide because I can't wait to tell Erin about this guy's aura. But when I turn back around, Erin and evil eyes are in their own lip lock. Her crystal aura is now completely matching his violet one.

My heart drops to my feet. Oh. My. God. Erin. . .and. . .this guy? No wonder she's acting all nervous. She'd better not use Splitsville.com again. One of these days I hope she'll find the right guy.

The time I told Erin about my little "gift" zips into my pounding head. She hadn't taken it well. "You mean you're a freak?" she asked. This was not the reaction I'd hoped for. Her words still burn.

"No," I spat out. "I have a gift."

Her eyebrows had angled into a V and she peered at me like I really was a freak. "So you're saying you can see an aura around me right now?"

I nodded. "Yes, Erin, I can see your crystal aura." I jammed my hands on my hips. "I don't get why you're angry."

"I don't believe you."

I hadn't wanted to, but I gave her proof by telling her about the time her high school boyfriend cheated on her.

She gawked at me. "Great, so you're going to know what I'm thinking or feeling before I do," she said after she got over the shock of her cheating ex. She'd been absolutely right. Erin has very few secrets from me.

Her reaction then hadn't been welcome. She'd thought I was a freak and started calling me her "freak friend" as a joke, but it had hurt and I don't want to relive that now by telling her that her boyfriend is a Romeo. By the way she is acting, she definitely won't want to hear anything I have to say.

Erin pulls away. "I see you met Kent," she says hesitantly. He, on the other hand, looks like he's holding a prize trophy. Erin is obviously his Heisman.

I look at Kent then back to Erin and ask, "So is this *your* Kent?" I'd hope the last break-up would've made her come to her senses. But with his aura, I don't think she has. I peak around them to see his friend continuing to walk away from us.

Interesting. I watch Kent's aura fade from magenta to yellow to violet. He's not crystal like Erin. I've never seen anything like this before. I make a mental sticky to ask Matilda what it means.

"Yes, uh, we met." He smiles like the cat with a feather in his mouth. Somehow he seems to know I won't tell her how creepy he is. "She was petting my little boy."

The lines between Erin's brows squeeze in tension and she points toward Kent's friend. "Was that…"

Kent interrupts, "Timmerman, yeah. He'll catch up with us later. He's got to go somewhere." We all look.

"I like Tramp," I say to break the tension. I bend down to rub the bushy eyebrows out of his face. I want to make sure his aura is okay even though his rough, shaggy fur is indicative to Irish Wolfhounds. "He seems like a nice dog." I smile when his aura tells me he's happy to be out of the kennel.

Erin fidgets with the strap on her purse. "Isn't he great?" I wonder who she's referring to, Kent or Tramp? "Kent adopted him today," she adds. Like she's a sales person and her client is her boyfriend. Only I'm not buying. Kent may have Erin fooled, but his aura tells me the truth about him.

"Yeah, great." I pat Tramp on the head and want to shake the shit out of Erin. Her boyfriend is a snake, and all her fidgeting makes me wonder if she doesn't think so too.

"I'm talking about Kent." She shrugs and wraps her arms tightly around his waist. He bends down to kiss her. She casts her eyes on me looking for my approval—another look I've seen one too many times. "We have to get going."

Erin's hands grasp Kent's and she pulls him toward the parking lot.

"Wait!" I put my hands up. One payoff to my volunteering is her taking me to dinner. "I thought we were going to eat." I can sit through a dinner with Kent, I think. I need food!

"Yeah, I'm looking forward to getting to know you," he says with a wink. "I'd like to see if everything Erin tells me is true. How wonderful you really are."

What the heck was that wink about? My distaste for this guy is growing at a steady rate, but my hunger pains are growing faster.

Erin begins to fumble. "I…I thought you might be tired and…" she says to me.

I rub my temples. "I am, but I'm hungry."

She knows what it means when my thumbs massage my temples. "You should probably go home."

"I'm hungry," I say again. She's not getting off the hook that easy. I need to spend a little more time with Kent to figure out what his game is. But suddenly Erin lunges and grabs the arm of a guy walking by. I stare. The arm of the cute guy who paid for two kisses. The one with the unbelievable blue aura.

"Hey Erin!" he says. "Great job today." The guy gestures around the park. "I think we beat last year."

"Oh, yeah, thanks. Um, Bradley, this is Olivia." She continues to hold his arm and nods toward me. "The Olivia I was telling you about."

I guess she didn't tell him anything good, because he looks as perplexed as I feel. She's never mentioned Bradley to me or described him. I would've remembered that.

"Umm…" Bradley seems a little flustered. "I'm sorry I don't remember you talking about..."

"Olivia, this is Bradley," she blurts, interrupting him.

"Yeah," I say. "We've already been intimate." All the color flushes into my cheeks and I smile knowing my aura is reflecting my bashful feelings. "It was *memorable*."

He laughs. "Yes it was." He flashes a crooked grin. "That's why I paid for two kisses." He holds up two fingers.

"Great." Erin steps between us. "I knew you two would hit it off." She puts her finger on her cheek. "I have a great idea. You two should go to dinner!"

My eyebrows cross. "What?" Erin completely catches me off guard. I have never seen her like this. I'm not used to her pushing me away. "But I thought…"

I hope it's not too late. Has she fallen hook, line and sinker for this guy?

"You two will have a great time." She hooks her arm through Kent's arm and hurries toward the parking lot.

"But…" I throw my hands up in the air. I definitely don't want to be a third wheel, but I do want dinner. I watch Erin walk away and resist the urge to yell, "Be smart! Don't do this again. Why are you treating me this way?" But I don't. Maybe my instincts are off today from all the kissing. Or maybe my instincts are on high alert due to Dabi's murder. Maybe Kent needs another chance. Maybe.

"Well," Bradley gestures toward the parking lot and continues, "I'm game if you are?"

I've studied every man in my life trying to find the one with the true blue aura until I've become blue in the face. Men with blue auras live from their hearts. They are the ones to hold on to and not let go: the nurturers, the caretakers. No wonder he's at the SPCA event—totally a blue thing to do.

I shake my head. "Oh no, don't worry, I'm not going to hold you to it. Obviously Erin didn't want me to go with them."

He shrugs and then he crams his hands in the front pockets of his jeans. He jerks his head flipping his floppy brown hair to the side, exposing his dark eyes. "I really would like to grab a bite to eat with you. Or are your lips too sore?" He laughs like it's the funniest joke, but the thing is, my lips really *are* sore.

"Funny." I laugh, wishing I had Erin's sexy chuckle. "All that kissing did make me hungry. I wonder how many calories I burned today."

"Too many, I bet. Let's see if we can put some of those calories back." He nods his head toward the parking lot again.

Maybe if you feed me chocolate cake. Without a word, I follow him to the lot. I love the way his pants drag the top of his feet, only his toenails exposed from his flip flops. His mop-top shaggy hair is begging me to run my hands through it, or maybe it's the other way around.

"Want to ride with me?" Bradley asks. I follow his toned tan bicep down to his finger, which is pointing to a tan convertible Mini Cooper. No wonder he's already golden. Why is he not taken? Hmm?

I hesitate, but only for a second. "Sure."

He smiles, opening my door. "I guess we should introduce ourselves since we've already been to first base."

Handsome, great kisser, awesome car. . .and witty.

"Are you a serial killer?" I question, half joking, half serious. The good old girl in me knows I should never get in a car with a stranger, but I don't feel like he's a stranger. Especially since we've locked lips.

"No. I just want to buy you dinner." He shuts the door and walks around the car. "I usually don't get to first base until a few dates in, but we can do this a little backwards."

I can't believe I'm in a car with a stranger. Well, practically a stranger. I put my head down and silently pray that I make it home alive. I admit, it's the stupidest thing I've ever done, but somehow it feels right. I sneak a peek at him. His aura doesn't tell me otherwise. Still blue. Even the throbbing in my head has subsided.

"How about Pete's?" Bradley is referring to the only pizza joint in town.

And on a Saturday night I know it will be packed. That's okay. I'd love for everyone in town to see me with this tall glass of water.

"Pete's is great." I look out the window. He might stop the car, open the door, and kick me out if he sees the excitement in my face.

Pete's Pizzeria is on the other side of town. Even though my stomach is grumbling, I have a secret wish that we get stopped by all the red lights through town. Being in the car next to a blue aura is a dream come true and I'm not ready to wake up.

"How do you know Erin again?" Bradley zooms under the yellow light right before it turned to red.

I adjust myself so I'm not completely staring at him. "We've been friends for a long time."

A few minutes later, and some fast driving, we pull into the parking lot of Pete's Pizzaria and park in the front.

"I hope you like pizza." He turns the engine off and we get out.

Of course I do, what red-blooded woman doesn't? "Sure, it's fine." I play cool. I avoid looking at all the people and seeing all the auras. Panic creeps through me, but I bury it. "Why did you come to the kissing booth?" I ask while we stand in line for a table. It's a valid question for a hot dude.

"I run the SPCA and one of the guys bet I wouldn't go up to the booth." He lets me walk first behind the hostess to our table, though I wish he would have led the way. Her aura is black. And it makes me wonder if she's divorced, abused, or some sort of addict. "Naturally I couldn't back down," he adds.

I'm not sure if I want the answer, but I ask anyway, "How much was I worth?" My heart beats faster with each second that goes by.

His hand touches my back and he pulls out my chair. I turn and look at him not in the least bit scared. Maybe aura reading has its perks after all. I know I'm totally safe with Bradley.

"Not nearly enough," he said. "It was one kiss for a fifty dollar donation to the SPCA. I would've done it if you were a mutt, but you aren't so I took the bet for one kiss."

"But you paid for two." I'm trying to figure out his math.

"Because I wanted the second one for myself." I swear I see some pink in his cheeks.

I nibble my bottom lip trying not to get too excited. I turn the menu over and focus on what to order. I'm already getting my hopes up about Bradley and totally don't want to screw it up. I calculate how much time I have before I have to tell him the truth about my gift. Not nearly enough, I decide.

My mouth waters as Bradley orders a large BBQ chicken pizza and a couple of side salads. It's fate, because it's exactly what I would've ordered.

I give my menu back to the waitress, trying not to think about her black aura, poor girl. "So you're the one who hires Erin's business every year for the fund raiser?" Even if Erin was just trying to keep me away from Kent so I wouldn't read his aura—too late for that, she did me a favor by hooking me up with Bradley. I'll thank her one day.

"Yep. Plan It is a worthy program and Erin is easy to work with." He takes a sip of soda. "But she never told me about you or we would've met a long time ago."

I don't look at him. If I do, I'm afraid I'll get my hopes up even higher than they already are, and I don't want to do that. I've been disappointed in love too many times to fall easily. But I think it's too late. I feel like Renee Zellweger in Jerry Macguire. *You had me when I saw your blue aura.*

I don't want to make it too obvious, but I need to find out more about Erin and Kent. "Erin and I've been friends for a really long time," I say between bites. "She loves her job."

"She should. She's good at it." Bradley points to my cheek.

"What?" I rub my fingers down my face.

Bradley reaches over with a napkin, and wipes my chin. "I got it. Your salad dressing dripped off your fork." His smile looks brighter with his blue aura surrounding him.

I look down before he sees me blush. "I guess you're the one Erin's been working so closely with on the fundraiser?"

He nods.

"I didn't realize Erin and Kent were so hot and heavy. Did she say anything to you about their relationship?" I ask nonchalantly.

"Not much. She always refers to him as her boyfriend." He shrugs. He waves his hands in the air, and makes a face like he doesn't get it either. "My boyfriend this, my boyfriend that. She's definitely into him."

He doesn't get the severity of his words. I roll my eyes. "I have no clue what she sees in him. I think it's weird how he came to the kissing booth and insisted on a kiss."

Bradley puts his drink down. His blue aura tones down a little as he's deep in thought. "He wanted a kiss from you?" His eyes narrow.

"Yes." My eyebrows rise. "Then he played if off when Erin showed up. Has she said anything about him?"

"Nope." He holds his glass up for the waitress to refill. "Just that she's into him."

I decide to drop it. I can tell by his tone that he doesn't care about Erin and her relationship.

"So what do you do?" Bradley asks as we make room on the table for the pizza the waitress is holding over our heads. I love how fresh baked pizza smells coming straight from the oven.

This is the question I have a hard time answering. "Dot com business," I say. It's my standard answer, even though it's vague. If I say it fast enough, maybe it won't stick in his brain.

"What?" He sucks up the cheese dangling from his mouth. "Dot com?"

"You know, internet stuff." I take a big bite of pizza stalling for time.

He takes a drink. "I know—Internet, but what type?"

I keep chewing as I think. As I see it I have two options. One, tell him the truth and watch him run away as fast as he can or two, tell a little white lie and keep him around for as long as I can.

"Well?" His interest isn't waning.

"Research. Boring old research."

"Sounds interesting. Like what kind of research?" He grabs another slice of pizza.

It's really a good sign that he's so interested in knowing stuff about me, but geez, I wish he'd let me off the hook. "Heart research. Let's not talk about my job. I get enough of that during the week." I get another piece, telling myself it's not really a lie. I do help people with their hearts. Heartache, specifically, but I leave that part unsaid.

We enjoy the rest of our dinner talking about the SPCA and his love of animals. Our glasses are drained, and the pizza joint is empty except for us and our morose waitress.

On the drive back to my car, I discovered there's more to Bradley than his blue aura. He talks about his family, love of animals and his zest in life. All of this is why I've always searched for a blue aura mate. Unfortunately I think I'm in—hook, line and sinker.

Four

I couldn't wait to get home to text Bradley after he dropped me off. "Thanks 4 dinner." My fingers can't type fast enough as I get settled at my desk before I check out my new dump clients. I don't want to seem the eager beaver, but I do want him to call.

My phone vibrates. "My pleasure. How about dinner tomorrow night?" My heart jumps as I read his text.

I hit reply. "Sure, where?" I play it casual. I look at the list of dating stages on my desk.

"We'll play it by ear. I'll pick u up." His texts are short and sweet.

With a few minor details on time and my address, we are set. As I push the off button, I see I missed a call. It's a number I don't recognize, and I panic. Maybe it's the police! Maybe they've already made a connection between Dabi's murder and Splitsville.com.

I read the number over and over in my head. My light isn't blinking so I know they didn't leave a message. Do I call the number back? Do I risk it? What if it's someone I've dumped using Splitsville.com or what if it was Bradley calling from a different number. Maybe the SPCA?

Without even thinking, I grab the phone and dial the number. It's as if my arm
and my brain are not even connected.

"Hello." A familiar voice answers.

I slam the phone. Stupid, stupid, stupid!

My phone rings. I look at the Caller ID on the third jingle. Damn caller ID. It's handy when I need it, but it totally sucks when someone else is using it.

"Hello?" I say. I sound all sweet and innocent.

"Did you just hang up on Kent?" Erin's voice on the other end of the line is loud and demanding. And all I can think is that she's already a goner. I just hope for Erin's sake this Kent guy isn't another gold digger.

But she sure does sound awfully defensive about him. "I didn't know who it was." I assure her. "What's going on?"

I can hear Kent in the background talking over her. "Did you forget that tomorrow night is the Spring Fling at Pleasant Ridge Park?" she asks me.

I slap my palm to my forehead. Yes, I'd completely forgotten about it. "Ahh…no." I say. Man I'm getting too good at this lying. Guilt coils through me. "Bradley and I are going and want you two to meet us?"

I'm one great best friend. I really wanted to have some alone time with Bradley, but I can't skip out on the annual Spring Fling with Erin. It's a tradition. We always go together, even if it means an evening with Kent.

"Oh!" she squeals. I wait out the long pause and she says, "Really? You want to go on a double date?"

"Yes." I'm surprised to hear myself say. "If you like him, I'm sure I will."

I can hear her in the background explaining to Kent what the annual Spring Fling is. "Yes, let's do it," she says after a minute and I can hear how excited she is. "We'll meet you there."

"Great," I say, though inside I'm dismayed.

"Oh, and Olivia?" Erin says. "I knew you'd get along with Bradley. He's great, yes?"

It's the perfect opening. "Why did you say you told me about him? Because you didn't."

"I didn't?" She plays coy, but her innocent act isn't sitting so well in the pit of my stomach.

"No. You didn't. It could have backfired." I want to clear the air before I see her. "Why did you do that?"

"I didn't *do* anything Olivia. Can't you be happy that he's into you and can't you be happy that *I'm* happy?"

Yes, I can be happy Bradley's into me, but I can't be happy about Kent. I don't like the sound of Erin's voice or the way she acts when she's around him. And I don't like that she's settling for someone who's not good enough for her—again. But now is not the time to talk to her about it, so I bite my tongue. "I am happy for you. I'm happy if you're happy. And yes, Bradley is a great guy."

I hear a chipper sound in her voice. "It all worked out. We'll meet you around seven?"

"See you then," I confirm.

I can't decide whether to call Bradley or text him. I dial. Okay, so maybe I want to hear his voice.

"Hi, Liv." Bradley sounds like he's smiling when he answers.

"Hi." I laugh at the sound of barking dogs in the background. And at the fact that he's already using my nickname.

"Are you canceling on me? Did I already scare you off?" he asks with a laugh.

I speak a little louder because I know he can't hear me over all the dogs. "No way!" I can't stop smiling. "You're not getting off that easy. I wanted to ask if we can meet Erin and Kent at the annual Spring Fling at Pleasant Ridge Park tomorrow night."

The sounds of chains and gates cause me to move the phone away from my ear. "Yeah, sounds great. What time?"

"Pick me up around 6:30," I scream into the receiver.

"Okay." He's yelling, too. "Gotta go toss some Frisbees. See you tomorrow."

My body tingles just like the first time he kissed me. "Bye." I linger a moment to hear him hang up the phone.

Aunt Matilda creeps down the hall allowing her cream gypsy dress to float serenely along the hard wood floors. The slight jingle of her bells use to drive me crazy when I was a kid when she would walk down the hall and check on me every night. But now it's a comfort.

"What's all the screaming about?" she asks after I hang up the phone. Then she nods like she knows. "Oh, how was volunteering? Did you adopt a cute puppy? Or something better, perhaps?"

Aunt Matilda doesn't like that I live alone and is always trying to get me to adopt a dog.

Maybe she's the one who needs a dog to come home to at night.

I ignore her comment because I don't have time for a dog and attempting to explain that is useless. I change the subject.

"You aren't going to believe what I saw today." My anxiety over Kent's aura is outweighing my giddiness about Bradley's. "A magenta aura."

Her eyebrows cock up. She takes a sharp breath and draws her hand up to her mouth.

"Don't worry." I reassure her. "It changed to violet right away." Which I still don't understand and which I hope to hell to make sense of—for Erin's sake.

Five

I had plans to clean my house before starting work, but since I neglected my dumps last night the piles of clothes will have to wait. I feel almost schizophrenic—or like I have multiple personalities. Half of me is on a high because of Bradley, the other half can't shake the chills after seeing creepy Kent and his aura, not to mention Dabi's death.

I grab a piece of day-old pizza out of the box and sit down at my computer to find all the lovely souls I'm going to come in contact with. Thank God Bradley is nothing like the people who use my service. Kent, on the other hand, is exactly like them.

The thought of going on a double date with them tonight puts me in a mean mood. A great mood to dump people.

I click on Splitsville.com emails to see what's in store. Wait! The threatening email (or disgruntled) I deleted yesterday is sitting in my inbox. "Didn't I delete that?" I mutter.

I scan the date and time to confirm that it's the same email. Holy moly. It isn't.

My finger trembles, hovering over the ENTER button. It's like pleasure and pain. I want to click it, but then again I don't. Finally, I let my finger drop. "End Splistville.com. Last chance." I read it out loud a few times. Each time I use a different voice. And I confirm, no matter what tone I use, sweet or evil, the threat sounds a little more real. I don't recognize the sender. Maybe a prank?

I take a deep breath. I have a sneaky suspicion this isn't a prank. My hands shake as I make myself open the next email. Work must go on. One good thing, I'm confident they don't know me.

At least I hope so.

I dial my first victim. "Hi, is William there?" I pull up William's picture and chuckle at the college student doing the infamous beer bong. The dumper is really getting her point across on why she wants to dump him.

"Yep."

"Hi, Bill, I'm Jenn from Splitsville.com and I am calling for Cecilia because. . .."

"You want Ceecee?" Of course he interrupts me. I hate when people interrupt me.

"No," I say slowly, "I'm calling because Cecilia hired me to break-up with you because you have no ambition in life and are unmotivated." I get the sinking feeling this call's going to take a while. I put my headphones on and pick up my house. It's a mess and quite frankly I haven't had anyone to clean it for or anyone to impress. But now that Bradley is coming over, the entire program has changed. I definitely don't want him to know what a messy person I am.

"Wait, wait, and wait." William stops me with his loud voice. "Did you call me Bill?"

Clothes and magazines are all around me. The more I pick up, the more I take my frustrations out on dear Bill. "You know, William or Bill, it's all the same."

"Listen, my name is William not Bill. And who are you again?" He's staying in stage one of "the process." No wonder he's in his sixth year of college. *You ain't too bright, are you, Billy?* I shake my head, taking another look at his photo. His eyes droop and scraggly hair is cemented to his head. Dumb as a post. I flip the radio on for background noise.

"I'm Jenn from Splitsville.com and Cecilia hired me to break-up with you because you are in your sixth year of college. She's getting ready to graduate dude. What the hell have you been doing the last six years?" A little part of me cringes, remembering Dabi and Michael. If my breakup call had unhinged Michael, I was responsible. Was I doing it again?

"What? Is this a joke?" His voice escalates, "Did she like Google you or some shit like that?"

"I don't know if she used Google or not, but she did hire me." Really I don't know how she found me, but it's worth putting the question on the form to see where most of my business comes from.

"I bet you are some big fat chick with dimples all over your ass that lives with your parents. Aren't you, bitch?" I hear a big thud and jump as he says, "I bet you can't even get a date."

WOW! I grab "The Process" checklist and realize he's the first dumpee that's completely skipping stages three through five. He's going straight for the jugular.

"Well, I don't live with my parents." I smile thinking about Bradley and my date for the night.

I walk over to the mirror and peer at my body image. I rack my fingers through my long black locks, turn my head and look down my body. *Sure I could tone a little in the rump area*, I think poking around on my back end. Nope, not fat either Billy.

"Listen man, she's getting ready to graduate and start grad school. What are you getting ready to do?" I turn around looking at the front of myself

I wish these people would listen to me. I separate the two big piles of clothes into three smaller piles: dark, white, and not sure. I briefly move the phone away from my ear when I hear the radio announcer mention Dabi's name. I drop the t-shirt and walk closer to the radio. I pull the phone from my head and put my ear up to the speaker only to hear they are going to reveal a suspect later in the day. My chest fills with panic. The missed call I'd gotten. Was it really the police? Was I a suspect?

"I'm getting ready to go to the liquor store because in about an hour I'm heading for spring break." William keeps his voice strong and steady. His masculine act makes me want to puke.

"Great, William! That's exactly why she's dumping you." I have to get on with this and Google Dabi. I continue. It's my job, I remind myself. "What is your major, dude?"

In my real life, I never use the word "dude," but in my job, I can be or say whatever I want. Although right now I'm not sure Jenn from Splitsville.com is a good person to be

"Paleontology. You know, digging." He sounds like a complete fool.

"Six years of undergrad?" I question, knowing full well he needs his undergrad classes and then a masters which means he's *far* from a degree. "Are you going to Africa to dig up some bones on spring break?"

"Naw. I'm going to Florida to dig on the beach. You know what I mean?" He snickers. "You want to come?"

"No, but I'm thinking maybe you should major in GET A CLUE BUDDY!" I'm growing tired of old Billy awful fast. "Cecilia has dumped you. Now move on."

"You know what?"

Oh goody, I'm about to get a life lesson from William. "What?"

"I'll accept what you're saying, but…"

I stop him. He has said the magic words. "Thank you Billy for using Splitsville.com." I have my finger on the off button and push. Quickly I type Cecilia a personal note to let her know her decision is wise and wish her good luck in graduate school.

I grab another slice of day-old pizza and flick on the television in time to hear the impromptu press conference on Dabi Stone. No suspect named yet, and new evidence coming in. My heart flips over like a dead fish. Oh God, oh God, oh God

I race around the house, throwing everything into an empty closet. I still have one more dump to do before Bradley shows up. And before I can really investigate the link between Splitsville.com and Dabi.

I begin my next call.

"Is Mac there?" I ask the voice on the other end of the line. This dump is particularly interesting to me. Carla's dumping poor old Mac because he's sensitive. Isn't that we are all looking for in a man? We complain we can never find the sensitive, caring type and when we have him, we don't want him anymore.

"This is Mac." His voice is curious. Maybe Mac should dump Carla.

I pull up Mac's photo. He looks like a nice guy. A little thin, but handsome. His teeth aren't perfect, but whose are?

"Hi, Mac, I'm Jenn from Splitsville.com and I'm calling on behalf of Carla." I wonder if she made him grow the goatee. I imagine Mac without facial hair. I smile at the baby face lurking under. Could Mac go postal?

"What?" Mac is quick to question when he hears Carla's name. "Splitsville.com?"

I bury my head in my hands and push the idea away. "Yep. Carla hired me to break-up with you because you are, well, just a little bit too sensitive for her." I begin noting the steps in "the process."

He laughs, "I'm what?"

"She says you're too sensitive. She says you cry during those animal commercials." I don't blame him. I have to turn the channel every time I hear Sarah McLachlan's song playing on the television.

"Of course I do. I can't imagine what an innocent animal can do to warrant such treatment." Mac is in the explaining stage of "the process." He says, "Anyone who doesn't is heartless."

"I understand that, but she's breaking. . ."

Click.

I stop and listen. He hung up on me! "Great!" This is not going as smoothly as it needs to go. I punch in his phone number.

"Hello?"

"Hey Mac." I continue with my break-up, "I think we got disconnected."

"Nooo," he groans.

It's not a good sign when someone draws out their words.

"I hung up on you." His voice makes a sudden change from groaning to commanding. Definitely not the shy guy I first called.

"You know, Mac, you seem like a super nice guy, but some women want a strong shoulder to cry on or hang out with. Not someone they have to wipe tears off of and babysit or someone who enjoys chick flicks." Of course, not me. I'd love a guy who's into *Serendipity* or *Say Anything*, my two favorite movies.

I can't help but give him a little advice. "You know the guy that just hung up on me?"

"Sorry."

"Don't be sorry. *That's* the kind of guy a woman wants. Assertive, aggressive." I continue, "Throw in a few of those episodes and a good mix of sensitive and a girl won't be able to resist."

Click.

"Jesus, Mac!" I shake my fist at his picture, scolding him for hanging up on me *again*. "Let's try this one more time." I jam my finger against the numbers on the phone.

"Whaaaat?" A sniffling Mac answers the phone. I clue in on the typing noise in the background.

"Did you find Splitsville.com?" This is where I usually hammer the coffin shut, but Mac might go all suicidal on me and I don't want *that* on my shoulders. Potential murder is plenty, thank you.

"Man. That son of a bitch." Mac mutters.

Son of a what? That's a little harsh for Carla, but I decide not to say so. He seems to be taking this harder than I expected, plus it's not my job to solve his life issues.

"Come on, Mac, pull yourself together. Can you tell me why I'm calling?" I want to plead with him to say yes so we can both be put out of our misery. I've been thinking. And planning. And now I have to get on with my next victim-Michael Schultz.

"No," he mutters. "I don't understand."

"Why can't you? How have you been treating her?" I never get personal, but he's bringing it out of me.

Oh no! I become a little shaky, fear radiating through my veins. Has Bradley gotten to me already? Am I losing my touch? Am I getting weak because Cupid has shot me square in my butt?

I read down the dump file a little more. There has to be more than this sensitive crap. B. I. N.G.O!

"Mac, Mac, Mac." I know I have something that will really get him to understand. "It says here that she's tired of you spending all her hard-earned cash on dates you asked her out on."

"She's the one who wanted to go on those elaborate dates."

I'm starting to hear the anger in Mac's voice. I take another look at his picture and the sensitive face that might lurk under the facial hair isn't so visible to me anymore.

"Plus I haven't seen her because she's been busy."

"She has been busy. Busy finding Splitsville.com. She's tired of your freeloading ways. She likes men Mac. Real, hard core men. Men who make money and can take her out for a good time. Not a man who spends her money." I have to dig down deep on this. "Do you understand?"

"You don't have to be such a bitch."

"It's a little too late to man up, Mac. Do you understand you are being dumped by Carla using Splitsville.com?" My harsh voice booms through the phone.

"I'm going to puke." Mac's voice sounds distant and muffled. "Who am I going to date now?"

"Okay well I don't know who you're going to date and I don't care. But before you blow chunks can you please tell me you understand?" I cross my fingers in the air.

"Yes." Mac cries out like a sick coyote. "I understand. I got it. I've been dumped by Carla, the rich bitch. Thank you and good night."

"Thank you, Mac, for using Splitsville.com." I hang up, feeling as sick as Mac sounded and stare a bit longer at his picture and his not so perfect smile.

I glance at my watch. Shit! The house is barely clean and Bradley will be here any minute to pick me up. I have no time to dig into Dabi's situation.

Six

"Let's go before we are late." I look up at Bradley and realize he's a good five inches taller than me. I scoot Bradley out the front door so he can't look at the mess I didn't finish cleaning up. I could have done better than my jeans and white t-shirt, but with no other clean clothes, my options are limited. Bradley seems to like what he sees, and I relax.

I catch my reflection in the side mirror. Not bad, like I've always belonged right there. I look back over at Bradley. His hair whips around as the air travels through it. I've known him for what, 24 hours? And I'm already falling hard for him.

"This is going to be fun." He flashes his bright smile while his blue aura shimmers.

Erin is more than eager to meet up with us at the annual Spring Fling our community puts on to welcome spring. Every year Erin and I go dateless, but not this year. She's been so far up Kent's butt, the only way for me to see her is to see her is when she's with Kent. I still haven't shaken the uneasy feeling his aura gives me.

This year I'll introduce Bradley as my date and other single girls will flash me those looks I give the couples strolling along the lake, hand in hand. I've always envied those couples who ride the ferris wheel and kiss when it stops at the top. We are going to be *that* couple tonight. I'm not even worried about the auras and all the people.

What a difference a year makes. What a difference a day makes.

Park City is so pretty in the spring. The city has gone through great lengths to beautify downtown area. They added a new sidewalk with patches of grass sprinkled all the way down the street. Old time carriage lamp posts are adorned with Spring Fling flags and hanging flower baskets.

I'm not sure if it's the renewal of spring or the beginning stages of a new relationship that's lifting my spirits, but I like it.

In no time, the car ride is over. We pull into the parking lot, only to be flagged over into the grass near the lake. The paddleboats are in full swing, with the waiting line all the way around the lake. I smile due to the collective aura around the crowd. If only people can learn patience. I especially love watching the mothers' auras. They have little tolerance, but quickly turn when someone compliments their child.

Bradley steps out of the car and motions for me to wait. He opens my door.

"A true gentleman." I take his hand and step over the mud created by a car before us. He has to be a good five inches taller than me.

"I don't want you to have muddy toes."

I probably shouldn't have worn flip flops, but they were the closest to the door and like I said, I didn't have time to find anything. I guess if I did pick up my messy house, I'd have my shoes in one place and I wouldn't have this problem.

It amazes me where all of the people come from. I know there aren't this many people living in Park City. Or if they do, I haven't seen them. The tilt-a-whirl is in full motion. I am enjoying seeing all the eager faces on all the kids. The smell of cotton candy brings back all the wonderful times that Erin, Aunt Matilda and I spent coming here. A tradition.

"Scream if you want to go faster," the Alpine Rollercoaster operator yells in the microphone, and blood curdling screams are heard throughout the park. "Louder!"

I clamp my lips together to keep from squealing out loud and point toward the photo booth. "I've always wanted to get a picture in one of those," I say hoping Bradley will catch on.

Bradley rolls his eyes. "Is that your way of telling me you want to take a picture?" He's caught me in my trick to trap him.

"Yes." I do my best school girl impression then dig out the change from the bottom of my purse. "Can we?"

Bradley stops me from getting money out. "No let me." He puts his hands in his pocket and pulls out some change.

He's such a gentleman. Not to mention he's hot, a great kisser, and mine. "Are you mine?" I blurt.

He pulls me close and plants a kiss on my ready lips. "Definitely," he says, and I melt a little inside.

I pull back the curtains exposing a tiny metal stool. So the photo will be of me sitting on Bradley's lap. Sweet.

Bradley goes in head first and pats his leg. "Just for you, gorgeous." His hand brushes my hair behind my shoulders.

I close the curtain behind me and take my rightful spot. I keep my weight on my toes. I don't want to make his legs go to sleep, but he pulls me back and I practically fall in his lap. His arms curl around me, and a fuzzy sensation climbs up my body.

I look in the glass box. His blue aura is lying up against me. I've never been fond of blue on me, but his blue looks great and I comment on how good we look together.

"Let's do a silly one first," Bradley says. He twists his lips and flares his nostrils.

The flash goes off.

"Let's stare at each other." Bradley turns his face toward mine and I do exactly what he says. We are nose to nose.

The flash goes off.

"Kiss me." Bradley whispers before his lips press against mine.

The flash goes off.

He deepens the kiss, keeping it gentle and allowing his tongue to find mine. His hands move along my face. I don't dare move as they tighten to hold steady so he can have the kiss just how he wants it. I am more than willing to give it.

The flash goes off.

"That will be the best one." Bradley smiles, pulling away.

"I already know it's *my* favorite," I say and go back for seconds.

"What?" Bradley pulls back with a questionable look on his face. "You have a funny look in your eye."

I bit my bottom lip. I wonder if Dabi Stone ever got the chance to get her picture taken in a photo booth. I know I should tell him about Splitsville.com and who I really am. Only, I don't know him all that well and frankly I'm not ready to give up a blue aura.

"Nothing." I smile and lean in next to his ear. I twirl a little curl of his hair around my finger. "I'm happy. That's all," I whisper and go back for seconds, *again.*

***

"See." I'm so proud to have the one-inch by one-inch piece of paper and hold it up for Erin to see.

"Oh fun!" Erin turns to Kent and begins to beg him with a whining voice, "Let's make one."

Kent scoots his chair away from Erin. "No way."

Erin's smile fades, but she doesn't give up. "Please?"

Her words make me cringe. I hate hearing her beg. Why won't he do it? Why can't she find a guy that'll make her happy like Bradley's making me happy?

"Eh." He has no problem letting us know his disgust as he takes a quick look at my pride and joy. "Don't you think you're a little old for something so childish?" His eyes stab me in my soul and I wince. I can't stare too long or his aura will ruin the entire night.

"No." Bradley takes the picture from my hand. "We love it." He smiles and leans down giving me a peck on the cheek. Bradley speaks softly into my ear, "Don't mind him. He's jealous."

I inhale, bringing life back into my deflated body. Even though we've only known each other a short time, somehow Bradley knows exactly what to say.

He'll never hurt me like Kent will hurt Erin. Or at least that's what his aura tells me. And auras are *never* wrong.

"We like to go to The Gallery." Kent puts his arm around Erin as if he owns her. "Besides, we have some things to talk about."

La-ti-da! Who gives a big crap about going to The Gallery? It's a swank art gallery in the newly revamped downtown area where you have to dress up, drink wine, pretend you know art, and act like you're somebody you're not. Besides, Erin hates The Gallery, or at least that's what she said when 'Plan It' did the grand opening for them.

Erin gives Kent a questioning look. "Really? What?" Erin looks off into the dark.

I hide my surprised expression as I watch Kent's normal aura turn a more dull grey. The only time I ever see this is when someone's trust is about to be broken. I wonder what he's keeping from her.

Erin shakes her hair out of her face and gently touches his forearm. "Oh, okay." She looks at me and raises her brows while lifting her shoulders. "I'll talk to you tomorrow.

"Goodnight Kent." Bradley shakes Kent's hand then nods at Erin. "Goodnight."

"Night." Erin takes Kent's hand and lets him led the way.

I have to do something to stop her. "Are you sure you don't prefer a caramel apple over The Gallery's day-old cheese?" I sympathize with her.

She smiles and shakes her head no-like a good little girl.

I'm disappointed that Erin and I can't spend more of the evening together. I can tell by the slump in her walk that she's going to miss our Spring Fling tradition eating cotton candy, popcorn, elephant ears and riding the tilt-a-whirl until we're sick to our stomachs.

"Off to the ferris wheel and then the space rocket." Bradley takes my hand and leads the way.

I look over my shoulder to a pursed-lipped Erin who loves to ride the Ferris wheel. Unfortunately, I'm sure Kent thinks it's childish. Plus apparently he's about to break her trust.

"Can you believe that jerk?" I shake my head and grumble to Bradley. "She deserves so much better. I know there's more evil to him than he lets on."

I look back at them again and read Erin's body language. She's standing still as a statue while Kent's lips move a mile a minute. I can't make out what he's saying, but her open-mouthed stare tells me she's not happy about it.

"Come on, Olivia." Bradley nudges me closer to the ride. "We don't need to be involved in their relationship."

All the white bulbs going off in sequence with the music stirs an excitement helping me resist the urge to run back to her. "We do if he's hurting her." I glance back in time for Kent to catch my eye. He must've told her what was on his mind because his aura is black and I sure don't want that to touch me.

"Why do you think he's hurting her? It's an argument."

I shrug, zipping my lips. Every time I've told someone about my "gift", they've run off. Invasion of privacy. Freak. You name it, I've heard it. Bradley is a keeper, so the longer I can wait to tell him, the better.

"He's not hurting her. She's a big girl, she'll figure out what a jerk he is." Bradley pulls me toward the Ferris wheel. We stand with our feet on the mat and wait for our seat to swing by so we can board.

"You're right." I slip back into the seat and peer over the lake on the upswing of the ride.

I see the back of Erin's grey aura walking toward the parking lot, behind Kent's red aura. Red is usually good. Great even. It means passionate. Kent's red is mad. This relationship is exhausting and her aura tells me so.

I point in their direction. "Where are they going?"

"Who cares?" Bradley pulls me close and kisses me. I know he's hoping I will forget about Kent and Erin. "I'm going to learn everything about you, Olivia Davis."

If only. I frown, wishing I could tell him everything about what I see or who I really am.

***

The carriage lights are burning bright on our way through the deserted downtown streets. When we pass the retirement community, I glance down the side street and make sure Aunt Matilda's truck is neatly parked in front of her house. This way I know she's safe and sound at home.

The Mini-Cooper turns onto my dark street. For years I've begged the city to put streetlights in my neighborhood, but it's not high on their priority list. It's the oldest section of Park City and they'd have to put in all new electric lines in order for it to happen.

I've taken great pride in my little cottage house over the past few years and the spring flowers popping up along the white picket fence and along the cobblestone walk add to the cuteness I've been trying to achieve.

When I painted my door red, the neighbors chuckled. "She's young. Kids now-a-days, they don't know what looks good."

I rolled my eyes and chalked it up to them being old. Thank God, Aunt Matilda isn't like them. She loved it and helped me.

Bradley parks the car in my driveway and asks me the question I fear most. "Are you going to invite me in?"

I panic.

Is he a neat freak? Will my messy side be a deal-breaker for him? I'd say we're on step two of my dating stage list and being a slob is not a good trait to have.

"Uh, sure." My brain scrambles to think up a complete lie about the state of the house. "I've been working so hard for the past couple weeks, I can't guarantee the house is spotless." A total understatement.

I slowly turn the key and pray it's not as bad as I remember it being.

It's worse.

"Oh, just step over it." I refer to the empty shoebox in the middle of the floor.

I flick on the light revealing the clothes piles everywhere. They're on the couch, on the floor. A blouse is haphazardly tossed across the lampshade. A bra hangs on the closet doorknob where I'd hung it to dry. Not to mention the dirty dishes piled on the coffee table plus the kitchen counter top.

"Sorry, I haven't unloaded the dishwasher yet." I grab an arm load of clothes off the couch, snatching the bra at the last second, and hurry back to my room.

There is no way any hanky panky will be happening here tonight. My bed is a rumpled mess. The beige, goose-down comforter in a heap in the center, pillows and shams scattered on the floor. The rest of my wardrobe was thrown all over the room. I dump the pile in my arms on the floor with the rest of them and close the door behind me.

I find Bradley sitting in the free spot I cleared, only he's upright and not lounging back.

"Sit back." I gesture and pick up the pile of plates. I take them to the kitchen and add to the pile on the counter. I might not be good at cleaning, but I am good at moving piles around. I peer around the corner of the kitchen door. "Do you want something to drink?"

He raises his eyebrows. "Do you have any clean dishes?" he asks, and I see the fear in his eyes and curiosity in his aura.

My shoulders slump. "Yes." I try not to be hurt by his jab, since it's true and all. "I've been so busy lately. . ." I trail off. By the look on his face I know I can't tell him the truth. If he freaks about my messy house, think what he'll do when he finds out I'm sort of psychic. The truth about my "gift" or my problem with trying to keep my house clean—which one will scare him off?

"I was going to ask how you can stand such a messy house."

An uneasy feeling bubbles up in my stomach when I see his beautiful blue aura turn more into the Delft blue that is on my Aunt Matilda's china.

"My aunt's been visiting on top of it all." I swing my arms out. "Most of this is hers." I bite my lip wondering if he'll buy it. I touch my nose, also wondering if it's growing like Pinocchio's. Small. Pert. Phew.

His jaw muscles relax. He bought my little white lie. At least for now.

My tall tale grows as his freaking strong clean house principles surround him and light up his profile. "I can't stand this mess." I fluff a cushion and fold a blanket to make my lie seem real. "That's why I'm taking off tomorrow and cleaning the house." I vow then and there to live up to my lie and change my attitude about clutter. I'm not too old to change. I've been meaning to clean up my act anyway.

Once settled, we chat easily about how lucky we are that we met, about dogs, movies, and the sex appeal of the Ferris wheel.

"Come by and visit me at the SPCA tomorrow."

"Absolutely, I'll bring coffee."

He smiles, sitting back and stretching his arm out behind me. "What exactly is your dot com job?" My mind comes to a screeching halt and he continues, "You said something about heart research."

Shit, shit, shit. There is no good way to say I run a break-up service. It makes me sound cynical. Greedy. Heartless. "Let's not talk about work." I hand him a glass of chardonnay in hopes he will forget about the mess around him and stop questioning about my job. "Cheers," I say.

"To us."

Us. I like how that rolls off his tongue.

We each take a sip, and then Bradley takes my glass and finds an empty space on the table. He turns toward me and leans in until his lips meet mine. Even though Erin is on my mind, this night is turning out perfect.

Seven

Every morning for the past couple of days, I've been dedicated to reading the paper and turning on the news, searching for anything about Dabi Stone. There are still no leads, no motives, nothing.

"Now Joyce and Dan Stone are making a heart moving plea to seek justice for their daughter death." I stop dead in my tracks, my hair brush dangling in my long hair. I take a long hard look at the television at Dabi's parents who are doing a press conference and pleading for any breaks in the case.

My heart aches for Mrs. Stone and I want to reach through the TV and give her a big hug. Tears pool in my eyes and slip down my cheeks. There's nothing natural about having to bury any child, much less your own. Our children are supposed to outlive their parents, not the other way around.

The same frail woman who's been splashed all over the newspapers glares at the camera. "Know we will hunt you down until we find you. Money is no object. Michael, where are you?" I jump because her eyes stare through the TV, piercing my soul.

The crowd immediately begins shouting, "Who's Michael?"

My tears turn to acid. Crap! She blames Michael! My mind races. I yank the brush out of my hair, taking a patch of blonde hair with it. I listen to see if anything else is said about him while I focus the rest of my attention on the squatty bald man with his hand lightly rubbing down Dabi's mom's back. I can only conclude, by the process of elimination, it's Dabi's father.

The way he consoles her doesn't look as caring as a man whose daughter has been murdered. I guess I picture an angry man who wants revenge for his daughter. Not a man who is scanning the crowd with a slight smile on his face and a few nods.

I shove the empty cereal boxes out of the way to find a pen and jot notes. Of course there's not a scrap of blank paper to be found. I have to protect Splitsville.com. It's my business. My baby. My livelihood. And if Bradley finds out about it, I might lose him.

Dabi's mother sobs and begins to gasp for air. She's disheveled from head to toe. Her hair looks like it hasn't been combed in days; her clothes look like they came off my floor. She's bent over, and sort of broken. I look closer and notice her buttons aren't even buttoned right. But underneath it, I know she means what she says about hunting down Dabi's killer. Dabi's father stands straight as an arrow, and is much calmer than his wife. Too bad I can't see his aura through the screen.

I rush back to my office and quickly thumb through my filing cabinet, the one thing I do keep organized in my life.

"Michael Schultz," I say his name and wait for my body reaction. "Michael Schultz."

Hmm. . .when I generally repeat people's names I get an instant vibe, but not this time. I wait for a sign, a shiver or a shake. Even a burp will do. I feel nothing.

I dig in my files. The reputation of Splitsville.com, and my new relationship with Bradley, is on the line. With the wonderful technology of the internet, I Google whitepages.com and run a reverse search on his telephone number which gives me his street address. I scribble the address on his file and grab the newspaper clipping, and dash out the door.

I check my watch once I get into the car. 6:50 AM. Way too early for me, but this way I'll be able to get it over with. I'll read his aura and hopefully clear my mind. He has to have a clear aura. He'd be the first one the police will suspect. Isn't it always the boyfriend? And a disgruntled one at that.

I can't shake Mr. Stone's TV demeanor. I know that if my loved one was murdered, I wouldn't be so—together. But he's the dad. Why would her dad want to harm his daughter? Who else would want her dead?

If my hunches are right, Michael didn't do it and Splitsville.com is free. I'll hunt the killer down because there's no way my company's going to be saddled with the word murder.

Plenty of time to stake him out, read his aura, come up with my next plan of action, and still get ready to meet Bradley at the SPCA.

My car hugs the road as I weave through Park City back roads, taking the quickest route from the westside to the southside of town. It would've taken me twice as long to get there if I'd gone through town with all the pedestrians milling around.

Michael lives on the outskirts, where all the old buildings have been turned into one of the trendy areas to live in. It's not expensive, but the park draws the walkers and animal lovers. It's the same park where Dabi and I made our distaste for each other known.

I pull into a spot right in front of his building. The yellow brick, three-story-tall apartment complex doesn't look like anything Dabi Stone would step foot in. Granted there aren't many high-end apartments in Park City, but there are a lot better looking buildings than this.

It's no big deal if he sees me. He'll think I'm here for the walking trail in the park across the street—another perk to being an anonymous name behind a computer.

My phone rings, signaling a new dump has been delivered by email. I ignore it. It's commute time. Wednesday morning. People pour out of the building, and if I don't keep my eye out, I'm sure to miss him.

I look at each guy carefully and back at Michael's picture. The first guy's nose is too long compared to Michael's button one. Michael's shoulders are definitely more slim compared to the second guy.

I sit up a little taller and crane my neck to see the third guy coming out of the building. I strain to see under his baseball cap, but the blonde curly hair sticking out the back is not Michael's black short spiky cut.

Nothing. Nada. Not a one of them looks like Michael Schultz. 7:15 AM.

I roll the ball on my Blackberry. Might as well read the email dumps I'm going to have to catch up on. I begin making up some of the conversations I might have with the dumpee, but a little black yapping dog breaks my concentration. The malti-poo is rushing across the street with Michael attached to it.

The real life Michael and the photo of him don't jive. He looks much smaller in the picture. With his muscular build, he looks like a guy who would own a larger dog, a little more masculine. I snicker at the idea of the pint-sized dog.

I slip my sunglasses down on the bridge of my nose and watch him. I've got one good shot at this. I fervently hope I'm not wrong and that he's not involved.

My eyes adjust to a pretty lavender aura surrounding him. It flutters lightly behind each step as the malti-poo pulls him.

I sigh, almost forgetting why I'm there. I look at my steering wheel so my eyes will go back into normal-vision mode and take notes on his file. First, he has a dog, which shows he's caring and so lavender. Second the dog is leading Michael so he's not tense, so lavender. His aura makes me feel good. He's a free spirit, a dreamer. Far from a killer.

He crosses the street heading straight toward my car. I slink down in my seat and pretend to bury my head in my BlackBerry to hide from him. "Shh Belle," I hear him say as he passes my open window. He's walking directly in front of my car toward the park.

Belle? Strange name for a man's dog. This guy is not what he seems.

Once he's out of hearing distance, I turn the key to start my old Toyota. Only it doesn't start. A flash of panic sweeps over me. I check the air conditioner to make sure it's not the culprit that drained the battery. The lights are even off. I take the key out and put it back in and turn. Still nothing.

Click. Click.

Great! Of all the times I need it to start, it won't. Dead as a cold fish, as Aunt Matilda would say.

Please start, please start. I beg to myself with my eyes tightly closed and turn the key one more time. If I need good karma, right now would be the time.

Click. Click.

There's a knock on the driver's side window. Startled, I practically leap across my seat. Michael is smiling down at me. "Do you need help?" he asks.

I glance out the window and see Belle sniffing my tires.

Click. Click.

"It's not going to start," Michael affirms what I already know, and reclines himself up against the car, arms crossed. He doesn't budge. He nods to a pedestrian passing by. For a guy who's just been dumped by his girlfriend who turned up murdered, he sure does have an upbeat personality. "I can check under the hood."

I glance at the photo wedged between me and the seat to make sure I've got the right guy. Yep, positive. The slightly turned front tooth is a dead giveaway as his lips turn up in a smile.

The steering wheel jabs my breastbone as I lean into it. Surely I misread his aura, I make my eyes to go out of focus and scan his profile as he picks Belle up. The overwhelming lavender confirms there is no way he killed Dabi. He couldn't kill a fly. I'd bet money on it.

With a groan, I get out of the car. Maybe my aura reading is a little rusty.

He puts the Belle back down and steps up on the curb away from my car. "Every morning Belle meets all her friends at the park," he explains.

He's much taller than I envisioned him to be from his picture. Dabi sent a photo from the chest up and it was definitely a few years old. His hair is much shorter and he's not as preppy in person.

I can see why Dabi's dad wouldn't approve. I'm positive he would prefer the clean cut type, not the disheveled Orlando Bloom look that Michael seems to favor. Plus the little tuft of hair under his lip makes him appear to be more of a bad boy than he really is. He's not fooling me. Or should I say his aura's not.

"Funny name for a man's dog." I want to get some answers and fast.

"My girlfriend, er, ex, er, dead ex girlfriend gave her to me." The look on my face must've said all the words swirling around in my head. "My girlfriend broke up with me and then turned up murdered."

His face turns solemn. He reminds me of the guys who cry during Barbara Walter's interviews. Nonetheless, I still don't let my defense down.

"Hh!" I gasp out loud. I can't believe he's just unloaded on me—a perfect stranger. What else will he tell me?

"What?" He stands up tall, and jabs a finger at me. "No, hell no. I didn't kill her, if that's what you're thinking."

"Well I'm thinking it." I take a step back closer to my car. If he's willing to talk about it, I'm willing to ask. "You don't run into someone who tells you their girlfriend broke up with them and then she's murdered. Are you a suspect?"

I want to tell him anyone with a lavender aura couldn't kill a spider, but I don't I stay on guard.

"I don't think so. At least no one's come to see me." He looks off into the distance. "I have my suspicions, but I'll leave it up to the police." His eyes dip. "Do I know you?"

Shit! Shit!

"Ahh…no." I change back to my girly voice and open my car door to retrieve my phone. I have to change the subject. I quickly dial Erin's phone number. "I walk the park."

"I swear I've heard your voice." Michael inquisitively looks me over. Now I know it's time to get out of here. If he recognizes me as Jenn from Splitsville.com, he'll know this isn't a coincidental meeting.

"Hi, I need you to pick me up at Pleasant Ridge Park." Erin tries to ask questions as to why I'm out at 7:30 in the morning when I never get up any earlier than 10 a.m. "I'll explain when you get here. Come *now*."

I turn back around coming face to face with Michael.

"I swear I know you." His eyes narrow and he scratches his head. "But where?"

"No, nope you don't." I shake my head. God Erin, hurry up. I rock back and forth on my heels out of nervousness and look side to side for any sign of Erin's car.

"Where do you work?"

"Daycare," I blurt out the only job I've never tried. All those little auras running around would give me vertigo. I wouldn't last a day.

"Hmm." Michael rubs his chin like he isn't buying it. "So you've got a ride?"

Relief flows through my veins as slick as blood. "Yes. I'm just going to wait inside." I open my door.

"One more question." My stomach churns when I turn back to face him. He points to Belle who's biting my feet. "Do you always come to the park in pink fuzzy slippers?"

I look down, flustered. Sure enough, my toes wiggle inside the fluffy slippers. "Uh, um. . .good-bye," I blurt out and shut the door on him. I don't have to answer him.

I did what I came to do. Read his aura. I'm just glad it's telling me he's not Dabi's murderer. I turn back to look at Michael walking to the park as if everything with the world is okay.

***

"God what took you so long?" I grit my teeth.

She doesn't answer.

"You okay?" I ask Erin once I gather all my stuff from my car and put it in hers. "Are you mad that I woke you up?"

"No," she finally says. She starts driving, her hands gripping the steering wheel. "Kent and I had a fight last night."

I seize the opening. "Well, his aura. . ."

"Don't start with that aura stuff Olivia. I'm not in the mood. His *aura* is fine." She tears up. Her voice breaks, then she says, "We went out for a drink last night. I came out of the bar bathroom and this girl. . .this girl said something about him only dating women for their money. Then she slapped him!"

"For their money?" I'm not really surprised. It's the story of Erin's life. Though I wish I was wrong. That explains a lot of Kent's aura color and changes.

She stops at the red light, turns to me with furrowed brows and says, "Don't even think he's dating me because of my money. That's what he wanted to talk to me about when we left the Spring Fling." She speeds the car up.

I'm cautious with the words I chose. "So initially he sought you out because of your money and then changed?" Yea, *right*! If only she'd listen to what I see.

Erin's quiet personality begins to seep through and a tear trickles down her cheek.

"That's what the fight was about. He said he wasn't a grifter anymore and was trying to change his ways." Her sad eyes want to believe him and every word he says. "I just don't understand why a man would do something like that."

I do. I break-up with on people on Splitsville.com for this same reason. Only Kent seems to be dating women for their money as a job. I think about the dumpee Mac. Carla dumped him for being a freeloader. It's an epidemic. What happened to the man taking care of the woman?

"Erin, you're better than these guys. You'll find someone better than Kent."

Erin's jaw clinches. "I thought he was different," she says. "I don't know what I'm going to do."

It's silent in the car for a few minutes until she finally says, "I didn't even ask you why you were at Pleasant Ridge Park." She sits sideways in her seat after she parks in my driveway. I guess we are done talking about Kent.

"Listen, I don't have time to talk about it now, but how about lunch later today?" I want to get inside to my file about Michael Schultz and write down everything he said before I forget.

"I don't really feel like lunch." Erin is the type who doesn't eat when she's depressed. Me on the other hand, I'd wolf down the couch if it was the only thing left in the house. "Let's do it tomorrow."

"Okay." I have to let her off easy or she'll completely shut down on me. "But if you need me, promise you'll call."

She nods quietly as I get out of the car. And of course I know she won't call.

Eight

Aunt Matilda's old red and white Chevy in the driveway is a pleasant sight.

"Hello?" I scream into the quiet house.

I toss my keys on top of the pile of papers on the kitchen counter. Aunt Matilda comes out with a basket full of clothes in her hands. I call the local tow company and leave a message on their machine where to pick up my car. They know my '95 Toyota better than I do. It won't be a surprise to them to get my message. They will be surprised at the part of town, seeing as I try to avoid the Southside as much as possible. Especially since I went looking for juvie and my mom there so many years ago.

"Where have you been?" Aunt Matilda asks suspiciously as she dumps the clothes on the couch and starts folding.

I won't be able to keep much from her for long. She can read me like a book—always has, always will.

"I had to run a couple of errands before I take coffee to Bradley at the SPCA. Can I borrow your truck? My car broke down this morning." I smile and dismiss her cautious eyes.

She stares at me like she's waiting for the right answer.

I break the silence. "You don't have to do my laundry." I notice she has completely picked up all my clothes off the floor, couch, lamps and tables.

Even though it's a big help, I don't want her to feel like she's still raising me.

"I think it's high time you started to keep a house." She gestures around the room. I was hoping she didn't pick up on that little detail.

I snort. Doesn't she realize that is the *last* thing I want to do, or the *last* thing on my mind is keeping house.

"You do, do you?" I walk in the kitchen and pour myself a mug of the coffee she must've made and continue back to the bedroom as I ignore her pouring over the clothes on the couch. I yell over my shoulder, "I went for a walk. Seriously Aunt Matilda, I will clean my clothes. Just leave the basket there. You should go out with some friends. Or on a date."

I throw it out there. She definitely needs to get out more. A little adult companionship would do her some good. I frown thinking about seeing her lonely truck parked off Main Street last night.

She wouldn't even flinch. "I've given up on men. Since when do *you* walk?" She's not going to let this morning's episode alone.

"Since I need exercise." I stop and realize I'm going to have to answer questions I don't want to. I walk back down the hall to be interrogated.

"And you don't wear tennis shoes?" Her eyes look down at my fuzzy pink slippers.

Leave it to my palm-reading Aunt Matilda to notice every inch of me. "It's all about comfort." I know she's trying to bait me.

"So. . ." she follows me back down the hall and asks, "Where did you go to walk? Why not walk outside on your sidewalk?"

"All right." I turn around and almost bump into her. "I went to Pleasant Ridge Park."

"Pleasant Ridge Park?" She's holding the laundry basket full of clothes. "Is that where your car is?"

It's not the closest park, but it is the park Michael frequents.

"Please leave the laundry," I plead. I set my coffee on my nightstand and take the basket from her. I dump it on the pile of clothes already on my bed. I pick up my mug and take a sip, hoping she'll stop questioning me. "Pleasant Ridge Park."

"Don't worry. I've got nothing better to do, except to find out who DS is in your journal." She walks out of my room and down the hall.

I almost choke on my coffee. I immediately turn, and rush back to her. "Give it over. You can't just read people's private journals!"

"Not until you tell me what you are up to." I can see the journal in her hand behind her back. "I know how your personality changes when you use your gift and I want to know what you're looking for."

"Give it to me." I hold out on her, but I know good and well she's going to win. She's relentless and knows me better than anyone. She plays hardball.

"Start talking or I won't let you use my truck."

"Fine." For free is a bargain, so I spew like a volcano. Just once I'd like to one up her, but that will be a challenge. "You know that girl, Dabi Stone, the one they found murdered?"

Aunt Matilda nods and mouths DS.

"Well, a few weeks ago she hired Splitsville.com to dump her boyfriend because her high falutin' father didn't approve. I wave my hand in the air and say, "The boyfriend, he was upset but was okay by the end of the dump phone call. But now she's dead. "

Aunt Matilda's skirt jingles as she shifts her weight. "And?"

"And her mom is devastated while her dad seems too quiet. Plus her mom mentioned Michael, the ex, during a news conference this morning. If they track down Michael, they'll connect the dots to Splitsville.com."

"If I recall, and I'm old, but I remember we don't have a good history with that girl. Leave it to the police." Aunt Matilda's tone is more threatening than comforting. "You're going to end up in over your head."

I know Aunt Matilda is concerned and doesn't want anything to happen to me.

"I can't. Then everyone in town will find out that I'm Jenn from Splitsville.com and I will have to get another job and you know how that'll go." I take a sip and look into my coffee. Anything to avoid her suspicious little mind. "Besides, I love my creation."

"What does your dream have to do with it?" she asks. I know she isn't going to let it go.

"I don't know yet. All I know is Dabi's initials are floating around like I need to dig deeper into her murder." I take a long slow breath because hearing it out loud only confirms that my dreams are back and in full force. "Only I don't think Michael did it."

"Of course he did. He's beyond hurt." Aunt Matilda sways side to side jingling all the way to the kitchen to fill up her cup.

I follow behind her.

"I didn't get that from his aura today." I throw my hand over my mouth. How could I be so stupid? Every time I say I'm reading someone's aura, there's a vested interest and Aunt Matilda wants to know all about it.

She points her finger in the air. "Ah ha! So that's why you went to Pleasant Ridge Park. I knew something was up because you only go there twice a year since your playground fiasco."

She's right. I go for the SPCA event for Erin and the annual Spring Fling.

"I had to, Aunt Matilda. I need to know if he killed her because of Splitsville.com."

"I can see we're going to lose sleep over this." She knows me all too well.

"I hope not." But positive thinking isn't going to help me now. The past has proven that. There is definitely more digging I need to do about Michael, but it's going to have to wait. "I've got to get my shower and meet Bradley."

Aunt Matilda puts her arms around me. Something I need. "Go visit Bradley and we can figure this out along the way."

Aunt Matilda always knows how to calm me down and help me figure things out. Today is no different.

Nine

"So what's the deal with Bradley?"

I jump, startled out of my thoughts. I turn to find Creepy Kent standing behind me in line at the gas station. It takes everything I have not to throw my high-priced coffee on him.

I turn back around and concentrate on getting to the front of the line so I can pay. "There's no deal." The quicker I get out of here, the better off we'll both be.

His aura flashes, shifting from red to orange causing his blonde hair to be tinted with a hint of brown. There is a tinkle in the corner of his eyes as they narrow. "Come on, you can tell me." The battle of the auras form around him. The red big 'ego' aura versus his orange 'determined' aura. Besides, why would I tell him anything? Especially since Erin told me all about his past.

I remind myself that Erin likes him for a reason. He must not be all bad. "No deal," I repeat.

He shrugs and leans against the counter. "If you say so. You and Erin have been friends for a long time."

It's a statement, not a question, and I'm not sure if he expects me to answer. I grunt noncommittally.

"Help a guy out," he says, his aura vibrating, shifting to a more rustic red. My radar goes off. Manipulator. "What's her ideal date?"

If I stare too long his aura will create a dizzy mess in my head.

He flashes his million-dollar smile and I get a glimpse of why women like Erin fall for him.

I threaten him through my gritted teeth. "I'm on to you. I know about the girl from last night. Erin told me." He needs to know that he can't get one over on me.

That shuts him up. His smile fades, but he recovers at lightning speed. "It was a mistake. I'm into Erin." Kent digs out money from his pocket.

Liar. Auras don't lie. I slam down my cash on the counter. "Keep the change," I tell the cashier, and bolt out the door.

I zoom out of the parking lot, resisting the urge to turn my car around and run him over. He's not worth a lifetime in jail.

I can't believe what a creep he is. But he's right about one thing, Erin will never believe me. Not yet anyway. I've got to come up with a plan to tell her about him and that aura. But carefully.

***

I spend the entire way looking in my mirror to make sure Kent isn't following me. "Slow down," Bradley mouths as I blaze into the SPCA lot. "Where's the fire?"

"I was afraid I was going to be late." I avoid his concerned stare. I smile and hand him his cardboard cup. "Plus I don't want our coffee to get cold."

Bradley's shaggy hair is still damp and his cologne trails him as I follow him to the front of the SPCA. I stop just shy of the door. The smell of animals envelops me.

He grabs the door and holds it open, looking curiously at me. "You okay?"

I'm suddenly afraid to go in. "Are they going to make me cry?" Images from the SPCA commercials of the dog's sad eyes resonate in my brain.

"No." He rubs his hand along my arm. "Remember we are a no-kill SPCA. All the animals here are loved and we have the staff to prove it."

He holds the front door wide open and I walk in under his arm.

There are people and their aura's everywhere, not to mention the dog's auras. The little girl holding on to the leg of an older woman wiggles her fingers at me. My gift attracts children. I wiggle my fingers back.

There seem to be a lot of adoptions going on and the atmosphere is almost euphoric. Every aura is happy and fulfilled with love, it knocks me for a loop.

I stop at the front desk and put my coffee down. I grasp the lip of the counter. All the auras of humans and animals begin to swirl causing me to lose my balance.

I've never been confined in an area full of dogs. The SPCA yearly fundraiser is outside where the dogs' auras breathe, but a confined kennel area might send me into a tailspin. Animal auras aren't much different from human auras.

Bradley drags me into another room and the dizziness immediately subsides. "Are you sure you're okay?"

"I'm fine." I sound as upbeat as I can. Being off balance, makes me more confused. I whisper so the girl who's cleaning the dog cage won't hear me, "I haven't slept well in the past couple of nights. Plus creepy Kent. . ."

I stand on my own, but once I let go of Bradley's arm, my legs wobble.

"Come on, Olivia!" Bradley grabs the chair next to the door and eases me into it. "I want a relationship with *you*, not with you and Kent. What's the deal?"

The girl at the dog cages glances over her shoulder like she's trying to hear what we're saying. She pushes her glasses up the bridge of her nose.

"No deal," I say under my breath. I really want to get my wooziness under control and thinking about Kent isn't helping.

"You talk about Kent and Erin all the time." Bradley looks over at the girl, who's now staring at us, and pulls me up from the chair and into the other room. "Listen, Olivia, I don't know you well yet, but I want to. Kent isn't part of that, so if this is the way it's going to be, then maybe we aren't going to work."

I look down taking in every crease in the old tile floor. I can't face him with all the lies between us. I can't tell him about the auras or he won't stick around.

Bradley tilts my head up to look at him. "I want to date you. Not you, Erin and creepy. . ."

"Ha!" I clap my hands together. The room has stopped spinning, and I stand up on my wobbly legs and hold onto the back of the chair. "You think he's creepy too."

"I never said I didn't, but I'm not going to waste every conversation on him and his creepiness." Bradley steps back and crosses his arms.

"I saw him at the gas station when I stopped to get our coffee. He knows you and I are seeing each other, so I got a little freaked when he wanted details of my relationship with you. It's like he has no boundaries." Bradley reaches out to take my hands and his warmth is a welcome touch.

"God, I wish that guy wasn't in Erin's life."

"Yeah, me too." I turn when I hear the shuffle of the dog cage girl coming into the room. "I promise, I'm going to tell Erin everything."

"If he doesn't stop harassing you, I'll take care of him." Bradley's blue aura began to darken around him.

"Wow, I hope I don't ever get on your bad side," I say half joking.

"Don't worry. You could never make me very mad."

Feeling much better, we walk down to the dogs that need to have their morning ritual.

"Every morning we get the dogs and throw balls or Frisbees. Sometimes they just want to be petted." He gestures toward a small grey dog.

"Hi there." I put my fingers through the cage Bradley stops in front of. I try not to look at all the other small eyes begging to get out of the cages. I don't need to see any more colliding auras today, especially animal ones.

"That's Herbie. He's a Schnauzer." Bradley opens the cage and Herbie jumps up on me. Bradley hands me the leash. "Put him on his leash and we can take him for a walk."

Herbie jumps up and down like he knows exactly what the leash means. Once I manage to get the leash on him, I take the ponytail holder off my wrist and pull my hair up.

"He likes you." Bradley smiles as I finally manage to get the out-of-control dog on a leash.

"I think he likes the idea behind the leash, not me." Still, Herbie is adorable with his grey hair and mustache, and happy about going on a walk. If only life was that simple.

"You need a dog." The delight in his eyes scares me.

"Forget it! I don't have time for a dog." I don't want any stinking dog to take care of. Or at least for Aunt Matilda to take care of.

I follow Bradley through the steel doors leading outside with Herbie close on his heels. It looks like a doggie daycare. All the dogs are running around, playing fetch or chewing on bones. Every one of them has a happy and healthy aura.

"Harmony." Peacefulness blankets me when I see how happy these dogs are. A sigh of relief comes over me. "Definitely not like the commercials."

Bradley smiles and says, "Nope. They love running around and playing with each other."

"Bradley, I hate to interrupt, but Sam doesn't look so good." The meek shelter worker from the dog cages can barely look Bradley in the eye, hiding behind her glasses.

"I'll be right back," he tells me. He puts his hand up for me to stay put, but I don't. "He's sick and we don't know what's wrong. You don't want to see him."

"I'll be okay." I'm certain I can tell them what's wrong with the dog.

Quickly we rush down the dimly lit hallway. The fluorescent lights buzz as we pass under them and the old tile creaks with old age. The oldness of it makes me think the sick animals are kept here.

The black lab lies on some blankets in the kennel, not moving. Bradley crouches next to her moving her stuffed animals out of the way.

"Sammy girl, what's wrong?" Sammy lifts her sad eyes up to him when he calls her name.

I crouch down next to him and touch her short prickly fur. Bradley stands back causing the timid girl to stand even farther toward the kennel door. His eyes are full of confusion, but he allows me to continue.

"Hi girl." I stare, allowing my eyes to go out of focus. I gently rub my hands down her back. Her spine feels good and she's not too thin.

Animals can sense when something or someone is good or bad. Sam is calm and relaxed, which gives me a good overall view of her.

She licks me and her black aura begins to surround her tongue and flows along her body. "It's okay, girl." I work to gain her trust. She laps at my hand. "I want to help."

Her ailments hit me like a ton of bricks. I inhale deeply and exhale slowly so I won't alarm Bradley or the other worker.

"I know. It's sad." Bradley put his hands on my shoulder.

"Shhhh." I look to see where Sam's aura darkens so I will know where to tell them to look. I know when I get home, I will be exhausted. Because this poor girl is really sick.

When she stops licking me, I slowly stand up so as not to disturb her.

"Do you have a veterinarian here?" I look back at Bradley and see the suspicious eyes of the girl. I ask her, "What's your name?" Bradley rushes to introduce us.

"Oh, Bree, this is my girlfriend, Olivia."

I put my fingers in my ear. All my energy has been zapped and I know I didn't hear him correctly.

Girlfriend?

"I'll get Dr. Versant." Bree takes off down the hall to get the house veterinarian. We bend back down to pet Sam.

"She's perked up a bit." Bradley allows her to give him kisses.

"No, she's just relived that I know what's wrong with her." My palms start to sweat. I can't believe I let that slip.

"What?" Bradley stares at me like I've lost my marbles.

A tall balding man in a white lab coat strides up to us. The quiet Bree is standing behind him. "What's the problem?" Dr. Versant asks.

I stand up, trying not to cower under Bradley's scrutiny. "I had a dog with Addison's disease and he looked a lot like Sam. See. . ." I have to find a good way to tell the veterinarian what Sam and her aura told me without them knowing. I take a couple of really deep breaths to gain strength to explain my findings.

It only takes a couple of minutes of explanation until Dr. Versant picks up on the symptoms.

"I think you saved her life," the veterinarian says while collecting the items he needs to begin treatment on Sammy.

Bree stands by the door with her hand firmly planted on the knob. "I'm going to finish up cleaning the cages." She quietly shuts the door leaving an eerie silence between Bradley and me.

"So." He keeps a good couple feet between us. I know where this is headed and it's no good. "You want to tell me what this is all about?"

He keeps his eyes completely focused on me. I crouch next to Sammy with my knees close together and my hands resting on them. I don't have a good excuse or an explanation at this point. My ruse with the vet didn't fool him.

"You've never had a dog. Or at least that's what you told me a few dates ago."

Crap! How could I forget that little detail? "I… I really have to go. I have to get to work." I check my watch.

"Olivia?" Bradley follows me to my car.

"I'm late," I say and pull my hair out of the ponytail. "See you tonight?"

He hesitates for a few seconds before saying, "Sure, okay. Then you can tell me what just happened in there."

I nod as I drive away, but inside I'm saying goodbye to the loveliest relationship I've ever had.

Ten

Somehow I have to get some work done today. And it's a good way to get Bradley, creepy Kent, and Sam the dog off my mind.

I pull up the next dump in line. This one has been hounding me for days. I scroll down the computer screen to read the reason for the dump and prepare my little speech for the dumpee.

I scan, then freeze.

"*What*?"

I re-read the reason out loud and slowly. "My boyfriend killed someone, and I can't take the guilt. I moved out of town and don't want him to know where I am. He doesn't have my cell number. Please do this for me. I am worried for my life."

Oh my God! Of course this has to be the first dump of the day. And someone wants me to dump a killer? I'm trying to stay out of jail, not get there. I can't do this even under the best circumstances-which isn't right now with the looming death of client Dabi Stone. I do not want anyone else's blood on my hands.

I quickly find Sabrina Reed's phone number on her file and dial the not so secret cell number.

"Hello?" I'm a little taken aback at her answering. I most certainly wouldn't answer any phone if I were privy to a murder. Sabrina's sultry voice throws a big red wavy flag my way. "Hello, is anyone there?"

Damn! I forgot to block my number by typing in star sixty-seven before I dialed her number. "Hi, is Sabrina there?" I decide not to hang up because she is going to have this number either way now. I kick myself for getting sloppy.

"This is Sabrina."

Okay, seriously Sabrina, I want to say, you're not good at hiding if you answer your phone and don't change your name.

"I'm Jenn from Spiltsville.com. I received a request from you to dump your boyfriend. You, um, you said he *murdered* someone." I can't stop myself from thinking she's an idiot. "I'm just letting you know that your request to break-up isn't going to happen. You have to go to the police."

"I can't do that, Jenn." Sabrina sounds like a strong girl, and awfully together for someone who fears for her life. "You have to break-up with him or he's going to kill me. Isn't that what your service is for?"

"No, as a matter of fact, my service is all about helping people get into better relationships by shedding the old ones. I can not be an accessory to any murder or put my company's name through the mud."

"So you're telling me that with all the crazy people out there, you've never had any request like mine?"

"Breaking up? Yes. Breaking up because you have pertinent information about the life and whereabouts of a human being's murderer? No!" I practically come out of my seat. I wish I had a picture of her. "Again, No!"

All the clues point to this dump as a fake. She did pay so it must be real. I pull up the picture of her murderous boyfriend. He looks more like a book nerd to me.

"How much?" she asks.

I rub my temples. "How much what?"

"How much more money is it going to cost me for you to dump him and not go to the police?"

"First, you can't bribe me." The nerve of her. Of course first I have to figure out exactly how I'm going to

alert the police without also alerting them that I'm behind
Splitsville.com, but Sabrina doesn't need to know that.
"And second, I am going to give all this information to the
police. I'm obligated to by law."

"Wow. Did you eat some bitch cereal today, Olivia?"

I fall off my chair. Oh my god! She'd picked up on the
fact I didn't hide my number and now she knows my real
name. Think! Think!

"What did you call me?"

"Are you referring to Olivia or Bitch?"

I'm just plain offended by her comment. It snaps me
out of my panic. "My name is Jenn and I do like bitch
cereal and not only did I have a bowl, I had two." I slam
down the phone and anonymously make a call to the local
Park City police department.

"911 what's your emergency?" the operator asks.

"Yes, I'm not going to say my name, but…" I use my
best southern drawl that sounds much like a dead cat.

I tell the operator the names and numbers of both
Sabrina and her murderous boyfriend and hang up. There is
no way I'm going to expose who I am or how I know the
information I gave her. Plus, if I keep it under a minute
they can't trace my call, right?

Or at least that's how it is on all the cop shows—under
a minute. God, I hope they're right.

"What are you doing?"

I jump around to find Aunt Matilda in a new tie-dyed
peasant dress. Her coal black hair is in two low pigtails.
"You scared me. I didn't know you were coming by today."

She makes her way back to the kitchen. "I didn't know
I had to call."

I follow her to make sure I didn't hurt her feelings.
That's the last thing I need to worry about. "No you don't,

it's just that normally I can hear you coming. I love your new dress. And your pig tails are very endearing." I see the sparkle come back to her eye. She can never turn down a compliment.

"Oh, just trying something new." She works her way around the kitchen like a busy bee making another pot of coffee, while wiping the counter behind her.

"I have another client, but I'll take a cup of coffee afterwards," I say walking back down the hall. That will be a good time to catch her up on Dabi, Kent and Michael.

Some dumps just have to be fast. There doesn't seem to be a lot of meat on this one. Michelle is breaking up with Keith because they aren't right for each other and they both know it. I can get this one over before the coffee is done brewing.

"Hello, is Keith there?" I ask when a guy answers. From his picture, he's boring as dirt. Blond hair, glasses, and no expression. No wonder Michelle's dumping him.

"Mm, yeah," he confirms.

"Hi Keith, I'm Jenn from Splitsville.com." *The place to come if you want to be murdered*, I think. "I am calling on behalf of Michelle. She hired Splitsville.com to break-up with you because she says every time she tries to do it herself, you get angry or depressed."

"It's a little too late for April Fool." Keith chalks it up to a joke.

"Keith this isn't an April Fool's joke. You know and she knows you aren't good for each other, so just let it go."

It seems to sink in. "How do you expect me to do that?"

"I don't know. That's beyond my realm of expertise. I do the breaking up, not the healing. I do know that you are going to call her when we get off the phone but don't. She won't answer." I convince him to just cut his loss and move on.

"Of course I'm going to call her."

"Don't do that. How would I know all of this if this was a joke? She's not going to take your call," I assure him. I can't bring myself to be a smart ass. Since Dabi, I'm afraid every dumpee might go cap the dumper.

"Keith today of all days, this needs to be really simple. All I need is for you to tell me you understand." I have to cut to the chase and finish this call so I can get all of my problems off my chest by talking to Aunt Matilda. The coffee smells delicious.

"I guess," he mutters, which is all I need to hear. If I look up "guess" in the dictionary, I'm sure affirmation would be in the definition.

I don't care. I take it. "Thank you for using Splitsville.com." I hang up the phone just as the doorbell rings. I hop up to answer it, but Matilda beats me to it.

"Hi Matilda."

I peek over her shoulder to see who's at my door that knows her.

The police officer standing in front of her catches a glimpse of me, then looks back at her. "Hello Carl, it's been a while." Either Aunt Matilda is eating a sour grape or she just sounds like it.

I stare at the six foot tall thin man and wonder what Aunt Matilda's distaste is. His salt and pepper hair is cut short exactly the way Aunt Matilda likes on a man, so it can't be his appearance. Maybe it's his aura?

It really it sounds like Aunt Matilda is a little hacked off at Carl. Never having heard my aunt speak to anyone in this tone, I want to stay and listen a little longer. Not that

I'm eavesdropping. It is my house, and wait. . .why is he here?

I keep silent, watching the ping-pong game going on between them.

"How have you been?" He takes his hat off in a well-mannered Park City man way.

"Fine. I don't believe you told me why you're here." She's so suspicious. Interesting.

"I didn't know you lived here." He looks back at me and then right back at Aunt Matilda. "And I *didn't* tell you why I'm here."

He glances over her shoulder to take another look at me.

"I don't. You remember Olivia don't you?" she asks. To me she says, "Do you remember Carl, one of the police officers I used to work with?"

I vaguely remember him giving me a doughnut once and his being one of the few nice auras around that place, but other than that, no. The muddy blue aura surrounds him causing me to wonder what he's scared to say.

I smile, trying to hide my nervousness, but my lip starts to twitch. "Hi, Carl. Good to see you." I nod, and have to close my eyes and steady myself by holding onto my aunt. His aura begins to radiate around me causing me to become dizzy and nauseous.

Not now. I repeat over and over in my head for this feeling to go away.

"I'm sorry Carl, my niece isn't feeling well." Aunt Matilda steps back in the room holding onto my arm. She begins to shut the door and I focus on *her* aura, not his. "We will have to continue our chat later."

He catches the door and pushes it a little wider. "I'm sorry, Matilda, I need to speak to your niece."

"Don't worry honey. I've been taking notes." Her eyes narrow letting Carl know she's not happy about this. Aunt Matilda can tell I've seen something, and walks me to the couch.

"I'm sorry you're not feeling well Olivia, but can you answer a couple of questions for me?" Carl tries to be as nice as a policeman can be.

"I'm fine," I assure my aunt. It's not like I wasn't expecting them.

Aunt Matilda jingles her way back into the family room with a cup of sweet tea for me. "Extra sugar, just like you." She pats my head.

Carl sits in the chair closest to the couch. "I'm sure you've heard about the murder."

Dabi Stone? What's this got to do with Dabi? I'm a bit confused, but I'm not about to confess to anything.

"I heard about it on the news." I have to admit I know about it, because I could fart and everyone in Park City would know about it.

"Did you know Ms. Stone?" Carl pulls out his little notebook. He clicks his pen and is ready to take some notes.

I tilt my head and give Carl a questioning look.

"Dabi Stone, the victim." Carl reminds me. "Did you know Ms. Stone?"

"Dabi?" I roll my eyes in my head. "Um…no."

"Really? You've lived in Park City all your life and don't know Ms. Stone? Dabi as you call her."

"Of course I know who she is, but I don't know- know her." I take a gulp of tea to get the knot down my throat. "We went to school together."

"I see."

I strain my neck a little to see if I can make out what he's writing on his little pad.

"I mean…" I sit a little taller. This is completely the truth if I don't count a few weeks back when I saw her at the coffee shop. "I haven't spoken to her in years."

Really it's not a lie, because she's the one who said hello to me and I didn't say anything back. I take another drink of tea.

"So how does Splitsville.com work?"

I choke on my tea and spray it all over Carl's face.

"Oh," I grab a shirt from the pile of clothes on the floor, and wipe at his face. "I'm so sorry."

Carl moves away from my dirty- well I really can't tell if it's dirty- shirt. "I've got it." He pulls a big hanky from his pocket and wipes off the dribbles of tea and pieces of lemon peel.

"Now, I guess you might have some information about Dabi Stone." He stands with that damn notebook in his hand. With a smirk on his face and a sarcastic tone, he says, "We took her computer from her house and noticed she used a break-up service. We staged a break-up and to my surprise, turns out it's you who's been breaking all these people's hearts. Talk of the town."

"I…" I take a gulp and proceed once I see his blue aura mutate into a bright yellow. He's aura tells me he's fishing for answers. "I've done nothing wrong. I told Sabrina I won't do the dump and I immediately called the police."

"Yes you did, and that's how we got your number." He isn't being so Mr. nice doughnut cop guy anymore.

"But I star-sixty-seven'd my number, and it was under a minute." Those damn cop shows are never right. Those producers need to do better research.

"Yes, but you didn't with Sabrina, and you were on with her for about seven minutes. Sabrina is an undercover cop with Park City's police. New girl, real nice and good at her job." He smiles like a teenage boy who just stole his mom's Victoria's Secret catalog out of the mailbox.

"We need to know everything about Miss Stone's break- up and would greatly appreciate all the files you have on her. You do have files on all your clients—right?" His salt and pepper hair glows brighter with his new silver aura.

"I do somewhere, but I'll have to dig them out and it may take a couple of days." Total lie, but his radiant glow says he's open to what I have to say. Plus, I want to gain more time to talk to Michael.

"I expect them at the police station by tomorrow or Park City's finest will be back with a subpoena. I'm sure you don't want the whole town to know who Jenn from Splitsville.com is." He reminds me of the Cheshire cat in Alice in Wonderland. I don't focus on any part of him or I just might break. Which is just what he wants, I know. "Good to see you again Matilda." He puts his hat on. "Oh, and Olivia-don't leave town."

I stay on the couch and let my aunt walk Mr. Cop Carl out. If I stand, I just might fall over.

"Sounds like you have some explaining to do?" I say when Aunt Matilda slinks back into the room.

She squirms. "No, little girl. You do."

There's no sense in trying to pry out why she acted like she did when she saw Carl. She's more closed up than Fort Knox when it comes to her personal life. And there's no way I can keep anything from her. She might be getting up in age, but her psychic instincts haven't gotten anything but sharper. Or maybe she's more in tune since retiring.

"Dabi Stone." I arch my eyebrows. I know she hasn't forgotten the incident with Dabi, her nanny and her mom. This isn't going away. Any murder in Park City has a tendency to hang around longer than the stench of the dead body itself.

Aunt Matilda creeps along the edge of the couch, sits and leans back making a nice cocoon for herself. "Yes, I remember her." She puts her hands in her lap and listens just like she always does.

I continue to tell her about everything I've uncovered including Michael and his aura. "I don't think he did it, but he is their number one suspect. Plus the police will let the world know that I'm Jenn."

And that would mean Splitsville.com would be *split up.* One, the people I've dumped will come after me, and two, no one will want me to know all their business. With Jenn, they trust her because they have no clue she's part of the community.

"If everyone finds out that I'm. . ." Big ole' James pops into my head and I look Matilda in the eyes, ". . .I'm afraid my murder will be featured on the six o'clock news."

Eleven

I'm surprised to see my Toyota back in my driveway. I must've slept right through Aunt Matilda's mechanic dropping it off.

Today's the day. I readjust the rear view mirror and check my face. I want to make sure it's compassionate enough for Erin when I give her the big news about Kent and his alarming aura. My eyes glisten like freshly cut grass, but my dirty blonde hair hangs like spaghetti noodles leaving me feeling the way I want her to see me—ugly. But my insides are smiling at the fact she will be rid of him good and for all.

She's meeting me at the SPCA so I can snag Herbie for a couple of days. Despite everything, that little pooch has been on my mind. If I know Erin, she'll be complaining about what happened at the bar, and her fight with Kent, giving me the perfect opportunity to tell her that her creepy, perfectly put together Kent is the real dog, not Herbie.

My BlackBerry blinks, but it's going to have to wait. Erin is more important than any dump on my email.

I pull into the SPCA parking lot, and see her at the entrance. I squint to see exactly what kind of shape she's in. She's smiling and waving at me with Bradley standing next to her. I squint harder, noticing that not a single hair is out of place and her clothes match. Plus the Starbuck's coffee she's holding is a sure sign she's in denial or something has changed since we talked. Every other time a guy has dumped her, she doesn't leave the house for days—not even for her favorite coffee.

Bradley hunches his shoulders next to her and lifts his brows. There is something too happy about her and we know it.

If Bradley told me he was a grifter, I'd kill him. I wouldn't be able to get out of bed. As I approach I turn down my lip and tilt my head letting her know she doesn't have to be so strong.

"What?" She gasps. "What's wrong?"

How sweet. I can't believe it. She puts all her needs aside, thinking something is wrong

with me. I stretch my arms out to comfort her. I'm ready with a strong shoulder for her to lean on.

"You don't have to pretend with me." I go in for the big hug and rub her back to let her know everything is going to be fine and she can rely on me. I'm determined to help her find a guy—a good one. "You're my best friend."

"Pretend what?" She shoots a look at Bradley. Bradley pretends like he doesn't know what's going on.

Okay, so she's lost it or she doesn't want to talk about it in front of Bradley. I can't believe she's in denial about Kent. Not twelve hours ago she was hysterical about what he did.

"Um, last night?" I reach for her hand. The last thing I want to do is make her uncomfortable. "We don't have to talk about this right now."

Bradley rolls his eyes. My heart takes a little dip. I know I told him I would drop it, but after all, she's my best friend.

She pulls her hand away. "Oh-about that. Kent explained everything, and he's changed. I really believe him. The entire situation has been totally blown out of proportion." She smiles, looking completely at ease.

Panic begins to curl inside my stomach. He did, did he? I want to say but decide to hear her out. "Really?"

"Yeah." Erin's happiness is making me nauseous. "Everyone needs a second chance."

I look over at Bradley, who's completely ignoring the situation like I should be doing, moving farther and farther away from the drama. Either that or he's doing a good job pretending.

I stare blankly. I can't help myself. "You mean he dates women to get a free ride and he told you he's changed?" How does someone change just like that?

"So," she continues waving her arms around as she explains, "it was a girl who accused him of using her. She's mad because he dumped her. He didn't take any of her money."

Now I know she's definitely lost it.

"That company of yours has totally zapped your faith in love," she finishes. Carefully she takes a sip of her coffee.

"Shh! Keep your voice down!" I look around making sure no one heard, especially Bradley. "No it hasn't. It's opened my eyes to situations people in love are oblivious to."

I reach down for my vibrating BlackBerry. I resist the urge to yell at her. I can't believe she is letting him off the hook this easy.

Erin drags me inside the front room where there's a little more privacy, and away from yelping dogs.

"I can't believe you haven't told him yet. Let me guess-dot com business? You know, you're like the pot calling the kettle black. Kent has a past, but he came clean. Can you say the same thing?" She shames me and shakes her head in disapproval. "Bradley has a right to know."

I smile, but what she said hits home. I'm no better than Kent. My friend knows me all too well, and she's called a spade a spade. I do wonder how Bradley will feel about my job once I tell him, but I can't worry about that right now. I have to figure out if Kent is using Erin or not. Plus if I think about Kent, I don't have to think about the end of my relationship with Bradley.

"Hey!" Erin twists her head around the door and yells out. Echoes bounce off the old tile floor and white walls.

"What?" I look around her shoulder to see who she's yelling at.

"That's her." She points in the direction of a completely empty hall. "Did you see her?"

I strain my neck looking down the empty hallway. "That's who? I don't see anyone."

"Great, thanks Olivia." Erin's frown is deep, and her forehead's crinkled. She points down the hollow hall. "I think I'm hallucinating. There was a girl there."

"What girl? I didn't see a girl." I look back down the hallway to confirm. Totally deserted. Bradley isn't even around. He must've gotten bored waiting for our little pow-wow to be over.

Erin looks concerned, but she shrugs it off and looks the other way. The sound of toenails tapping on the old tile makes me smile.

"Cute dog." Erin meets Bradley and Herbie halfway. I take one more look down the hall. No girl, only old tile that's yellowed over time and the curly-haired silver schnauzer sniffing my shoes.

"So I've talked you into getting a dog?" Bradley is pretty proud of himself.

"We'll see." I smile, knowing Herbie will be right back here this time tomorrow. Politely I bend down and pat him on the head and confirm, "Just a test."

"You'll fall completely in love with this little guy." Bradley kisses me and hands me the leash.

"Mmm, which little guy would that be?" I swear I see a spark in both his and Herbie's eyes.

Bradley hands me a bag with enough food to keep Herbie fed over the next few days.

"Oh, Tramp loves that food." Erin has her nose stuck in the bag.

"How is Tramp?" Bradley hands her a few treats to stick in there while I continue to pet Herbie. "I kinda miss the big lug around here."

"He's great. Kent said he keeps him company." Erin smiles at Herbie, and continues to look in the bag. I remember how excited she was when Plan It landed the SPCA account. She's always wanted to help out the animals, and the annual fundraiser landed in her lap. I chalk it up to good karma. She deserves some after the crappy family hand she was dealt.

Bradley focuses on Erin and his eyebrows narrow. "What does Kent do?"

I pull Herbie closer to me as a pink band surrounds Erin's usual crystal aura. It's no secret who she's being nice about—Kent.

She puts her head farther into the bag like she wants to crawl in it. "Um...he's between jobs right now."

I carefully watch the bantering auras between my two favorite people. Blue versus pink. Blue wins! "Hey I can always use another volunteer around here and he can bring Tramp."

"Yeah, I'll tell him." But by the tone of Erin's voice, I think she might forget this conversation and I can't shake the uneasy feeling I have.

* * *

Erin leaves the SPCA ahead of me to get a table at the restaurant while I take Herbie home. I laugh as he hesitates to jump into the Toyota.

"I know boy." I run my hand along the top of his silky head and then pat the seat. He jumps in like a champ. "Your kennel is nicer."

I roll the window down so he can hang his head into the air as we drive, but he just curls up on the seat and looks at me with his big brown eyes. My heart melts. I already know it's going to be tough to take him back to the SPCA. Bradley was right. How does he know me better than I know myself? I put the window down a little more to coax him, but nothing.

"Listen Herbie, you better take advantage of what works in this car." Because the only thing working is the automatic windows. I hit the dash just in time to hear the new Eminem song. And off we go.

Herbie gets up and looks out the window when I pull into my driveway.

"We're home." I laugh watching his little stub of a tail wag back and forth. I open the door and he jumps out, trotting like he's been here before.

"Hey, hey!" I snap my fingers trying to detour Herbie from peeing on all the flowers I've planted along the white picket fence. "Come on."

I herd him into the yard and shut the gate behind me.

"How much pee can you have in you?" I ask in disbelief as he continues to go around to every bush, blade of grass, flowers and the ornamental rocks.

I've taken a lot of time in creating a beautiful yard, all the way down to the window boxes. At least he can't pee on those. Is this what happens when you own a dog?

Yep, I watch him shower my gnome, he's definitely going back.

Worried, I stay on Herbie's heels as he runs around the house, and smells all the piles of clothes, trying to figure out where he is. As much as I hate to admit it, he really does look at home sitting on the couch among the clothes, *and* he isn't complaining about the mess, which no matter how I try, never goes away.

I make a quick water bowl from the only remaining clean dish in the place. He jumps down and begins to sniff it. He takes a few licks and looks up at me with a wet beard.

"You are cute." I quickly rub him and make a mental note to pick up a dog bowl.

My heart tugs. I don't want to leave him here alone, but I have to meet Erin for lunch and get her on the straight and narrow.

He yelps when I shut the door, and he begins to bark. Halfway down the cobblestone walk, I turn around and laugh. Herbie is standing the in the bay window looking like a child yelling at his mother.

I wave. "Bye, buddy."

I don't have time to feel guilty about a dog. I jump in my car and start to prepare my speech for Erin.

I'm hungry, tired, and now worried about why Erin is still in love with a guy I'm getting uncertain vibes from. Plus I have to go talk to Michael, and give the file to Carl.

I pull in next to Erin's Lexus, her pride and joy. She said, "If people are going to have me plan their parties, I have to show up in something professional."

I look up in time to see Carl coming out of the restaurant. Fiddling with my phone is the best strategy to keep my head down so he doesn't recognize me. I want to give him the file on my terms. Not his.

When the coast is clear, I head in and spot Erin in the back corner booth. She still has the same happy face she had this morning. And it's time I find out the truth behind it.

My phone gives a steady stream of email notifications as I slide into the booth.

"Let me see." Erin leans across the table and tries to read my emails upside down. "What's the reason now for the latest split on Splitsville.com?"

"Let's see." I roll the ball with my thumb, randomly picking one of the five.

The waitress fills the glasses with water, and stands with her pad ready for our order.

"Hold on," I say, and we quickly scan the menu. But my attention is still on my phone.

The waitress taps her pad with the tip of the pen.

"We'll have the oriental salad with grilled chicken." Erin hands her the menus.

Her nose crinkles in disgust. "Are you sharing?"

"No. Two." Erin laughs self-consciously. She even wants the surly waitress to like her. I still don't understand why Erin needs reassurance from everyone around her.

One certain email stands out, and I click on it. My heart pounds, and my palms sweat more and more with every word I read. My pasty thumb rolls the ball to scroll through the text. Then the panic hits.

"What's wrong with you?" Erin is searches my face for answers. "You are scary, chalky white."

The waitress leaves and I watch as though she's in slow motion. Everyone around us looks like someone pushed the slow forward button on a DVD player.

I turn back to Erin with my eyes wide open, words finally leave my mouth, "Did you tell anyone I'm Jenn from Splitsville.com?"

Her lip trembles, a dead giveaway she's stressed. "Why? What's wrong? Let me see." She holds out her hand.

"Answer me. Did you tell someone about Splitsville.com?" I shake the phone at her. She had to. There's no other explanation. How could she? She may as well have stabbed me in the back.

I've been so careful to keep my identity a secret. This could be the end of Splitsville.com or worse—*me*. "Erin?" I ask, warning dripping from my voice.

She twirls her hair with one finger. Her cheeks turn pink and her aura has gone orange. And the last time I saw her with that color aura was when she was sixteen and she told my aunt about me sneaking out to meet someone my aunt didn't approve of. Of course I found out later that my aunt was right, he did turn out to be a snake. "I might've mentioned it to Ke…"

I run my hands through my hair. "How could you?" I feel my anger swelling up inside.

"What were you thinking?"

I get money out of my bag and slam it on the table. There is no way I'm able to compose myself. My identity has now been compromised.

I stand up slowly so I don't faint, and take my purse. "You know what? You weren't thinking. This is my life. You've taken years of friendship and gambled it on that no-good piece of crap boyfriend of yours who just might take you for all you've got."

Erin mouth flies open. She opens and shuts it like a fish out of water.

Not looking back, I storm out of the restaurant.

I find my car and head home, but when I get to the intersection, I slam on the brakes. I have to stop. I can't wait. I have to know about this email *now*. The one bad thing about having my out-of-date BlackBerry, the emails have limited access.

I turn into the closest neighborhood and pull over. I look around to make sure no one is following me.

And then I stare at my laptop. Do I dare?

Hell yes I dare, especially if my life is on the line. I open it. I boot it up, and start driving slowly in front of every single house until I get a wifi signal.

UNSECURE NETWORK. Music to my eyes. Desperate times call for desperate

measures. "Okay, come on," I beg my laptop to connect fearing some rogue PTA mom is going to come out, guns blazing because I'm stealing her internet.

I look in the rearview mirror to see if any internet sniffing dogs or FBI are on my tail for

Internet theft. I look at the two story red brick colonial with the free wifi, and watch to see if there is any movement past the windows. Any sign of life, dog, cat, or people.

The coast is clear.

This is good, I tell myself making me feel a little better about tapping into their system.

"It will only take a few minutes to clear all of this up."

I know there has to be some sort of mistake. I hadn't really given Erin a chance to explain or deny. Maybe I'd jumped down her throat too quickly. A wave of guilt washes over me. Carefully I type in the login for Splitsville.com. Due to the case sensitive passwords, I take my time because I have no time to spare.

Get it right the first time.

Enter.

I smile, knowing I imagined the whole thing. The dump emails pop up and I run my finger down my laptop screen. I stop when the tip finds "you" in big, red letters.

"No, no, no," I moan. I close my eyes, and slowly inhale pressing the return button so I can read the entire email.

Name: You'll find out soon enough.

Type of Dump: Death.

Dumpee: Your body in a deep lake.

Reason for Dump: I am going to take *your* heart and smash it into bits like you do to others.

Picture Attached:

"NO!" I scream slamming the laptop shut. This day started out to be about Erin, and now my email threats have gone from bad to worse. First Dabi Stone. Now me. And all for helping people end bad relationships.

"Oh God." I groan as I recognize I've hit stage one in "the process." And I know

what's next on *my* checklist that *I* made up.

Quickly I peel out.

"This is not happening," I repeat over and over, "This can't happen." I check my

reflection in the rear view mirror. I wish I could see my own aura, I know what's coming next. Unfortunately I have no idea what to do about it.

Twelve

As far as I can tell, no one's following me home. I take the long way around Park City to my house, just in case. Keeping my eye on any car that gets behind me. I hit the garage door button, slip my car in, and shut it before I even get it into park.

I've got to be better off in the house than out, I think, slinking out of my car, and running into my kitchen in a crouching position. I lock the door behind me, and prop a chair up against it for extra protection. I lie on the floor only to be pounced on by Herbie, who's trying to give me kisses or telling me he's really thirsty.

Damn! I forgot to get him a bowl. It's the *last* thing on my to-do list right now.

I army crawl to the first set of windows. I slide up the wall and pull on the blinds. Only it takes me a couple tries to figure how to get it down. With the distraction of Herbie jumping on me, I figure out I have to turn the stick to close it before I can put it down. I slide back down the wall and army crawl to every single room, taking all of thirty minutes to get the house dark.

I jump at the vibrating BlackBerry in my pocket. My hands fly to my chest. "God please don't let me die," I whisper in fear that someone is outside my window listening, trying to torment me, and sending a new email when they see I am home.

My phone is like a hot stone in my hands. I don't want to look at the email. With my hands shaking, I scroll down the menu. Slowly I click on the envelope icon.

"Two new messages?" One is from PayPal signaling the other email is a valid dump.

I slide back down the wall with my knees propped up like a tent and read the dump. My mouth drops open and I know my eyes are playing a trick on me.

Name: Kent Goodwin

Type of Dump: The General Break-Up

Dumpee: Erin Lee

Reason for Dump: Not exactly what I thought she was.

I hardly register what I'm reading. This doesn't make sense. Why would he use my service when he knows I'm Jenn from Splitsville.com?

"Ah!" I gasp. For a moment I forget about *my* death threats. I close my eyes trying to remember the day's events. What are the odds of Erin telling me she told Kent, me getting a death threat and Kent dumping Erin—all in one day? Herbie licks the back of my hand, and I absently pet his head. "I know, I'm going to get to the bottom of it."

"Okay. Think, Olivia!" I tap my temple and pace the hallway. I take a deep breath realizing there are no windows in the hallway. I breathe in relief, a little more at ease. I speak out loud, processing what's happened.

"One, I went to meet Erin because she was upset."

"Two, I get there and she's happy."

"Three, I get the death threat."

"Four, Erin told Kent I'm Jenn."

A light bulb goes off in my head. "He knows my identity and made the death threat to scare me. And then he sent the dump email knowing who I am." I bite my bottom lip. I can't believe he would go to such lengths to break-up with Erin or go to make me uncomfortable. He is a jerk.

I have to call Erin immediately. No! I have to see her and show her the dump. It isn't right to tell her over the phone. I need to see her expression. I need to tell her everything. She has to know. I have no time to spare.

Knowing Kent won't really cap me, I move the chair away from the door and jump in my car. Then I realize I have no idea where Erin is.

Her apartment. She'd be home by now I think.

There are more people walking around town than normal. Each time my car passes someone, they look at me. Paranoia sets in, and for a brief moment I fear each one of them might be the one who's sending the threats.

Deep down I know they are enjoying the nice spring day, and I don't make eye contact with anyone else.

A few minutes later, I'm driving up Erin's street. Blue and red police lights flash and a vice clamps around my heart. Am I too late? Are they here for Erin or her crazy neighbors?

I always tell her, "Why are you living here, Erin? You've got money. You could live in the Hyde Park area." Every week the police are here on a domestic violence or disturbing the peace with all the loud music. I've tried to get her to move, but she loves the comings and goings of apartment life. "It's like the childhood I never had," she always says.

Whatever's going on this time is big. It's like a circus on the sidewalks of Park City, Ohio.

I have to park halfway down the block, and hoof it the rest of the way, thanks to the lookie-loos. "Excuse me." I walk past the police officer who's standing outside Erin's apartment building.

I actually feel much safer here with my death threats looming over my head. Being surrounded by police isn't a bad thing right now. If only I could tell them and get real protection.

The metal stairs creak underneath my feet as I ascend to Erin's apartment. Each apartment door has the number either missing or hanging by a thin nail. The concrete flooring is cracked in most places and chipping beneath my feet.

I deduce that it must be Erin's neighbor and his yahoo girlfriend who are fighting because the police officers are lined up along the outer wall leading toward Erin's apartment.

"Excuse me." I smile at the officer standing outside apartment 8A-Erin's place. The tag on his shirt is not from the Park City's PD. It must be a really bad domestic violence case to have neighboring police. I reach for the doorknob.

The policeman puts his arms out to the side to block me from passing him in the hallway. "You're not going in there," he says. His voice is sharper than a Ginsu knife.

"I'm going in there." I point to the door behind him. "If you'd be so kind to move a little that way." I notch my head in the directions of the Erin's noisy next door neighbors. "I'll just slip right by." I smile. He may be dealing with domestic violence, but I've found a little sugar goes a long way.

I reach for the door knob.

"No, you're not." He steps in front of the door to completely block it. "No one is going in there."

A cold sweat begins to gather at my brow as I quickly realize the police officers aren't there for Erin's neighbors, they are there for her.

"Why not?" Where's Erin?" I become frantic. I peek over his shoulder into her apartment as another officer comes out the door. My blood pumps behind my eyes as I try my hardest not to read any aura's in the room. The mixture of black and grey hangs in the air.

"Are you family?" The officer at the door asks.

"Sister," I say. How's a little white lie going to hurt *this* situation? She doesn't have a sister so technically I'm the closest thing.

"She's down at the police station being questioned."

"She's okay?" I look for any clues in his eyes. "I swear if that guy did anything to hurt her, I'll kill him."

He just stares at me, like he's trying to read my mind.

"Is she okay?" I demand. His lips are sealed. He isn't giving me any more information. He keeps his lips tight, but finally nods.

I breathe out. Erin's okay.

"Fancy seeing you here." Carl walks up behind the officer.

"This is the renter's sister," the police officer says, gesturing to me.

One of Carl's eyebrows lifts. "Sister? Is that right?"

Shit! I don't have time to sit here and explain while Erin's off being questioned for who knows what. I glare back at Carl. "Might as well be. Why's Erin at the station?"

The police officer stood a little taller and puffs out his chest like a banty rooster. "Sir, I did not tell her anything about the shooting."

I jerk and poke a finger in my ear. Did I hear right? "Shooting? Who was shot?" A wave of nausea flows through my stomach. I clasp my hand over my mouth.

Carl gives the guy a look that says, "You're an idiot. You just told her."

"If you want to see your friend, er, sister, you can find her down at the station." Carl has become as tight-lipped as his buddy. I turn, ready to bolt down the stairs, but he stops me with a hand on my shoulder. "Oh, we may want to talk to you about this too. You being the renter's sister and all."

Goosebumps cover my legs and arms. He can talk to me all he wants, but later. Right now I need to be by Erin's side. I nod, jerk free, and rush back to my car.

My mind has a field day, racing through the possibilities. Robbery? Rape? I have to get to the police station as quickly as I can. Kent? Oh god! I think of every possibility. Maybe he admitted the girl in the bar was more than right. Maybe she was threatening him. What if Erin lost it, they got in a fight, and he hit her? Or maybe Kent didn't wait for me to do his dirty work. Maybe he totally dumped her, they argued and he threatened her. Or. . .my imagination ran wild. Maybe he told her he contacted me at Splitsville.com.

The fact that it's a shooting, throws me. Erin doesn't even own a gun let alone know how to shoot one. Who did she shoot? Or who shot at her?

I peel out of the parking space, and head east to the Police Department.

My phone chirps from the depths of my purse. With one eye on the road, I dig, my hand finally finding it. I rush to answer when I see Erin's cell number pop up on the screen. "Erin, I'm on my way."

"How do you know where I am?" Erin's voice is trembling. I can picture her clutching the phone in one hand, her other one twirling her hair out of anxiety.

"I stopped by your place to tell you." I stop. There's no way I can add to whatever she's going through by telling her what a first-class loser Kent is. "The police have it surrounded. They told me you're making some sort of statement."

"Olivia." She begins to sob, heaving so I can hardly understand her. "Kent is dead."

My vision blurs, and my foot lifts off the gas pedal. I've heard people talk about out of body experiences. And I'm definitely having one of those. This isn't making any sense. Kent was the bad guy, not a victim.

"He was at my place." Her words are barely audible. "S. . .someone came in and killed him."

"That can't be right." He sent me a dump.

"Can you pick me up?" Erin sniffs, her crying under control. "I can't go back to that apartment. Ever. Olivia," she whispers. "What if Kent was just in the wrong place at the wrong time? What if-what if I was the one who was supposed to die?"

The dark sky seems to be folding around us on our drive back from Park City's police department. The sky looks bruised just beyond the hilly park the closer we get to the middle of town. The only noise is the sound of Erin's whimper.

There are two deaths in Park City and both can be traced back to me. My heart palpitates at the thought of how cop Carl is going to love throwing this at me.

Slowly, I descend through each stoplight. I glance down Aunt Matilda's street to make sure she's tucked in for the night. The old rusty Chevy isn't there. I put the pedal to the metal. If Aunt Matilda isn't home, she'd better be at my house. With murders and death threats looming around this city, I need to make sure she's safe.

My heart melts when I pull into my driveway with Erin next to me, and see Aunt Matilda's truck. The lights in the kitchen signal she's made a new pot of coffee which means she knows about Kent's death.

Aunt Matilda is reaching for a couple of coffee mugs as we walk into the house. "Just in time. How you doing, sweetheart?" She pours the coffee while keeping one eye on Erin.

Erin walks right into Matilda's arms, and gets wrapped up in her love.

I bend down and pick up Herbie. Having his little heart beat next to mine makes me feel better.

Erin lets go of Matilda, slumps down on the barstool, and leans across to take a cup of coffee. "I guess you heard about Kent."

Aunt Matilda puts her hands around Erin's which are cupped around the mug. I look at their intertwined hands and recall the same scene when Erin's parents died. Funny, I never realized that Aunt Matilda has also been there for Erin all along. I only wish we were enough for Erin and that she wouldn't seek out these men that are no good for her.

"Yes, honey. Carl told me all about it." Aunt Matilda brushes Erin's bangs out of her tear-stained eyes.

Both Herbie's and my ears perk up at the mere mention of Carl's name. "Why? Why are you talking to him?" I blurt out shocked that Aunt Matilda would be the first person Carl would call. Especially when he was giving me such a hard time.

"Let's just say he wanted to see if I'd come out of retirement." She jingles her way back to the coffeemaker to refill her cup. Hmm…her sway has a little too much sashay for me to believe that's all the contact was about.

"And?" I have to wonder if Carl has an ulterior motive.

"And, I told him no." She turns around and she puts her nose in the steady steam to smell the fresh brew. "I'm officially retired."

I watch her make her way to the couch and sit down with Herbie right alongside. "Are you sure that's all he wants?" I don't even bother to be subtle. Aunt Matilda should have a social life, but Carl?

She gives me the look I know all too well. The stepping-over-the-boundary look.

With a stiff upper lip, I sit on the stool next to Erin. She seems to be comatose, unresponsive. I break her silence. "Think Erin. Is there any reason why someone would want Kent dead?" I have to get to the bottom of Kent's murder.

She looks up and her eyelids are as red as blood. "No. Nothing."

"No conversations? Nothing?"

"No." Her whisper is barely audible.

I think back to what few conversations she and I have had about Kent or what little I know. "There's only one path to pursue. What about the girl who slapped him?" There's a motive. "Who was she?"

Her eyes widen like she just remembered something, and then they dim again. "No. She was mad because he dumped her. He said she was the first girl he dated after he stopped ...um...that other life. He started his straight and narrow act with her." Erin takes a sip of her coffee.

Hmm, so this girl really doesn't have a reason to kill him, but she could know something.

"Wait!" Erin stands up and paces between the couch and the bar stool. Aunt Matilda peeps up from the couch to hear. "He did say something about that heiress from Macro Hard. You know, the one who died."

"What?" I lean a little closer to hear her ramblings.

"I don't know. I was so mad at him that I didn't even listen to what he had to say about her."

"Erin this is crucial. You need to think." I grab her by the shoulders to steady her. Her bouncing aura is starting to make me sea sick. "This could be life or death for both of us."

She closes her eyes, and a tear trickles down her cheek. "I can't remember."

I drop my hands to my side and let her go. She turns around and saunters down the hall to the bathroom. I look at Aunt Matilda just as I hear the shower turn on. Aunt Matilda throws her hands in the air like she gives up.

Thirteen

Herbie doesn't make a peep all night long. Last night he jumped up on my bed and curled into a ball after a vicious cycle of going 'round and 'round only to lie at the foot of the bed like he's been there his entire life.

"Good morning, Herbie." I run my hand along his wiry hair and yawn. I'm already tired and my feet haven't touched the floor. Herbie's eyebrows stick up all over the place, "It's a shame you'll have to go back to the kennel today," I say, bending over to scratch his head.

He looks at me like I'm crazy.

Maybe I am. All night I wrestled with whether or not to tell Erin about Kent and his aura. Even if she doesn't want to hear, I'm obligated by the rules of the Best Friend Handbook to give such privy information.

It's far more likely that someone would want him dead than Erin. But he was killed at her apartment, so none of it makes any sense to me. Dabi's smile keeps circling in my head, but unlike Herbie who finally settles down, her picture never fades. Two people I know have been killed. Two people who've sent dumps to Splitsville.com are dead. What's their connection?

I sneak a look through the blinds to make sure no one is lurking in the yard. All night long I listened for someone or something to brush up against the bushes or the bricks of the house. Nothing. But of course not. I'm sure Kent was behind the threats and I am pretty sure he can't send any more from the Great Beyond.

I feel a little more confident, but the bags under my eyes say a completely different story.

Herbie follows me to the kitchen, leaping over piles of magazines and dodging the occasional dust bunny. "I wish you could stay, but I don't know how to take care of a dog. Plus you have all your friends at the kennel." He tilts his head like he understands every word I'm saying. "If I keep you, you'd have to wear an ascot." I crouch down and laugh out loud, as he jumps up and licks my face.

"Okay, let's see how well you perform today." He accepts my answer. I open the door and he runs into the backyard.

I start the coffee. My cell rings. It's Bradley.

"Hi." My voice sounds the way I feel. Tired. Worried. Exhausted.

"Well?" he asks.

"Well what?" I don't know what he wants me to say.

"How did Herbie do? Did he pass your test?"

I glance out the window. He's running around the back yard like he owns the place.

"He's okay." I play if off to prepare Bradley for the return of Herbie. Aunt Matilda barrels into the house, slamming the door behind her.

"He's got eyebrows like your dad did." She chortles. She's right. The one thing I do remember about my father is his bushy eyebrows.

I put my finger up to my mouth. "Shh." I point to the phone.

"Are you going to keep him?" Bradley asks.

It's a good question. As cute as he is, I just don't have a place in my life for a dog. But somehow I can't bring myself to give him back quite yet. "No comment. I'll let you know after I take him for a walk in the park with other dogs." The whole reason I got Herbie in the first place is to take him back to the park so I can meet up with Michael again.

It's time for Herbie's starring role.

"Right," Bradley says, but I hear the smile in his voice. I think he knows I actually like the little mutt. "Talk to you later, Liv."

A warm feeling seeps through me. Liv. So maybe nicknames aren't so bad after all.

Bradley and I hang up and I turn to Aunt Matilda. "Well?" she demands.

"Well what?" I ask walking over to kiss her.

"How did Herbie do?" she asks.

"Just using him for Splitsville.com and Dabi's murder." Knowing her disapproval, I try not to look at her.

She glances at me with a lingering eye. She is in full jingle regalia. She has bells on her shoes, scarf and edge of her shirt. I sing the Grateful Dead ballad, *She has rings on her fingers and bells on her shoes. . ."*

Erin stumbles out of the guest room. She rubs her eyes, big black bags deep underneath. Looks like she didn't get a wink of sleep. "I guess Aunt Matilda is here. Did Olivia fill you in?" She blinks under the waterfall of bangs hanging down her forehead.

I haven't, but I do right then and there. Matilda listens intently, nodding every now and then. The only things I leave out are the threatening emails, the dump request from Kent, and his shifting auras.

"Do you have any advice?" Erin asks with tears sitting on the rim of her eyelids like water getting ready to spill over a dam.

Herbie scratches on the door to come in. Even though Kent is dead I still look around the yard before quickly shutting the door. Even if he sent the threats, there's a live killer out there in Park City.

Matilda pushes her bracelets up her arm, and looks at me. "I think you need to check out something of Dabi's.

Something that might give you a clue why someone would want her murdered."

She's right. That something is Michael. Somehow I have to get him to open up about Dabi and what she was like. Things she liked to do.

"Do you think the same person killed Kent?" I question Aunt Matilda. She has these certain feelings that are generally spot on. I don't know how she knows and I don't want to know, but they are remarkably accurate.

"If we put our two heads together," she winks, "like old times, I bet we can come up with the killer."

Herbie rubs up against Aunt Matilda's legs, making the bells on her shoes jingle. He cocks his head to the side trying to figure out if it's a toy or something he should steer clear from. Regardless, he breaks our conversation and leaves us with our separate thoughts.

"I think you found yourself a man." Aunt Matilda catches me off guard a moment later. Is she talking about the killer?

Erin leans over the kitchen sink and looks out toward my cobblestone drive. She's oblivious to what Aunt Matilda and I have been talking about. I don't think she's looking past the tip of her nose.

"Who?" I question Aunt Matilda. "What man?"

"I'm talking about Herbie." She points toward the little grey guy on the couch like it's been his spot the entire time.

I must admit, his pink aura goes great with his grey hair. I smile. I'd never have guessed his green stubborn aura at the kennels was a cover-up for his real pink, sweet, loving, happy, well-balanced color clinging tightly to his sleeping body.

"Not a good sign." I smile toward my new friend who's already made my home his new home. I'm afraid whatever he proves today while visiting Michael and Belle won't determine the spot he is carving out in my heart.

***

Pleasant Ridge Park is filled with animals and their owners. Trying to find Michael and Belle might be my big feat for the day. Herbie is a champ. He walks with his head held high as though he is showing me off. I notice he isn't trying to pull me in the directions of the other dogs or trying to sniff every pee spot in the park.

"Hi."

I stop short and look up. Michael and Belle are standing before me. Super sleuth I am, I've been paying so much attention to Herbie that I almost miss my target.

"Oh! Hi Michael." I bend down to pat Belle. "Hello Belle." I stand up to let the two dogs acquaint themselves as dogs do.

"How do you know my name?"

I tap my tongue on my teeth trying to come up with a quick response. "Um…" Nothing is coming to mind. It's time to fess up. "Actually, that's a funny story. I wanted to talk to you about."

Michael tilts his head like a curious dog. I look around to make sure cop Carl isn't hanging around looking for Michael. There's only a few girls crossing the street in their skimpy t-shirts and tight black stretch pants with their designer dogs. I glance down at my oversized University t-shirt with a coffee stain the size of a tennis ball, and my cut-off sweat pants with my dingy white kickers where the color has faded with time. Oh well. I'm not trying to impress anyone. I'm just trying to save my life.

"Maybe we can talk inside your apartment." I know I'm taking a gamble. He might be the killer, but that's what

I'm here for. I'll take my chance because the blue glow surrounding him is definitely not threatening.

I slip into the apartment unseen. I don't want Carl or anyone connecting me to Michael.

"Can I get you something to drink?" He takes water out of the refrigerator and fixes a fresh bowl of water for Belle and one for Herbie. "Water? Coffee?" He points to the coffee maker. The freshly brewed coffee scent lingers in the air.

"I'll take a cup of coffee with sugar and cream." I can't believe I'm going to have coffee with someone who could be a killer. Okay, again, his aura tells me no, but at some point in my life, I've got to be wrong.

I walk around. There is a picture of Michael and Dabi on the mantel. A picture of Belle and Dabi. And a couple of Polaroids without a frame of Michael, Dabi and Kent.

My mind screeches to a halt. *Kent*? What the hell is Kent doing in this picture? His arm is loosely draped around Dabi's shoulders. He is wearing a black tie and so is Michael. Dabi and Michael have on the same outfits as the other pictures. I pick it up to get a closer look, but hear Michael's footsteps. Instinct kicks in and I slip it into the waistband of my shorts.

"She was beautiful." Michael's eyes are on the picture of him and Dabi.

"Who is she?" I ask, noticing he said "was" and not "is."

"That's my ex-girlfriend."

"She is beautiful," I say. I steady my shaking hands, put them around the mug. I pray the fear in my belly won't show. I want to steer him away from the mantel. What if he notices there's a picture missing? My eyes lock on a silver candleholder. The perfect weapon if my instincts and aura reading prove to be wrong and Michael comes after me. "Why are you dressed up?"

"Company function." I take note that he doesn't smile then he looks at the pictures. "He's the guy they should be questioning." Michael points to Kent, and then turns his back on the memories.

"Why?" But I really want to say, well, there's no way in hell now. The guy is deader than a doornail. "Who is he?"

"Her ex." Michael's nose snarls in disgust.

Ex? Dabi and Kent? Did Kent scam Dabi out of her money?

"You look pretty chummy to me." I try not to give a hint in my voice that I know, er, knew Kent was a piece of crap.

My thoughts go rogue. Somebody wanted Dabi and Kent dead. But who? They were lovers. Coincidence? I take a long look at Michael's profile. He loved Dabi. She broke up with him. He hates Kent. Could Michael have killed them out of jealously? Isn't jealously the number one reason for murder? Or is it money? I frown. *CSI* sure does make this look easy.

I take a step toward my weapon of choice. The tall candlestick on the coffee table looks like it could do some damage if I need to use it. "Why did you break-up?" I question him because I need to make sure my "gift" is giving me the right aura and not something I can't see. I'm not really listening because what if Kent killed Dabi and then killed himself. Why?

"Her family." Michael takes a big gulp.

"What do you mean?"

"Are you a cop or something? First you show up in pink fuzzy slippers, and then you show up with a dog and know my name." His eyebrows arch. "It didn't take you guys long to suspect me. I didn't kill her. I could never hurt her."

"No, Michael. I'm not the police."

"Okay, then what do you want? Why are you asking me so many questions?" There's escalating irritation with each word.

It's time I come clean. "I'm Jenn from Splitsville.com. The online break-up service Dabi used to break-up with you."

Michael backs away. "What?" The color drains from his face and his eyes are slits.

"It's true. I heard about Dabi and the police called me. I know you're innocent, but. . ."

"This is sick Jenn, a…Olivia. Whatever your name is. You can leave now." He bolts for the door. This is not the way I planned this. Actually I never planned this.

"Wait, Michael. It's only a matter of time before the police come. They know Dabi broke up with you using Splitsville.com and you are the perfect suspect. They just don't know your last name yet." This means they're either horribly terrible police officers or they're following other leads at the moment. "If they find out you also know Kent, well, that's not going to look good."

His knuckles turn white on the door handle. "You know Kent?" He stands still. His aura begins to have breaks all over and sadness covers him.

"Think about it Michael." I say. "The disgruntled ex-boyfriend did it."

He turns with a look of death in his eyes, and an aura to match. I put my hand on the mantle to steady the spinning room.

"I didn't do it."

I hear Michael's feet speeding toward me and I focus. He puts his hand on my arm. I jerk away.

I push him aside and make my way to the door, only to fall on the couch to help stop the world spinning around me.

"Are you okay?" Michael rushes past me back into the kitchen and back again. He hands me a glass of water. "Here."

"I'm fine. Thank you." I take the water and drink small sips. "I know you didn't do it Michael. But with Kent dead, too, things are not looking good for you."

"K-Kent? H-he's d-dead?"

Either Michael didn't kill Kent or he's an Oscar caliber actor. "Yes."

"I have a few ideas, but I can't discuss them with you right now. You need to hide yourself for a few days until I come up with something to help save me and *you*."

"Olivia?" I turn after I put Herbie's leash back on him and look at Michael. He asks, "How do you know I didn't do it?"

"I don't," I say. There's no way I am going to tell him about my "gift." I continue, "Let's just say innocence surrounds you." I walk out the door and have a sudden thought. "Michael, you don't have keys to Dabi's apartment do you?"

He looks around his apartment darting from one drawer to the next. "I can get them. Meet me at the park tomorrow afternoon."

That is something I can definitely do. "I'm hoping I can find some evidence to help us both out."

I turn just before walking out the door. "Do you have a job?" Maybe his occupation has something to do with Dabi and her dad or Kent. Hell, I really just want to know.

"I'm a dog walker." There is a grin as wide as the Mississippi across his face, "Wealthy people will pay a ton of money for their four legged creatures to be walked. That's how I met Dabi. She hired me to walk Belle." He bends down to pick up his precious pooch. "To bad you can't talk to Terry."

I turn and he's holding Belle in the crook of his arm, the picture of him and Dabi in his hands.

"Who's Terry?"

"Oh, Kent," he says. "He used different names for different people. He hated to go by Terry."

Fourteen

The entire way home I can't get over the idea of Dabi hiring Michael as a dog walker. "No wonder her father didn't want her to be with him." I tell Herbie who's sitting straight up in the passenger seat and looking at me like he knows exactly what I'm saying. "There can't be that much money in it and Dabi's dad, I'm sure, didn't want his precious daughter with the ultimate pooper scooper. And when did Kent date her?"

I smack the dash for a little background music. Gloria Gaynor is belting out the mantra of my life. "Sing it Gloria." I turn up the volume and sing *I will survive* all the way home.

With Herbie settled at home, Erin back to sleep, and Aunt Matilda nowhere to be seen, I head back out. I like Michael and want to help prove his innocence. Not that anyone thinks he's guilty, but once the police figure out the connection between Dabi, Kent/Terry, and Michael, he'll be at the top of their list. I pull the picture out of all three of them and put it on my dashboard. Maybe if I stare hard *enough* something will come to me.

I stop my car next to the chain link fence parking lot where it looks like all three of Park City's pigs haven't left for the day. I look for the entrance for normal citizens, but wonder if I'm considered a normal citizen or a suspect?

I grab the file off my passenger seat and get out of the car.

I walk in the squeaky door to find all of Park City's finest eating their doughnuts and drinking the stale-smelling coffee. It's exactly the way I remember it from when I was little and Aunt Matilda would bring me here. The flickering lights hum and are still barely hanging by their electric wires. I have no clue what my taxes are going for because they obviously haven't been used to spruce up the joint.

I lightly tap on the sliding glass window where the receptionist sits, but I'm sure it's too early for her.

"Hello, Ms. Davis." Carl stands up from his desk and licks his fingers. "I didn't take you for an early riser." His eyes focus on my hands. "Is that the file I asked for?" He tries to slide the glass, but it gets stuck on the track, causing the window to stay put on the bottom, but go cockeyed on top.

I notice the young policeman look up from his desk and snicker. He continues to watch Carl communicate through the glass and laughs.

Carl points to the door next to the window. He turns the handle, but it seems to be stuck. I pull the handle, but it doesn't budge. Carl's mouth becomes tight as he jiggles the door-knob and pulls with all his might. He is flung back and takes a few steps backwards so he won't fall flat on his ass.

I purse my lips in an attempt not to laugh. By this time all three officers snicker and snort, but don't dare release the pastry goodies from their fingers.

"We need to get this door fixed!" Carl doesn't look back at his colleagues. His face is as hot as a piece of sizzling coal.

I hand him Dabi's break-up file. Of course it's not the *original*. "I'm sure there is nothing there to lead you to the killer."

"Now, now." He looks suspiciously at me. "Don't put your nose where it shouldn't go." He opens the file and thumbs through it. "If you're anything like your aunt, I'm afraid I'm wasting my breath." I notice his face relaxes when he talks about Aunt Matilda.

I smile and do not reply. I can't lie to the police—again.

The young officer gets up from his seat. "Is this the Dabi Stone file from the on-line breakup service?"

"Splitsville.com." I pop my head over Carl's shoulder and correct him. Break-up services sounds awful compared to Splitsville.com.

Carl nods and hands it over. If this were a doughnut, he wouldn't have given it up so easy.

"I'm Olivia Davis," I say, holding out my hand. I've never seen him around and everyone knows everyone in Park City.

"This is Officer Ian Parker." Carl pats Ian on the back. Ian's electric blue eyes catch me off guard. They are much brighter against his sulfur aura. "He's new to Park City. Specializes in murders."

Pride emanates from Carl's eyes. If only Carl could read Ian's aura, he'd know Ian is *not* a happy employee.

"Are you here investigating Dabi's murder?" I wonder how long I'm going to have to deal with this clown.

"No, I'm here for good. It's just a coincidence this happened my first week." He gives off the police air that leaves a bad taste in everyone's mouth. He even looks the stereo-type with his high-and-tight hair cut, stiff collar and shiny shoes.

Great! He's hungry to get this solved and prove his worth. I don't need another officer on my tail.

Okay, whatever pig! I want to yell, but I don't. I have no intention of being a guest at Park City's jail today.

"Nice to meet you." I smile and look at Carl. "Let me know if you need anything else."

"We will," Ian confirms.

Again, *whatever, pig!* Of course I don't say it, but I want to. Like a good girl, I turn and start out the door.

"Did your aunt look at this?" Carl hollers after me. I'm sure he would've asked her to if I hadn't been around yesterday. There hasn't been a double murder in Park City in a long time.

"You'll have to ask her that." I throw my head back and laugh. If only they knew the truth and how I was a big part of Aunt Matilda's job with the Park City Police Department.

Fifteen

Aunt Matilda is outside with Herbie when I get home.

"Dang, he's cute." She pats her leg and Herbie jumps up to get a good dose of loving.

I smile, watching Herbie rub his head around her ankles. Her long brown gypsy skirt floats around his head as he darts in and out. "He is," I say. I'm starting to get attached to him and that's not what I intended to do.

"How was Carl?" She looks over at me.

He's a jackass. That's how he is, I want to tell her but I hold my tongue. "He's fine. They have a new police officer. And boy is he eager to solve Dabi and Kent's deaths." I recall Ian's strong authoritative aura.

I walk over while thumbing through my BlackBerry to retrieve a dump file.

"What's wrong?" Aunt Matilda stops petting Herbie and leans over to see what's on my screen.

I tilt my head and my eyes come face to face with Aunt Matilda's. My eyes sting from not blinking or being able to blink. "I'm watching you. You better shut down Splitsville.com or else." I read the screen a couple of times in my head then look down the street for any sign of a car, a person, anything that may be stalking me.

The street is dark and silent.

"Is it another threat?" Aunt Matilda quietly asks, as if it's no big deal.

"What?" I know I didn't hear her correctly. How does she know?

Immediately I want to think Erin told her, but she hasn't gotten out of bed since we came home yesterday.

"I know about the threats. You forget, little girl." She embraces me and my soul begins to feel a little better. "I know you better than you know yourself. I've had the gift longer."

"The gift! The damn gift!" I pull away and march over to Herbie. I pick him up. "I'm so sick of having this gift that I don't even understand!" With Herbie in my arms I stomp around the house. "I read auras, I have night visions. What kind of gift is that?"

I plop on the couch and the piles of clothes puff up around me and Herbie. He runs off.

"Do you ever question a gift Erin gives you?" Aunt Matilda begins to pick up clothes and put them in the empty laundry basket.

I jump up and grab the basket out of her hands. "Don't do this." I can't tell if I'm completely irritated that she's cleaning up or these threats are getting a little old. "No, I don't question those types of gifts." But I have definite questions about this dump.

If Kent's not behind the murders, since he's in the great beyond, who is?

I walk over to the window and peek out to make sure the killer isn't standing on my walkway. My reflection stares back at me. The dark eyes run deep. I shiver. The threat in my inbox did say someone is watching me. Granted, they didn't give details to what I'm doing, but eerie nonetheless.

"A gift is a gift." Matilda nods. "Don't question your gift Olivia. Once you accept and embrace it, you will have a much better life."

I grab Herbie's leash. "My gift might get me killed."

*　*　*

Bradley called early to see if Herbie and I want to meet him at Pleasant Ridge Park with a few of his other shelter dogs for a morning walk. A walk might do me good. Plus it's too late for Michael Schultz to be there so I don't have to worry about running into him.

With one eye on the road and one eye in the rear view mirror, I drive to Pleasant Ridge Park. I don't see anyone following me or anything out of the ordinary, which puts me a little more at ease.

The streets are filled with people going to work or taking their morning strolls. I pull into the closest spot to the coffee shop so I can grab a couple cups, one for me and one for Bradley.

I leave a crack in the window for Herbie, so the cool brisk breeze won't chill him too much. He sits there like a human when I get out. I look back to make sure he's okay and stop. How did I miss this? I walk back toward my car.

Herbie is as happy as a lark. "Oh no." I hang my head and groan. A brown aura surrounds Herbie, meaning he's become addicted to something and unfortunately the something happens to be me. How am I going to give him back now?

I put his aura in the back of my head and turn toward the coffee shop. I don't want to be late meeting Bradley.

I believe in signs and the blinking one in the store next to the coffee shop is telling me something! According to the window, they sell guns, nunchucks, stun guns, mace, and personal alarms. If there's a killer after me, I'm going to need more than a dog that acts like a human and thinks he's human.

I look at my watch.

9:20 A.M.

I don't have time to check the store out, but I will put it on my priority list. Right now, Herbie is in the car waiting for me and Bradley might be at the park waiting on me.

***

I find Bradley standing next to the gazebo in the middle of the park, holding tightly to three leashes. His blue aura dances around his shaggy brown hair. I smile, taking in his every drop of him as he is trying to keep the three dogs from barking.

"Hey Olivia!" His teeth are almost blinding. "Over here!" He tries to put a hand in the air, but flings forward as his dog lunges at a passing pooch.

I walk with my head high, two coffees, and a leash attached to the best dog in the world. Herbie doesn't pay any attention to the others we pass. He seems to know we are on a mission and he's not straying from it.

"Thanks." Bradley looks between his hands to see which one is freer for holding a cup. He points to a bench next to the lake. The shade will be nice for the dogs and us as we drink our coffee. "Let's sit over there."

"Hey Herbie." Bradley pets Herbie once the other three are situated. "How's your new mommy?"

Herbie wags his tail and his aura is as brown as mud.

"Wait a minute." I remind Bradley. "This is a trial. *Remember*?"

"Sure it is." Bradley nods slowly. I can tell he already knows Herbie and I are a good match for each other.

Michael's voice comes out of nowhere. "You're early."

I cringe at the sound. I ignore it and pretend I am someone else or, at least, let him believe he has the wrong girl. I continue to ignore him and sit with Bradley while we enjoy our coffee.

"Olivia?" He yells even louder, "Okay, Jenn!"

Sharply I turn around on the bench to face Michael walking across the grass toward us. What is he doing here? I look at my watch and confirm its past 10 A.M. I made sure I'd miss him. He's supposed to be meeting me here tomorrow, not today.

"Do you know that guy?" Bradley, looking a little confused, points to Michael. "He knows you or someone named Jenn."

Michael trots up, out of breath. "Hey, I didn't think you'd be here until tomorrow." He seems more relaxed than earlier in the week.

"I'm here with my boyfriend enjoying a quiet stroll." I hold up my cup and give a shit grin, "I'll see you tomorrow."

"Cool. Hey, Herbie." Michael put his hand out to Bradley. "Michael Schultz." He snorts, "Thank God, Jenn, er, Olivia volunteered to clear our names because I wouldn't know where to begin."

Bradley takes his hand. "Bradley." He looks over at me but I can't look him in the eyes. I take a drink of coffee. "Yeah, it sure is nice of her."

"Just in case I saw you walking, I've been carrying these." He pulls out the set of keys and begins to tell me which one goes where. I follow along, but there are too many. I can picture myself having to try every key when I break in. Now what kind of image is that for a sleuth?

He continues, "This is the entrance to the garage, this is the entrance to the building, this is the apartment and this is the mother of all mothers." He holds up a key much larger than the other ones. "The office key. Don't ask me how I got them because I'm not telling."

"Fine." I take the set of keys and try not to look at Bradley. I feel his stare and it's about to burn a hole the size of the National Geyser in my head. "I'll let you know what I find out."

He begins to walk away. "And Michael?" He stops and turns. "Remember, you can't tell anyone!"

"Oh I won't. My life depends on it." He smiles wanly and takes off running back to wherever it is he came from. His life and mine really do depend on it.

I still feel Bradley's stare. I head back toward him, nervously sipping my coffee, no clue what to tell him.

He launches in the second I'm next to him. "Are you going to tell me what that was all about?" Sparks shoot from his eyes as he leans in front of me. I gulp and almost spill my coffee on a perfectly clean t-shirt—even though it did come from the basket of laundry I took from Aunt Matilda. I can tell him that Michael is a dot com nerd like me...or I can tell him the truth.

"What, *what* was about?" I say, totally stalling, but I can see he's not going to budge one bit. His aura still radiates as brightly as the big blue sky.

I grab Herbie's leash and start hoofing it down the sidewalk, my coffee close to sloshing over the rim of the cup. I don't even care. "If you really want to know," I say as he falls into step beside me. "I'll tell you, but you have to tell me one thing first."

He nods, eyeing me warily.

"You can't hold it against me." I have no idea if what I'm asking is really possible, but I hope against hope that it is.

His nod is slower this time, but he's agreeing, so I feel a tinge of relief. Still, part of me thinks I should warn him that he better be careful, he doesn't even know what he's agreeing with.

"You see," I keep my voice and walking pace steady. "I have this thing..." I trail off, not even knowing how to say it.

"What kind of thing? Like an STD?'

"God no! More like a "gift"...or a curse. Kind of depends on how you see it."

He's slowed down, so I slow down. He is staring at me. "I don't get it."

"Have you ever heard of people's auras?" I smile trying to take the sting out of my shocking words.

He stops and takes a couple of steps away from me like I have leprosy. "I don't know much. Only that it has to do with voodoo or witch-craft."

"No, it's not witch craft or voodoo," I snap. Ugh! Why does reading auras have such a bad rap? If I didn't like him so much. . . "You can learn a ton about someone by the color of their aura." Like how his has changed from vibrant blue to dusty gray, meaning he's completely doubting everything about me.

"Hold up." He laughs, his aura sliding back to blue. "Are you telling me you have an aura *thing*?" He continues to snort but abruptly stops when he sees I'm not laughing. As a matter of fact, my insides churn and shrivel up and die with this conversation. He's back to gray and I'm sure he's going to run as far away from me just as fast as he can.

He laughs one last time and I can tell he's trying to figure me out. "Wait, you're kidding right?"

"I wish." My mind goes blank when he begins walking in circles like he's trying to digest everything he's just heard. I imagine it spinning around in his head like a tornado.

Bradley suddenly wheels around and faces me. "So when we met at the kissing booth, you knew I was attracted to you from my...my...my aura?" I can see the light bulbs going off in his head. I shake my head, but he's already onto another thought. "And Sam. That's how you knew she was sick?"

I nod this time. "Sam's aura color deepens in the spot where she's sick. That's how I knew where it was." I rub my hand down his arm to comfort him and let him know I'm not some freak. "I couldn't tell one aura from the other at the kissing booth."

"What about that guy?" He points to where Michael and I were standing a few minutes ago.

"Oh, that." I take another deep breath preparing for what comes next. So far Bradley's not running, but if it's not the aura thing that's going to kill us, it's the Splitsville.com. It's what I fear most. I take a deep breath and just blurt it out. "My dot com job is really an on line break-up service called Splitsville.com."

He takes another step back. His aura goes from grayish blue to baby blue. And then, God love him, he starts to laugh.

"I don't have face-to-face contact with anyone who uses my business. I use an alias," I whisper conspiratorially. "Jenn."

Bradley is nodding and listening to every word as I tell him about my life. He seems to be taking it well. He's breathing slowly, even if his nostrils flare a bit, but he's still next to me and hasn't run for the hills over my secret identity or pessimistic break-up service

"That's why I know who Dabi Stone is and why I need her keys. I need to clear not only Michael, but Splitsville.com." I carefully explain everything. "Dabi used Splitsville.com to break-up with Michael. The police linked Dabi to Splitsville.com and I had to check Michael out."

"Why?" he asks, shaking his head. "You shouldn't get involved. Why not leave it up to the police?"

Damn good question. I've asked myself that several times, but keep coming up with the same answer. "The thing is. . ." I choose my words wisely, "with this aura thing I have going on. . ." I circle my hands around the top of my head like a halo. "I can't work in an environment with a lot of people."

His eyebrows narrow and his mouth is slightly opened, like he just can't believe we're having this conversation. And truthfully, neither can I.

"Aura's collide and it makes me dizzy. I do okay if it's for a short period of time, but basically my college education was a big waste of cash."

"What about now?" He points around to the people in the park. "Does this bother you?"

I shake my head. "If I'm outside, it's better. Not confined. Like the SPCA fund raiser." I know it's hard for him to understand, but it's the best I can do.

"And if Splitsville.com is implicated in Dabi's murder, or if my identity's revealed, there goes my business." A lump settles in my throat. I can hardly get the next words out. "I don't know what I'll do if that happens."

He bends down and his warm breath on my neck sends a comfort that tells me he is man of honor. I don't have to look at his aura to know the truth about Bradley. "Well, if what you say is true, I will not let you do this alone. Why didn't you tell me earlier?"

"Because I was scared shitless you'd bail? Because I didn't think you could handle the truth. No one else has been able to." I smile at him and settle into his arms. "But now you know the whole story."

"So let's go save your business." I don't dare tell him about the photo with Dabi, Michael and Kent. I can't add thief to my laundry list of quirks.

"Olivia," he says as we walk back to our cars. "Just don't ever use your break-up service on me, deal?"
I snuggle closer. "You have a blue aura. I love blue auras." I roll up on my tiptoes and kiss him. "It's a deal."

Sixteen

Is it really breaking in if I have a key? I'm not going to break anything to get in, so it's definitely not breaking and entering. Only entering, so I feel a little better about the whole thing.

Bradley pulls into the garage. "What do these people do for a living?" Mercedes and BMWs line all the garage parking spots like a high-end dealership.

I shrug. "I have no idea. But the rate I'm going, I'm never going to get a car like that." I point to the little black convertible Mercedes. "I'll stick with my Toyota. You know, throw people off when I work on spying." I smile over at Bradley.

"When you spy?" He continues to look for the visitors parking spots, "This is the last job you're doing."

It's cute how Bradley is nervous about me going into Dabi's apartment to find something, anything, to help Michael and Splitsville.com.

The visitor parking is right next to the security guard office. I can see the glow of several small televisions lined up on the desk. His back is to us.

Bradley turns off the car and points in the direction of the security office. "Do you see those TVs in there?"

I look again and the security guy motions for us to get out and walk over there.

"Those are security cameras. You be careful. I'm sure this place is lined with them." Bradley puts his hand out for me to stay put while he walks over to the guard.

The security guard looks official in his *Paul Blart Mall Cop* security get up. He stands a foot shorter than Bradley which makes me feel better. If we need to take him down, I think we can do it.

I really wish I'd gotten something from that store to protect myself. Its times like this I need to carry some sort of weapon.

I roll down the window to see if I can hear what they're saying.

Bradley flashes his SPCA badge. "Here to see about taking a dog back to the shelter. Apartment number 203." Bradley is charming the attendant.

"I didn't know they had a dog." The guard seems a little suspicious.

"They brought one home from the shelter and I'm doing a visit to make sure it's a good fit." I smile. Bradley can tell a lie without flinching. I had no clue. Bradley isn't bad at this sleuthing stuff.

The attendant pushes the gate open and points in the direction of the visitor entrance. There is a security station right before the glass doors.

Bradley comes back to the car, the security guard is watching, and retrieves a fold-up kennel. "I have to pretend to check on a dog, and this will distract the guard." He reminds me of Frank Hardy in the Hardy Boys Mysteries.

"And how exactly are you going to do that?" I'm no big sleuth, but I don't understand how a kennel is going to distract *Paul Blart*.

"You have to get up to Dabi's apartment, right?" He waits for me to agree, "I noticed the cameras aren't in the stairwells. They're focused on the building entrances and the floors themselves. If we go up in the elevator, we can find the stair entrance on that floor. I'll hold the kennel up in the air to shield the camera as you slip into the stairwell."

I smile. "You *are* Frank aren't you?" I recall him being the logical Hardy Boy.

"Frank who?" Bradley asks.

"Frank Hardy, from the Hardy Boys." I smile.

"Never heard of him." He isn't fooling. "This is serious Olivia."

"I know, but you're so cute." I get out of the car and keep my face turned away from the security guard.

Bradley walks around the car. "One thing first." He holds my head and kisses me like it's the last kiss I will ever get. His aura is so strong and red, I squint from the glare. "What?"

"You're aura is blinding." I smile.

"I hope it is." He gives me another kiss before we make our way into the visitor elevator.

There is silence between us. I think we are both nervous about our first breaking and entering, well my first breaking and entering. He's just an accomplice. I wonder how much time he can get for that.

We get off on the second floor and turn left and spot the stairs sign down the hall. Of course there is a security camera stuck right in the corner. True to his word, Bradley holds up the soft tent kennel for only a second as I slip into the stairwell. My stomach turns. I sort of wish Bradley had come, but I know he'd be in the way. Besides, he needs to keep watch.

I look around for a camera before taking my hike up the stairs eight more flights. Bradley's right, I don't see any.

I climb to the fifth floor on a mission and have to stop. Beads of sweat form on my upper lip. I pull my hair up into a ponytail. I know I can't stop, but my legs and butt don't feel the same way.

Five. More. Floors.

Slowly I climb, letting my adrenaline take over.

A sigh of relief escapes my lips. Bradley and I never talked about how I'm going to get to Dabi's apartment without being seen by the camera.

I take the key Michael told me belonged to the stairwell and open it.

"Yes," I say in a hushed whisper. He didn't tell me it opened up in her *penthouse*!

Michael failed to mention she had the best place in the joint. She definitely had the prettiest view in Park City. Briefly I look out the glass-wall window that overlooks the square. I can see the entire town gathered for the annual Park City Public Servant fundraiser. Twinkling lights hang around the gazebo where the band is playing and the food line is all the way down the street.

I totally forgot about the fund-raiser. Relief settles in my stomach because I know the police won't be snooping around Dabi's apartment. There is no way our finest are going to miss out on their annual hot dogs, beer and apple pie. I went once and won't be going back. There is nothing more unappealing then a bunch of men who think their shit doesn't stink sitting around and belching. Not my idea of fun.

I turn back to look for any type of clues Dabi might have left behind.

I'm pleasantly surprised to find a couple of lights have been left on. I twist the cap on my keychain flash light. I don't know what I was planning on doing with it because it gives off as much light as a lightning bug.

Dabi's place isn't ransacked, as I pictured it would be. I thought there'd be clothes all over, drawers hanging open where deputy dog and his hounds might've trashed the place. Nothing. It's spotless.

I walk in the kitchen and my eyes follow up along the oak cabinets to the glass ceiling. My mouth drops open. I've heard of these but have never seen one. My eyes cross the ceiling and down the glass wall that overlooks Park City square.

I run my finger along the bookshelf wall where Dabi kept her awards, some knick knacks from her travels and a few photos. She was beautiful. I don't recall her being this pretty when we were in school. Granted she's younger than me, but I'd put money on it that she was one of those gals who would have gotten prettier as she got older.

She has the same picture where she's posing with Michael and Kent. There isn't anything else that catches my eye as a clue. I don't know what I'm looking for, but there has to be something.

I hear the band playing in the square. I walk back over to the floor-to-ceiling glass wall and look out. I know Aunt Matilda doesn't ever miss a good time. She has to be in that crowd somewhere.

I look hard to find her and smile as soon as I catch a glimpse of her Bohemian strapless dress. What seventy-year-old woman wears a strapless dress? Aunt Matilda. She looks divine with a big smile across her face as she chats it up with cop Carl. I'm relieved to see her happy, but ecstatic to see her talking to Carl. I know he's not working.

Quickly I scan the crowd to see if I can count the rest of Park City's armed forces. "One, two." I count the two who are gathered near the watering trough, aka, beer keg. "Where are you, Ian?" I whisper and continue to look for him.

"Shit! Shit, shit." I grab whatever I can when I see Ian walking across the street toward the apartment building and enter under the awning.

With a couple photo albums under my arm, I grab the dog bowl by the door, spilling the contents all over the tile flooring, and take the stack of mail on the counter before I leave the exact way I entered. Through the back.

"Did you find anything?" Bradley's waiting in the stairwell outside of Dabi's penthouse.

"These." I hand him the photo albums and start running down the stairs. "Let's go. I saw Ian enter the building."

"Pictures? Who's Ian?" Bradley huffs down the steps on my heels. "What's up with the dog bowl?"

We make it back to the car. I turn my head away from the window when I see Ian's police car pulling out of the garage. "That's Park City's newest." I point in the direction of the cop car. "I met him when I took the file down to Carl. He claims *Ian's* real good at solving murders and that's why I have to get Splitsville.com cleared before Ian snoops around too much."

I watch Ian's taillights turn the corner. Maybe I did have a little more time in Dabi's penthouse. Maybe the garage let them park there for the fund raiser. Either way, I'm sure there may be some photos linking Dabi and Kent. Besides, I can always go back. I have a key.

"My brother-in-law is a cop out west. He owes me a few favors, if you ever need anything." Bradley nonchalantly throws it out there like no big deal.

"A cop?" I immediately think about the emails. "What about tracing emails?"

"I don't think he can trace the person, but he can get a location by the IP address."

My phone rings putting my ideas about using Bradley's brother-in-law out of my head. I look at the screen and see it's Erin.

"Hi." I'm glad to see she's awake. "Why is Herbie barking?"

"Can you come home?" I'm alarmed by the sound of her frightened voice. "A policeman is here and he's asking me all sorts of questions about Kent that I can't answer."

Bradley punches it to make it home. I leave the photo albums in the car. There is no way I am going to give them up or let the police know I let myself into Dabi's apartment.

"Why aren't you at the Park City fund raiser?" I bend down to pick up Herbie, whose aura is completely beige. I shudder. He's feeling upset and irritated by the presence of Ian.

"There's been a murder, Ms. Davis, and police work is never done." He looks toward Erin. "Don't you find it interesting that two murders have turned up and you knew both of the victims?" He points to Erin. "And that your friend here was dating one of them?"

I don't know what he's leading to, but I don't think it's nice. "You'll find the town of Park City is very small and everyone knows practically everyone."

"I'm just asking questions." He steps back toward the door. "Trying to figure this out. That's all."

"I turned over all my files to Carl." I'm letting Ian know we don't trust him yet. "He has everything I know. Unless you have a warrant, you can leave now."

He rests his hand on his Barney Fife gun and turns to walk back to his car.

I watch the police car turn the corner and I quietly shut the door. With Ian on the job, the stakes are higher and I have less time to figure this out. I have to get some real clues if I'm going to save Michael, Splitsville.com, and now Erin.

Seventeen

"TKG...." I roll to my side. "TKG..."I wake myself up muttering these three letters. I groan and roll to the other side. I need to reach for my notebook, but I don't have the energy to write it all down. Breaking into Dabi's wore me out and I just need a little more shuteye.

I reach down and feel around for Herbie. It's a comfort just having him by my side. I slightly open my eyes to see the time illuminated in green dots on my clock.

"TKG." Aunt Matilda scares the bejesus out of me, standing there scribbling away in a notebook.

"Aunt Matilda! It's in the middle of the night. How long have you been here?" I sit up and put my hand on Herbie. "Some watch dog you are." He doesn't even lift his head.

She closes the notebook and sits at the edge of my bed. Her hair's pulled up in a bandana and the dangly earrings in her ears are the same bells that are on her shirt fringe. I smile at the memories of waking up several times over the years with her staring at me. Only this time I see the worry in her eyes. The worry about how this is about me.

"A few different times over the course of a few days." She takes out her notebooks. A ritual I know all too well.

Sometimes, well, most times, it had to do with a recent crime in Park City. She'd throw me a bone to get me to dream. She would mention things like a suspect's name, or conveniently take me to see something, and the dreams would begin. She can read auras, but she doesn't have dreams.

I didn't mind. I was a mini sleuth, a Nancy Drew and for a kid that's kind of cool. Plus I was helping out.

"Well?" I question what she's overheard and point to the book she has behind her back.

"Something about lipstick and TKG." She reads her cryptic writing. She quietly closes the door. "It's all I can make out." She turns toward the door and then back. "The older you get, the more you mumble."

I roll back on my side.

3:30 AM.

I close my eyes and let my mind wander. I know I saw something else, I can feel it. But what?

I relax more. I take a deep breath in my nose and let it out slowly through my mouth. My mind begins to see the three letters. TKG. Suddenly they are printed across Erin's face and her words become tattooed on my brain.

"You're jealous because I was happy. You are jealous of my relationship." Her eyes are dark and scare me. I know it's only a dream, but I know all too well that sometimes my dreams are meant to tell me something.

I reach for my notebook, but pull my hand back.

"No." I shake my head. "Those words never came from her mouth and I refuse to give them life."

I squeeze my eyes together to make them go away-permanently.

***

This is the first outing for Erin since being named a suspect in Kent's death. It's taken me all day and a bribe of ice cream to get her out of the bed where she's made a cave for herself. The lack of sleep and lack of food have taken a visual toll on her. Her black bob reminds me of a coarse horse's tail that's in bad need of a brush and cut. Her split ends are killing me!

Her blue eyes have deepened to grey or maybe the one-inch black circles make them look darker.

"I guess I should check my messages," she says, turning her phone on. She's taking a leave of absence from her party planning business until this mess is figured out. Trust me, no one in town wants their party planned by a murderer. That would definitely dampen any party excitement.

With the new no-text law, I look around for any cops, mainly Carl or Ian, before I check the vibrating cell phone between my legs. Coast is clear. I pick it up and scroll down to my messages. I'm sure it's a new dump. All this dying business has made me virtually ignore my real business.

I stop at the red light. I know I only have a few seconds before the light turns green to read the dump and put it back between my legs.

"Are you comfy in your office? Not for long. Stop breaking people's hearts or yours will stop beating altogether. Are you scared?" I read out loud.

"Oh my God! Let me see that." Erin's mouth is wide open. She grabs my phone.

The guy behind me in a pickup starts to beep, "Go! Green means go!" he screams and continues to lay on his horn.

I put the pedal to the metal and give a couple friendly birds to the guy behind me.

"Let me have your phone!" I grab Erin's phone out of her hands before she can object and immediately dial Bradley's number. I continue to drive and hold Erin's phone to my ear all at once. So much for the new law.

"Hi, Erin." I ignore Bradley's happy greeting. I glance between the rear view mirror and ahead of me, making sure there are no cops around to pull me over for being on the phone.

"No, it's me. Listen carefully." I need Bradley to concentrate on my words. "I just received a new threat and they obviously don't know where I live because they said 'I'm watching you in your big office right now. Are you scared?' And I'm driving."

I know I didn't get the threat word for word, but he gets the gist of it.

"Hold on. I'm on it." I can hear Bradley clicking away on the computer, getting into my website, where he can pull up the information he needs to send to his brother-in-law to trace the email. "Coffee Bean."

Without looking I make a complete illegal u-turn. Thank God no one is around.

"I'm not even a minute from there." Thank goodness for quick technology, favors and a good brother-in-law. I hurry, knowing I will soon be face-to-face with the person who's threatening me. And without the police's help.

Bradley's voice quivers, "I can't come. I'm the only one here." He is still at the SPCA.

With no time to spare, I punch it. I am going to end this once and for all. My poor little Toyota. I rub the dash. "Don't fail me now."

I pull into the parking lot on two wheels and find a spot right near the door. I run into the Coffee Bean as quickly as my feet will carry me and wend my way through the lunch crowd line. I know exactly where the computers are.

Back corner.

I've used it before on a couple dumps when my computer was getting fixed.

The chair is pushed back, a steaming cup of coffee sits by the keyboard and no one is there. It's like they vanished into thin air. Like they knew I was coming.

Surely one of these customers had to see someone on the computer. "Did you see who was on the computer?" I grab the guy's arm at the table closest to the monitor and point to the full coffee mug.

"No." The man sounded annoyed, and jerks his arm out of my grip. "What's wrong with you?"

I turn to the rest of the table. "Excuse me; did you see the person who was on the computer?"

Everyone shakes their head no and I notice the people at the next table talking about the crazy girl.

"What crazy girl?" I ask one of the women who are staring at me. "Was she at the computer?"

"No honey. They're talking about you." She gives me a sorrowful look.

I take the mug of coffee and head to the exit. Cop Carl is standing with his arms crossed and legs spread apart.

"What's the rush?" He doesn't break his stare.

I snarl and then laugh. "Aren't those a little too Starsky and Hutch?" I point to his black driving gloves. I remember Aunt Matilda loved watching that show every Wednesday night. She would squeal like a little girl when they caught their man.

"You aren't tracking your own email threats are you?" He peers over his 1980 Ray Ban sunglasses with a smug look on his face.

The look is enough to send chills up *and* down my spine, but I have to look away in fear of seeing his aura. I don't have time to play around when I know his aura is totally authoritative.

"How do you know about those?" I growl and worm my way around him. "If you want something productive to do, besides following me around, you should solve the unsolved murders."

I can't believe he knows about the emails.

On my way out the door, I dump the contents of the mug and take it with me. I don't know why, but it seems the thing to do. Evidence, test it for DNA like they do in CSI. One small problem, the only science kit I have is the small test tube kit I got has a kid.

"Olivia." Carl steps outside the door and jerks my arm to stop me. "You need to leave any threats to us to solve. This isn't for an amateur." He takes his sunglasses off and gives me the sternest fatherly look. He shakes the piece of paper in his hands at me. "I know you're trying to save your business, but you're also getting death threats."

I tighten my lips together and wiggle my arm from his grip and storm back to my car.

"Did you see that woman in the baseball cap?" Erin turns completely around in her seat looking out the back window.

"No." I keep my eyes on Carl who continues to stare at me. I look away and take a closer look at the mug.

"I swear it was *that* girl." Erin turns around and puts her head next to mine and looks at the mug. "Ugly lipstick."

"Look! Lipstick!" I hold it up and put it back down. I see Carl straining to see what I am talking about. I'm not about to do all his work.

"I know, I just said that." Erin backs away like I'm crazy. The rose color is stamped on one side of the mug. The left. So she is a right-handed coffee drinker.

"The girl that slapped Kent. I swear she walked out as soon as you walked, er, ran in the Coffee Bean." She points to the door.

"What?" I jump back out of the car and look for the girl she's talking about. Is she the one sending me death threats? Is she the one who killed Kent and Dabi? "Oh my God!" I stop for a second and stare out the front window. "TKG." I whisper out loud.

"TK who?" Erin questions.

I get back in the car and ask Erin, "What's Kent's full name?"

"Terry Ken…"

I stop her. I know exactly what she is going to say. "My dream." I slowly turn my head and my mouth flies open. "The initials in my dream and the initials Aunt Matilda wrote down. TKG, Terry Kent Goodwin."

"What does Kent have to do with your dreams?"

I have no way of explaining how my brain works. With the mere mention of Kent's name, those initials pop in my head like hot kernels of corn. "Terry Kent Goodwin used Splitsville.com to dump a girl named Brittany because she had Obsessive Compulsive Disorder."

"Shut up!" Erin begins to scream and bounce in her seat. "Do you think she's the killer? Do you think she set me up because he was dating me?"

"I don't know." I start the old Toyota and put Ian out of my mind. "But we are about to find out."

I pull out of the lot and head back home. I'm quickly finding out there's more to solving a murder than putting names together. I know I have the baseball-cap woman's information from using the website. It shouldn't be hard tracking her down.

"What about the ice cream?" Erin asks.

"I think we have sherbet in the freezer." I assure her. I'm not about to stop now. We are on a roll.

**

"Terry Kent Goodwin" I repeat as my fingers touch each file tab.

I glance over at Erin who's looking through the files on the desk. Herbie stares at us.

"Got it!" Erin screams and holds it up in the air.

We hunch over my desk. "Let's find out about this dump." I open the file and immediately remember what a pain in the ass Brittany was.

Oh, how I remember that perfectly put together redhead. I also recall what some people think about redheads, "they are hot-headed" and "a woman scorned is worse when she has red hair." Brittany's definitely been scorned.

"I remember her." I rub the photo in the file. I pull the file up on the computer.

"OCD?" Erin laughs, "No wonder he loved hanging out at my messy apartment. I think I need to rest."

I continue to read through the file and ignore Aunt Matilda as she jingles into the room.

I pull up the audio and the first words out of her mouth sting just like they did the day she said them, "Is he cheating on me with you?"

Aunt Matilda grabs my arm as soon as the words leave Brittany's mouth. We continue to listen.

"That first line is haunting." Aunt Matilda reminds me. "There are no better motives for murder or threat than a jealous woman."

I look into Brittany's eyes. Aunt Matilda is right, it *is* the reason for the death threats. But murder?

I click off the file because I think we have everything we need.

I look at Aunt Matilda. "Did you tell Carl about the email threats?" I'm hoping she didn't, but deep down I know the answer.

The answer is written all over her face before she even says it. "You're all I've got and I'm not going to sit around while someone threatens your life. I don't care how much a job means to you. Your life means more."

I can't help but have some sense of relief. I thought I'd be mad, but she's right. She's always right. Still, someone's still trying to link me to the murders and I'm going to find out who.

***

While everyone's still tucked in bed, the early morning sun wakes me up. I let Herbie out in the backyard, but not before looking to make sure no one is out there. I make my way to the kitchen to start the coffee.

Brittany's dump file is right where I left it. On the counter. I thumb through it again, hoping something will jump out at me.

I hear Erin shuffling down the hall. "Can't sleep?" I ask her and take a mug out of the cabinet. "Do you want some coffee?"

She still has the hollow eyes and the faraway look. "No. I checked my messages and the police want to see me. I'm definitely a suspect. They said someone came forward. The person heard us fighting at the bar that night." Slowly she lifts her face and looks at me.

"Do you remember what you said?" I can't imagine what she'd say to make her a suspect. "Of course you were angry, but it doesn't mean you killed him. Heck, I'd be angry too if I saw Bradley kissing some girl."

"I…" she sobs, "I didn't tell you about all of the fight." She pulls out the bar stool and sits down. Her shoulders are slumped.

I lean over and pat her hands. Her crystal aura is a clear as ever. "Nothing can implicate you."

"I told him I hated him and could kill him for what he's done." She puts her head in her hands and continues to cry.

I hand her a paper towel to wipe her face because it's the closest thing to a tissue I've got. "What did he say?" I know he got himself out of it.

"I told him he was right." She stops and looks at me.

I can't recall what she's talking about. "Right? About what?"

Her words sting me like a bee, "You couldn't stand him, but I think he was right. You can't stand to see me have a boyfriend. You are so jealous."

I quickly blink to make sure her aura isn't turning grey. I take a deep breath. Erin's entire aura is ashen, almost black. And black auras mean she's got an uneasy heart which makes her unable to forgive in this moment. But I don't stop even as her aura darkens.

"Jealous? Of what?" I stand taller and defend myself-forgetting all about her aura. I remember my dream and the words she said in it.

"I was finally happy and you flaunted yourself in front of him." In shock, I watch her storm down the hall and disappear into the bedroom. She rushes out, arms loaded with her things.

"That's not true," I yell out after her, "I have Bradley. Remember? And he doesn't want me for money!"

She peels out of the driveway.

I can't believe this. How did her becoming a suspect turn into me wanting Kent dead? I put my head down on the kitchen counter. Kent is ruining my relationship with Erin from the great beyond.

I reach for my cell when it rings. I hope it's Erin. I don't even check to see if it's her.

"Come back," I plead. "Please, we can figure this out." I want her to know that no matter what, we will get to the bottom of this. "Erin?"

"No, Olivia." I recognize Carl's voice before he acknowledges who he is. "What are you going to figure out with Erin?"

I close my eyes, plop on the couch and wonder if I can start this day over. "Nothing, Carl. What do you want?"

He exhausts me.

"I need to talk to Matilda and I can't find her. I thought she might be there."

"No." I hang up the phone. I don't have time to worry about what he wants. I have to use what time and energy I do have to solve my own problems.

***

Dabi's life is—or was—picture perfect, or so it seems from her photo album.

The first page is an antiqued Dabi as a baby, with pink highlights around the picture. The crinoline on her dress is much larger than her tiny frame. Neatly written under it in calligraphy: *Dabi's first picture.*

Perfectly posed Dabi, even in her play date and playground pictures. Her hair bows match her shirt, skirt, socks, shoes and nail polish.

I smile looking at the tiny nails, "Nail polish?" I hold the album closer and check out each finger. If Aunt Matilda had tried to put nail polish on me, I'd have thrown a mammoth-size fit.

When my first tooth fell out, Aunt Matilda took a picture with my hands cupped around my mouth and blood slipping through the cracks. My nails had remnants of the day before dirt pile.

All of Dabi's firsts. First parade, first dance, first boyfriend, first prom, first day at Harvard business school, first. . .

I gasp, "Kent?" My mouth flies open and I frantically turn the pages to see what comes next. Kent is everywhere. There isn't a single picture without him.

I slowly turn the last page in the album. My stomach churns. The smiling Dabi in her beautiful white gown, next to a dapper Kent in his tuxedo, in what looks like a. . ., wedding? I whisper as fear sweeps over me.

"Hello?" I blindly pick up the phone while I continue to look at the happy couple.

"Hey." Bradley's voice is a welcome sound. "What's going on?"

"A lot actually." I tell him about Erin, but not about my dream, and I tell him about Dabi and Kent's marriage.

"Really?" He's surprised. "Does Erin know?"

"I don't think so." I set the album back down. I know what I have to do. I have to find out what's going on. I have to find out how Dabi, Kent and Brittany know each other. I just have to find Brittany.

"Did you see the paper today?" Bradley brings me back into the conversation.

"No. Why?" My feet are chilled from my findings, plus the cold hardwood floor isn't helping. I hastily walk over to the door and find the paper has been stepped on—by Erin I'm sure. I pick it up, and as big as day the headline reads: *Splitsville.com isn't only breaking hearts…it's breaking up a community.*

Anxiously I scan the article. There is no substantiated evidence to pinpoint Splitsville.com as the reason for the murders, only for connecting them. My heart floats in my throat. Who sent in this article? Is it another scare tactic? Or enough information for the police to suspect Splitsville.com, even more?

You never know with Park City's finest. But I do know the article doesn't say who's behind Splitsville.com and I have little time to waste. I have to get to the bottom of this.

Eighteen

I pull into the visitor parking of Dabi's father's company, Macro Hard Internet. If I have a shot to learn who these people are in Dabi's life, I'll have to go into her life and see for myself.

Aunt Matilda tried to prepare me before I left the house. "Here's a cup of coffee with an extra shot of juice." She refers to the extra espresso I only use when I need to stay up a little longer. "And it should give you a hard time concentrating on just one thing."

I pull up to the guard station, relieved that Aunt Matilda knew exactly what I needed so I can't stare at people's auras. The caffeine alone will keep my eyes jumping. All I can rely on is my intuition and the images of the people in the photographs. Especially the ones with Kent.

"I'm here for the interview in housekeeping," I tell the guard and point to the big glass building ahead. My goodness, I can't even pick up my own clothes, much less clean an entire building.

He takes the paper I fill out and looks it over. He fumbles around the sliding glass window, obviously looking for a piece of paper.

"Listen, I don't work in this department." He fiddles around in the little guard booth. "You're like me, a guy who needs a job, and I'm covering for my buddy, so." His shoulders take a move up to the tips of his ears, his lips pucker in a curious way.

"Where's your friend?" I'm not sure if he's covering for him or working for him.

"He's with the boss's secretary, if you know what I mean. I'm on lunch, but with the hat they don't know it's not him." He weakly smiles. "I kind of owe him."

"I see." I nod. "Since I'm here for the cleaning department and you're security, we're on the same level and I should understand?" This situation is quickly taking a strategic move in my favor. "Sure, I won't say anything if you give me a couple of days-passes so I don't have to stop at this little station every time I come."

"There you go." He hands me the passes, winks and asks, "Are you single?"

"Yes, but you're not." I point at the big shiny gold band. "And by the size of the ring, your wife wants everyone to know."

"We're having troubles." His eyes show a twinkle of hope.

I hand him a Splitsville.com business card. "If you're unhappy, call that number. I hear they do a bang-up job on breaking up marriages." I should be ashamed, but I'm not. It's all about business. I put my hands on the wheel and slowly drive to the last spot in the lot.

My phone rings and I pick it up to see who it is. Bradley.

"Hi." I crane my neck to see how many entrances are near my car. For some reason I have a fear these people will recognize me and trap me. Knowing all the escape routes somehow soothes me.

"I don't like the idea of you doing this." I like the tenderness in Bradley's voice. I know he doesn't like it, but he does understand.

"Well, you can stop saying that because I am here. I've got to go."

"I have some news." He has no shame. He'll use whatever tactic to get me to stay on the line. "My brother-in-law tracked down the locations of all the threatening emails."

I keep my hand on the keys in the ignition. "Great!" A little glimmer of hope creeps into my body, stirring up a bit of excitement.

Bradley sounds very confident. "I gave him the codes from the sender and he got back with me. And he told me we need to call the police if you're getting threats."

Here we go. He's not a big advocate of my Nancy Drew ways.

I cut to the chase because I don't really care about the particulars; I just want to know who. "Who? Who sent them?" I stop. My life is way more important than illegally going for a job interview.

"I don't know." His voice goes flat. The confidence he had a few seconds ago has completely forsaken him.

"What do you mean you don't know?" If he doesn't know, why did he tell me this bit of information? Some cop his brother-in-law is.

"They are all from different public computers. One from the library, one from the internet café and the last one is from the Coffee Bean."

"So this person is going around using public computers?" Someone must really be serious to go out of their way to find public computers. Plus those are places I go. I wonder if I've seen them. I look off at the glass building, digging back in my memory at someone who might've stuck out. You know, like the crazy lady at the supermarket or the bum in the park – they stick out.

Mmm...nope. Nothing. I can't even remember what I ate for dinner last night, much less the people standing in line at the Coffee Bean. I'm even more uneasy now. I can't help but wonder if this person really is watching me. "We have a smart one on our hands," I say to Bradley.

"The police will have to subpoena the library, Internet Café or where ever else the emails are coming from to see who's using the public computers." Bradley pauses. "I really think you need to call the police."

"Right now I need to go into Macro Hard and fill out an application." There's no need to talk about this.

"Fine. Call me as soon as you get out of there."

I put my phone on vibrate and place it in my purse. The rear view mirror squeaks as I position it to see my face. Lipstick—check, brushed hair—check, clean teeth—check. I'm ready to go in.

I'm not sure what I'll find out at Macro Hard, but being around a lot of people in a closed environment, I'm a little worried about colliding auras. I don't care how many espresso shots Aunt Matilda gives me.

I stop shy of the entrance. The sun reflecting off the huge glass building makes my eyes scan up to the top. There have to be at least ten floors. It's definitely the tallest building in Park City.

For a brief moment I reconsider applying. How can I possibly clean an entire building this size when I can't clean the five room cottage I live in. With a deep inhale and steady exhale, I walk straight through the door.

"May I help you?" I watch the words leave the petite brunette's lips and realize I can't back down now.

I blink several times to keep her aura at bay.

"We have a bathroom over there if you need to fix your contacts."

Contacts? I don't wear contacts. I can pretend to wear contacts. I put my fingers up to my eyes like I've seen Erin do when her contacts are bothering her.

"I'll be fine. I'm here to apply for the cleaning position." I keep fidgeting with my lids pretending to fix my contacts so I won't see her aura.

"Take the elevators next to the bathroom up to the third floor. You'll find the HR department there." She picks up the phone and says, "Thank you for calling Macro Hard. How may I direct your call?"

HR? Those are two letters that haven't floated around in my dreams. What's HR? I wonder, while keeping my eyes low. Thank God I'm the only one in the elevator. I run my fingers down the index next to the buttons and push three. "Human Resources. HR." I snicker at my stupidity.

The entire third floor is covered in a thick fog of hovering auras. My head begins to get light and dizzy. I grab the receptionist's desk and hold on for dear life.

"Are you okay?" I don't even look up at the voice coming from the other side of the cheap laminate desk.

I put my fingers back up to my eyes. "Contacts." I grimace, hoping it will work a second time. "I'm here to apply for the cleaning position."

"Nightshift, right?"

I perk up when I hear night shift. Nightshift equals no people, which mean no auras. Perfect! Suddenly my pretend contacts are much better. For a nightshift position I can keep my dizziness in check long enough to interview.

"Yes, the nightshift." I ignore her white cloudy aura, and do my best shit-eating grin. "I'd rather clean toilets than sleep."

"Here." She hands me a clipboard with an application. "Fill it out and take it down to the second door on the right." She scans me from head to toe, checking me out.

I want to say, your aura color does nothing for your bleached out hair, but I don't. Like a good girl I take the clipboard and head over to the seating area to fill it out.

"What's your name?" She hollers after me.

I almost spit out Jenn from Splitsville.com, but catch my tongue. "Olivia Davis."

She picks up the phone and says, "Olivia Davis is filling out paper-work for the cleaning position. She'll be down shortly."

I fill out everything on the application like a breeze until the previous experience part throws me off. I tap the clipboard with the pen top. "Hmmm, previous experience." I guess I can put that I clean my house every few days which would be a gross exaggeration.

"I'm sorry, is there a problem?" I look up at the tall Amazon women towering over me.

Of course there is a problem. I've never cleaned a toilet in my life much less a urinal.

I politely smile. "No problem."

She puts her man hands out and says, "Great. Sandra Jones, HR manager." My eyes follow her finger as she taps on her prestigious HR manager nametag.

"Nice to meet you." Obviously this is the butt I need to kiss in order to get in here and figure this mystery out.

"If you're done, you can follow me." She takes the application and hands the clipboard back to the receptionist.

I follow her down to the second door into her office. She gestures for me to sit on the loveseat next to her chair, with a small table between us.

"We like it cozy, like a home." She touches the picture hanging on the wall. "We are all family here, no matter what job you have."

I stand back up and mosey over to the picture. Immediately I spot Dabi in the framed 11x14 photo. I make a mental note of all the people, but Sandra Jones's fat finger is too busy pointing herself out.

"Very nice." Again I politely smile.

"Let's get back down to business, shall we?" She points back to the love seat.

I agree as she goes through my application starting with the verification of my name. It's all smooth sailing until I see her eyes focus on a particular part of the application.

She taps the page. "I see you left out previous experience." She looks at me wanting an explanation.

Nervously I say, "There's so much to put down and so little space."

"So you've scrubbed floors and toilets and used a feather duster before?" Sandra Jones mocks me. I want to snarl, but decide not to be a smart ass because I need this job to further my Nancy Drew skills.

"Yes."

She places the application on the table between us. "Here's the deal. We need someone tonight. Every floor has its own cleaning person. You will be cleaning the executive offices." She hands me a map of the executive floors. Dabi's name jumps out at me. "Let's make this a trial week."

Trying hard to control my excitement and the luck of having this handed to me is almost too much to bear. "Yes, I will do a great job. Trial week."

With a few particulars discussed and a couple different pieces of paperwork filled out, Sandra gives me a temporary name tag and free pass to Dabi's office...er...make that free reign to learn how to clean a urinal.

Pushing the heavy glass door to the outside with one hand, I reach in my purse for my phone with the other.

"I start tonight," I say to Bradley when he answers the phone. The phone jiggles as I run to my car to get out of the pelting rain.

"That was quick."

My hair is dripping and my clothes are soaked. I take it slow around the back roads making my way home and tell Bradley about the entire interview.

Nineteen

The rain is coming down at a steady pace, which puts me in a crabby mood, and having to stay up to clean is the last thing I want to do. I had no clue they were going to hire me on the spot. That was something I wasn't prepared for. I'm tired and my shoes are soaking wet, I want to go home, crawl into my bed and pull the quilt Aunt Matilda made me, over my head, with Herbie lying next to me, and sleep the night away.

But if I want to save my entire life, I have to learn how to work a mop bucket. How the hell am I going to pull this off? I'll have to work and work fast. Get in and look around.

I find the closest spot to the door because I definitely have no desire to clean an entire building with sopping wet shoes. Or snoop around in wet shoes.

"Welcome to the night shift." The elderly gentleman checks my badge and makes some type of mark on a piece of paper. "Here's your uniform and your cart closet is over there."

I take the blue jumpsuit from him and hold it up to me. It's something straight out of the eighties only a little less attractive. "You've got to be kidding me?" I fold it back up. "Are you?"

I eye the security guard. He eyes me back.

"Nope, not kidding." His small frame is exactly how I'd picture a grandfather to be. His white hair is neatly tucked under his security cap and his matching mustache is equally maintained. "Everyone in housekeeping wears one. Just be glad no one has to see you in it."

"Precisely!" I slap the get up on his counter. "No one will see me so I don't have to wear it." It's bad enough I have to keep myself awake for this.

"No." He slides it back toward me. "You have to. Or my job will be on the line. And you aren't looking like you'll be here long. So it's not worth it."

"What does that mean?" I curl my nose.

"You don't look like much of a cleaning person. Or at least one that usually works those kinds of jobs."

"I don't know whether to take that as a compliment or insult," I shoot back at him.

"Let's just say you don't look like you get your hands too dirty." His suspicions are right. I don't plan on being here very long. A few nights at best, enough time to find some clues to who the people are in the photos and their relationship to Dabi and Kent. "Enough chit-chat, young lady. It's time you get to work or you'll never get these executive offices cleaned tonight."

Reluctantly I take the jumpsuit to the closet and put it on over my clothes. It's bad enough I have to clean; wearing this is plain humiliating. Even if it is just me and the security guard.

I open the door and back the cart out of the closet, only it doesn't budge with a little pull. I grab the handle and slide while pulling at the same time. I turn when I hear laughter.

"What?" I glare at the security guard who's bent over laughing.

"Yep, I knew you weren't cut out for this work," he yells just as I fall to the ground. He points and doubles over again snorting. "There's a brake on the side."

I brush myself off, hoping it will help with the humiliation, but it doesn't. I fiddle with the brake and it pops free, causing the cart to slide forward, and I have to throw my body in front to stop it. It's the battle of me versus the cart and I'm going to win or at least I try. "Ouch!" I jump around on one leg while holding my foot in my hands. The cart rolled right over my foot and continues to roll until it stops smack dab into the wall.

I don't look at the security guard, who is giving his full attention to details about me, as I gather the cart. Once I have it back on track, I push the squeaky thing down the hall.

Every other light down the hallway is just enough for me make a mental note of all the rooms and the name plates. And if I count correctly (I did pass third grade math with flying colors) there are eight executive offices and a conference room.

I quickly maneuver my way around two offices doing the basics—vacuuming, light feather dusting and empting the garbage cans.

"You okay in here?" A flashlight blinds me.

I hold my hand up to block the light. "Do you think you could kill the light?" I blink trying to ignore the black dot in the center of my vision.

I hear Harold click the flashlight off. "Sorry, job hazard." He flicks the overhead lights on.

"I'm good. You didn't have to turn all the lights on. The corner lamps are fine." Every office is laid out the same. There is a big cherry desk in front of the windows and a wall full of cherry shelving on the opposite wall. Which stinks because all this dusting leaves me little time to snoop, and Harold following my every move doesn't help.

Harold sits in one of the cigar chairs.

"What are you doing?" I dust around the lamp on the table next to him. "Don't you have to walk around and point your light in a corner somewhere?"

I don't bother waiting for him to get up before I exit the room.

Nothing seems suspicious until I hit Dabi's office. I back the cart up to the door and look down the hall. The coast is clear. I back into her office pulling the squeaky cart. I grit my teeth hoping it will miraculously stop the god-awful sound coming from the wheels. I bend down and spit on the wheel for some lube but of course it doesn't work.

Dabi's office is a little bigger. It's a lot more feminine with window treatments and corresponding decorations. The closet door is open and I look in. She has several jackets hanging up, an armoire full of accessories, and shoes to match. A tinge of jealousy makes my stomach churn. The closet is bigger than my bedroom.

Everything seems to be in place. Her desk looks as though it hasn't been touched. I use my keychain flashlight, which only gives me pin-sized amount of light, and read her day calendar. There are business meetings penciled in dinner dates, a couple of different parties but nothing out of the ordinary for a businessperson.

Footsteps and voices coming down the hall cause me to stop. The doorknob squeaks as I turn it and quietly shut the door. I put my ear up to the door. The footsteps seem to be getting closer. Quickly I grab my cart and head toward the door next to the closet.

"Please be a way out." I close my eyes and open it. "Crap," I whisper, "a bathroom." I notice my cart and I will barely fit in there.

I squat down praying that whoever is coming into Dabi's office doesn't have to pee.

"I guess if anything good can come out of my dear sweet Dabi's death, it's Kent can't get any of her money." I hear the voice loud and clear coming from under the crack in the bottom of the door.

I barely crack the door to see who's talking. It's the bald guy from the press conference—Dabi's dad. I can't see the person he's talking to because the opening isn't wide enough and if I move a single millimeter, I'll fall out of the bathroom and blow my cover. I keep my knees bent clear up to my ears and stay as quiet as possible.

"It is a shame." I barely make out the whispers of the other person. I can tell it's a man's voice. I close my eyes and strain harder to hear him, but he's a dark shadow. "I can't believe he killed her and then himself."

What? Killed himself? How does this guy know Kent killed himself? That is not what Carl is telling everyone.

"They don't know that for sure. But it all makes perfect sense." I have perfect view of Dabi's dad putting a file in the drawer. "No one will come in here, so it will be safe."

They continue to talk about some business that I don't understand—expanding the company and working late nights. My eyes feel heavy. I push the indiglo on my watch and notice its one AM and way past my bed time. I think I hear the door close.

***

"You can come out now." My knees fling out from my chest as the bathroom door opens and the security guard startles the crap out of me. "They're gone." He leans the right side of his body on the door handle.

"I…" I have no idea how I'm going to get out of this one. I blink several times to figure out where I am. I can't believe I feel asleep. "I'm not used to this night shift thing."

"I don't know who you are but you better get to the job they're paying you for." He points to a small camera hanging from the ceiling. The camera I didn't see on my way in. He nods toward the cart. "You need to oil that thing when you're done snooping."

"That's what I want to ask you about." I grab the cart and pull it out. I whip it around and push it after the security guard.

"I don't know anything about carts. I'm the security guy and I should be calling you in right now, but I didn't see you do anything wrong yet." His eyebrows narrow. He stops at the security desk and pushes buttons to bring up the camera screens.

"No, not the wheels." I lean over his desk. He's got a complete smorgasbord laid out in front of him and it looks really good. Ham sandwich, potato salad, regular salad with ranch dressing, and I'd know ranch dressing from anywhere. There are several snack baggies full of cut up veggies, a thermos for something hot, diet coke and a bottle of water. I can almost taste the cold water. The cold sweating down the side makes it look so refreshing. "Your wife afraid you aren't eating?"

"My wife is dead."

A knot instantly forms in my throat. His eyes warm.

"It's all right. My daughter takes real good care of me." He holds up a snack bag of carrots. I take it. "Harold."

I smile pulling apart the bag. Harold is trying to make nice.

"I'm sorry. I have a habit of putting my foot plus my leg in my mouth." The carrot crunches between my teeth. "I guess I better get back to work."

"What did you want to talk to me about?" The sandwich he took a bite out of makes my mouth water.

"We'll talk later." I decide I'm not ready to confide in Harold yet. I've little time to discover whatever it is I'm trying to find.

The little nap and carrots did me good. I've got a little giddy-up back in my step and with the building empty—well, I guess Harold is watching me I can get back to business. I continue down the halls, making a mental note of where all the rooms are.

I push my cart down toward Mr. Stone's office.

I take out the vacuum and try not to look at the camera hanging in the corner of the room. I keep my back to it most of the time and move my arm back in forth as I read Mr. Stone's calendar. Barely sticking out is a piece of paper.

I turn off the vacuum and shuffle the paper on his desk around with the feather duster so I can read it. Of course the paper is heavier than the little duster so I swing causing all the papers to catch the wind and float to the floor.

"What are you doing?" Harold is standing with the door wide open. "I don't think this room needs to be cleaned." His brows draw together, making the creases deep between them. "Mr. Stone's wife cleans his office."

"They didn't tell me what I couldn't clean." I scramble to the floor to pick up sheets of paper and quickly slip the one with Dabi's name on it in my jumpsuit pocket.

"Well, this one and Ms. Stone's are off limit." He holds the door wide open, "As a matter of fact, those are the only two rooms you've attempted to clean tonight. If I didn't know better, I'd think you were a cop. Now why don't you start with the bathrooms down at the end of the hall?"

Meekly I follow him out and get to my next stop. Bathrooms.

I push open the first stall with scrub brush in hand and Harold standing over me. I go in for the kill. Harold hands me some scrubbing foam stuff in a can. I bend over and scrub as hard as I can.

"That's cleanser. Use it." He shuffles off, hopefully back to his desk. After he talks to management, I'm sure I'll be fired, so I need to get all the information I can now.

I take the foam and spray it all along the edges. As I'm scrubbing the piece of paper falls into the toilet and I plunge my hand in after it.

"Ewww." I pull my hand and shake it as soon as I realize what I've just done. I look down in the bowl at the only words visible left on the paper. *Dabi Stone: Last Will and Testament page 3* is all I can make out. The cleaner eats it faster than I can read it.

***

"Dabi's last will and testament is what it said." On my way home I call Bradley and tell him about my night on the job. "It was in Mr. Stone's office and only one page. That means there are two more pages somewhere else."

At least the sun is coming up and no rain in sight. I'm exhausted and ready to hit the sack as soon as I get home.

"Where do you think they are?" Bradley is practically yelling over all the dogs barking in the background.

"I have no clue. But if they don't fire me first, I'm going to find them. They're somewhere in that building."

I'm glad to be home, in the cozy confinements of my house. Aunt Matilda has left a note saying she has taken

Herbie to her house so I can get some sleep and will bring him back later in the day. I check the caller ID to see if Erin has called, and feel sad when I see she hasn't. I resist the urge to call her and ask her about Kent. One thing's for sure, he is someone none of us knew.

I turn on the TV and settle into the couch with a cup of hot tea. Reruns of *Bewitched* put me sound to sleep.

***

I feel like I just went to sleep when Herbie jumps on me giving me kisses, and Aunt Matilda stands over me with her notebook.

I blink several times and feel the sweat on my brow. I have been dreaming about Dabi Stone's office, which meant one thing. I had to go back in there.

"What did I say?" I question Aunt Matilda. The notebook in her hand is one sure sign I've been talking in my sleep.

"Something about a file." She sticks her pen in her up-do.

Dabi's father's words begin playing over in my head. "No one will look for it in here."

"Let's break this down." I sit up and think out loud as Aunt Matilda takes a seat. "What are the motives, reasons why someone would kill Dabi and Kent?"

Aunt Matilda was always good at this part of our game when I was a kid and I need her to be this good now. "Money, greed, betrayal."

"But…"

"If this picture of Kent and Dabi is real, and it sure looks real," she opens up Dabi's photo album to the wedding picture, "maybe there is some agreement on alimony or he opted out and wanted part of the company."

Ah-ha! Kent really did seek out and marry Dabi for her money.

"So Kent really did kill Dabi because he would get some part of the company upon her death, and then her dad killed him out of revenge." I tap my temple with my finger. "Maybe Mr. Stone knows about Dabi using the service and Kent being dumped by the service. So to buy time, he's trying to pin the murders on Splitsville.com and trying to scare me."

I know there is something to Dabi's dad being involved. There has to be.

"Maybe you should get your hands on the other part of the will."

Aunt Matilda is right. I need to get my hands on that will to make sure my hunches are right. Only I feel like there is much more to it. But what?

Twenty

Herbie licks the blisters on the palm of my hand from pushing that big-ass cart around at Macro Hard. "I know, buddy."

If I'd read the job description of housekeeping, I might have gone for the mail job. Only it's during the day and sleuthing isn't as easy as I thought. So I'll stick to the low key.

If the chowder chomping old lady from *Murder She Wrote* can do this, so can I. Speaking of which, I remember I have the Sleuth channel and maybe I can catch an episode of *Snapped*. I twist my body around and find the remote on the table under a pile of clothes.

I rub my rough hands along Herbie's silky fur. He stands up, circles a couple times and finds a nice comfy spot on the cocoon of blankets.

I point the remote and press on. I hit the guide button and on the corner of my screen is a live press conference featuring none other than Officer Ian. I make the guide go away and the press conference a bigger picture. It's the same old song and dance.

"We have a few leads." His eyes bleed into the screen like he knows I'm watching. "A few witnesses have come forward in both murders." My eye catches a shadowy figure in the back in the crowd. I lean closer to see if I can get a better look, only the camera pans in the other direction and focuses on Michael. Michael who is supposed to be in hiding, but he's there in plain view.

I jump up and say to Herbie, "Come on, boy. We need to make a surprise visit to Michael and Belle." I have to make sure our agreement is in hand. What if he told the

police I've been snooping in Dabi's apartment, or worse—
Macro Hard! Why else would he be there?

I dart around the house looking everywhere for the
blue leash. In, under, on piles of clothes, in the closets,
under furniture, and it's nowhere to be found.

I grab a belt off my bed. "Come on." I pat my leg for
Herbie to follow me.

My phone and keys in one hand, Herbie in the other, I
head out to the car.

Herbie takes his usual spot on the passenger seat, I hit
the dash just in time to hear Elvis belt out *Suspicious
Minds*.

I stop in front of Michael's apartment and hook the
belt around Herbie's collar. "I know, buddy. I'll clean the
house, I promise." I have to say something to those little
black eyes when I know in my heart I'll be doing nothing
about the piles of laundry.

I check my watch and make a mental note: I have one
hour before I need to be home and put on my lovely
jumpsuit and head back to Macro Hard for, hopefully, what
will be my last night.

The park isn't as crowded as usual. Probably because
everyone is getting home from work and relaxing before
they take their dogs for a walk. I instantly spot Michael
with a few dogs and make my way toward him.

"Michael," I whisper, walking by. I'm not about to
stop and watch him pick up poop.

"Follow me." I walk to the wooded area of the park. I
don't want anyone seeing us together.

"What's up with the leash?" Michael laughs. I swear I
can see the embarrassment on Herbie's face. Belle growls
and tugs at the belt. The dogs do their usual dance of

getting reacquainted. The harder I tug Herbie away, the more he fights me.

I ignore Michael's question. I'm not here for pleasantries. "What where you doing at the press conference today?"

Michael kicks the dust around with his shoes. "I know I should've left, but I was returning a client's dog to their house and there they were, setting up the conference." He looks up, "I'm like a cat. Curiosity got me."

I feel like his mother scolding him, "I told you to stay clear. What if they saw you? Then I couldn't help you *or* me." I'm not about to let all that hard work I've done go right down the drain.

"Fine." Michael wraps the leashes around his hand and begins to walk back, "You know, you better hurry up. We won't be able to find clues in jail."

I look around to make sure no one sees us or is taking a picture, "You keep your end of the deal and we won't go to jail."

Michael heads one way and I head the other. He is right. If I don't find anything out tonight, this whole little investigation I've got going on might be a dead duck in the water. I check my watch and hurry back to the car. I've got just enough time to get Herbie home, find the awesome jumpsuit and get to work.

***

I have to find that stupid jumpsuit. I pick up piles of clothes and let them trickle back down to the floor hoping the jumpsuit will fall out. "Hush, Herbie." I yell over his bark. "I'll let you out in a couple minutes."

His bark gets louder. I stop. I slowly walk out of the bedroom and down the hall where there are no windows. I tilt my head around the corner and see Herbie standing at the door growling and barking.

He follows the shadowy figure between the door and the window. It looks like the intruder is trying to peek in the window.

I stand up against the wall and don't move. What if it's the killer? I pat my pockets for my phone, but it's not there. I must've left it in the bedroom.

The person knocks on the door. Cautiously I look around the corner at the door. The figure is knocking louder than Herbie's bark. Damn! I'm regretting I didn't get some of that protective spray. It would come in handy today.

I get down on all fours and crawl over to the window. I slide up the wall, and barely open the blind. My heart falls back down to where it belongs when I see Carl standing at the door.

I pick Herbie up and open the door, "You scared me."

Carl gets right down to business. "Looks like you two had some sort of spat." Ian stands beyond Carl's shoulders, holding up a picture of creepy Kent and me with a very noticeable look of disgust on my face. "You want to explain what this is all about?"

I'm already running late for work and I can't find that goofy jumpsuit anywhere. I've spent the last ten minutes picking up loads of clothes and throwing them in a basket. Herbie needs to go out, and standing here defending myself and my actions to Carl and Ian are the last things on my agenda.

"Look Carl. That was the first time I ever laid eyes on him." I can't believe the killer has gone to such great lengths to take my picture. This is total premeditation. I've been worried about my business this entire time when I should've been worried about me.

"Do you have anything else to say?" Ian puts the picture back in the breast pocket of his coat. I shake my head. I'm thinking I might need a lawyer. "Did you become friends with Goodwin through Splitsville.com and when he started dating your best friend you became jealous?" Carl is hammering the questions.

Ian chimes up, "Did Erin take this picture?"

What? Jealous? Erin? Oh. My. God. They think I did it. They think I killed Kent.

"What does Erin have to do with this?"

Ian doesn't take his eyes off me. I keep a straight face. I don't want to show any fear.

Carl steps around Ian. "Leave the questions to us." He puts his hand on Ian making Ian take a step back.

"Am I a suspect?" Being a suspect was the farthest thing from my mind when I started my investigation. Now it's the only thing on my mind.

"Let's just say, don't leave town." Carl tips his hat and heads back to his cruiser with Ian in tow.

Twenty-One

My tires squeal as I pull into Macro Hard's parking lot. The rate I'm going, they're going to fire me before I can quit—another reason to save Splitsville.com. There is no way I'll ever be on time for work. Granted, if my house— or really, my clothes—were organized, I would have been here earlier.

"Running late?" Harold bends the paper down and looks over it at me. "Not a good sign for the second day."

I hold my hands in the air, looking for some sympathy as to why I'm late. "Look, calluses." No amount of lotion is going to help with this. Another good reason I don't clean, or at least a good excuse for now.

Harold doesn't budge. "Calluses or not, this place isn't going to clean itself."

I go over to the closet to retrieve the god-awful cart and refill all the cleaning supplies. I've devised a plan to keep Harold busy looking for bleach. What's the use if it isn't hidden?

I eyeball the row of paper towels on the top shelf near the back of closet. Hoisting the bleach over-top my head, I stand on my tiptoes and push the bottle until it hits the wall.

"There." I push the last paper towel roll in front of the bottle. "He'll have to search all over this place," I whisper and pull the piece of paper out of my pocket.

Last night I drew a map of all the offices at Macro Hard. Dabi's office is going to be my first stop. The paper I grabbed was the last page of her will. By the way her father was talking, the will might have something to do with Dabi and Kent's murders, so I have to get the file her father put in filing cabinet last night.

I lay a cloth on the handle of the cart. I don't want any more calluses pushing this thing around.

Harold is watching the monitors, and now would be a good time to put my plan into action. I'll clean the restrooms first then nonchalantly work my way to Dabi's office, or file cabinet. I didn't fill up the bleach bottle all the way so I can yell down at Harold to bring me some more. Finding it should take him awhile since I used my best hiding skills.

Believe it or not, the women's bathroom is nastier than the men's. Or maybe it's the fact that I only want to deal with my feminine hygiene and not the rest of the company's.

I cup my hands over my mouth. "Harold?" I call out.

"What?" He startles me by creeping around the corner when he's supposed to keep watch at his desk.

"What are you doing?" I find it a little odd he's keeping an eye on me.

"Walking around the halls." He points to the badge on his security jacket.

"Part of my job."

"Oh! Well, can you go down and get me the bleach out of the supply closet?" I shake the empty bottle in the air. "Please?"

"Now that's not part of my job." He points to the badge on my jumpsuit.

"I know, but I was late, and I need to get going on these rooms."

With a suspicious eye he says, "Fine. Ain't got anything better to do." Harold turns back toward the closet.

I'm actually glad he's here, because it'll take him a little more time to get back down the hall, open the closet and search for the bleach.

Just as Harold turns the corner to the supply closet, I rush down toward Dabi's office and use the key Michael gave me.

I find the flashlight on my keychain and turn the cap so the light comes on. Barely. "A firefly is brighter than this," I mumble to myself.

Another mental note, get a bigger flashlight.

I thumb through the files looking for I don't know what, but I figure it'll jump out at me. There is one folder with a handwritten label.

"Hmmm." It's strange how all the rest have typed stick-on labels. I pull it out and put it on Dabi's desk. I dangle the flashlight up to the title just before the battery dies. I twist it back and forth hoping it will work. I shake it, but it doesn't come on.

"What are you doing in here?" Harold startles me when he flips the lights on. "Put that back, and come with me."

I do exactly as Harold asks. I've no way of finding out what's in that file, well, not tonight anyway.

"Exactly what are you doing here?" Harold plants my butt in a chair, and walks around me in circles. "I knew something was up with you the first time I laid eyes on you. You don't have a cleaning bone in your body. You can't take the brakes off the cart, and that's the first thing you should know."

Fast, think fast, but nothing is coming. It's all blank.

He takes my hands and rubs his fingers over the rough dry patches on my palm. "Look at your hands. Soft as a baby's bottom. Do you have anything to say or should I call Mr. Stone?" He picks up the phone.

I grab the receiver out of his hands. "No." Fear jumps into my spirit. I'll for sure be waking up in jail instead of next to Herbie if he calls Mr. Stone.

Harold takes the receiver out of my hands, and puts it back on the counter. "Well? We've got all night." He sits back at his desk, pours two cups of coffee into the Styrofoam cups. One for me, and one for him.

I tell Harold everything, well almost everything. Not about me and my "gift" or my death threats. Everything about Dabi and what I know so far. Even the part about Mr. Stone's conversation with the mystery figure in Dabi's office.

His eyes soften and he folds his hands in his lap.

"I'm not saying I haven't seen anything funny, but it's none of my business." He picks up his cup and slowly takes a sip. "No business is worth going to jail over."

"Splitsville.com is." I know he doesn't understand, but I don't want to tell any more people about my "gift." I want to get this solved and move on with my life.

Harold puts his cup down, puts both hands on the desk and pauses. He stands up and begins to rub the back of his neck. "I'm going to the bathroom and take a stroll upstairs. I'm not going to monitor the cameras for at least twenty minutes." He set his big mag flashlight on the desk.

In disbelief, I watch him turn the corner. He's giving me permission and free rein of the executive offices. I grab his flashlight and quickly make it back to Dabi's office, locking the door behind me.

Just as I pull the file out, the handle on the door starts to jiggle. It's not been twenty minutes so I can't be Harold. I push the drawer back with the file barely sticking out of the top, turn the flashlight off and crouch under Dabi's desk.

Another flashlight is heading straight toward the filing cabinet. The glare coming off the white Puma tennis shoes is enough light without the flashlight. I strain to see who it is, but can't without moving the desk chair I'm wedged up against.

The file drawer slowly opens. The wheels creek with every roll they make. I look again, but still can't make out anything above the knees. Only the Puma's and blue jeans.

The shuffle of papers, the wheels rolling back in place, the click of the file cabinet being shut, the door quietly closes, the jingle of keys locking the door, and the thud of shoes walking away and the intruder is gone. All in less than five minutes.

Someone with a key knew exactly what they were coming for. I open the cabinet all the way and search through the files—twice. It's gone. The intruder got want I need. The hand-lettered file.

I open the door and look both ways. Nothing but an empty hallway and noise to match. Slowly I tiptoe my way down the hall without the flashlight on. I'm not going to bring attention to myself.

The exit sign illuminates the hallway. If I take the stairs, I can make it up to Harold faster. Taking two stairs at a time isn't for someone who sits in a computer chair all day. I stop for a brief second at the top and catch my breath.

Harold stands at the end of the hallway, looking out the window.

"I'm so glad I found you. Alive." I grab and hug him.

"Child, what's wrong with you?" Harold pulls away like I have the plague.

I explain everything that happened while I hid under Dabi's desk. "You keep a running video right?" The intruder has to be all over the camera footage. You can't walk an inch without seeing a camera in this place.

"It would've been running, but I gave you twenty minutes. *Remember*?"

"What?" I can't believe it!

"If I gave you twenty minutes to do whatever it is you need to do, I'm certainly not going to keep the camera's rolling for the world to see it." He shakes his head. "I need my job."

"Did you see anyone?" I ask.

"No. I was busy trying to ignore the executive office so when the police come snooping I won't be able to answer any questions." Harold starts down the hall. "I'm going to walk around and see if I see anyone."

Why in the world would he go look for the intruder? What if they're still here? "Wait. I'll go with you." There's no way I'm letting him go alone or even worse, leave me here.

He jingles the key ring hooked on his belt. "It was probably Mr. Stone."

Harold has a point. I never thought about that. I guess I'm the intruder.

I walk behind Harold the entire time, like a shy child. Even with the lights on, this place is a little creepy.

I jump when my phone vibrates in my pocket. Splitsville.com is hopping and I've totally neglected all the dumps in the past couple of days. I thumb through them hoping to take my mind off my present situation.

Great! I read the email. I don't need anything to add to my night.

I've been watching you sleep all night. You better watch yourself. Or you just might find yourself DEAD, like your client.

Obviously this person doesn't know where I live, because I've been here all night and secondly "client" is really "clients."

Harold helps me tidy up the joint as we go along looking for any intruders. It's only surface cleaning. No one will really notice if the boardroom wasn't vacuumed or the top shelves weren't dusted.

"Almost quitting time." Harold points to his watch.

Leaning in closer, I read the time, "4:30 already?" It's funny how time flies when you're up to something you shouldn't be doing—I mean the sleuthing part.

We quickly finish up the offices.

Harold's yawn is contagious. Or this nightshift might be making me tired. I promise Harold I'll be back and do a better job even though the file I need is no longer in the building.

***

I stop in the coffee shop to grab a cup on the way home. There's no way I'll be able to go home and fall asleep. The file being taken and the threat are weighing heavy on my mind. With a cup of joe, I can stay up a few hours and start on the dumps that have accumulated over the past couple of days.

The red-lettered sign on the coffee shop reads closed. I didn't take into consideration they might not open at 5:00 a.m. But a cup sounds great right now.

I walk over to *The Surplus* where I saw the protective spray. The neon sign blinks open. I've regretted twice not buying something to keep me somewhat safe, or something that makes me feel safe. This may be a good time.

I pull the door open and look in before I cross the threshold.

"What brings you in here so early?" The woman standing behind the counter chomps on a piece of gum. The chalk from her fingernail file is dusting the top of the counter. Those nails can take my eyeball out in one quick stab. Her long black hair is sleek and beautiful as silk, but the puff on top is pulled back in a clasp and makes it look like she is housing acorns under it. "Who you wanna hurt?"

"Aww, Vive, shut up." A guy slinks up alongside of me. "How can we help you?"

I look along the wall. "I'm just waiting for the coffee shop to open. I have some time to kill." I can't believe I just walked into a gun store. I move over to the area labeled protective sprays, I snicker. When did everything become so politically correct? The man follows me.

"*Killing* time huh?" Vive seems to take amusement in my choice of words.

I nod because I need to look into some sort of protection. I'm conducting my own spy jobs and receiving death threats. Why not? It may come in handy.

I shy away from the gun side because I know I can't shoot someone. With my hands locked behind my back, I scan the wall.

There are several different types of sprays to choose from. I always thought there were two types. Mace or pepper spray.

"Those are good for any single woman," the guy says looking down at my ring finger. His brows lift with anticipation. "And it looks like you're single."

"Let's say someone is making threats and…" I stop myself. I don't need to tell anyone about the threats, and I don't want Carl or Ian to find out about them.

"What kind of threats honey?" Vive went from leaning on her elbows to standing tall in her high heels.

I don't make eye contact with her; I say, "Just every day threats."

Vive walks over and takes a can of spray in her hand. "Like 'I can't stand you' or 'I'm gonna hurt you real bad,' 'threats?" Vive tugs at the bottom of her jean mini skirt. Her big toe sticks out the front of her shoes as if it's begging to be let out. I hold in my laughter once I see her toenail is bedazzled.

I pick up one of the sprays and say, "Something like that." I want to see how it feels in my hands.

"Well?" Vive begins to take down some of the sprays. "Which one?"

"Which one what?" I check my watch because I know the coffee shop is open by now. "Which threat?"

"Honey if you have to pick which threat is worse, you need pepper spray *and* a gun." Vive hands me the smallest little pouch with the teeniest nozzle sticking out the top.

It fits perfect in my hand. The scent of leather swooshes up to my nose when I pop the snap open to take the small can out. It's no bigger than my pinkie.

"I know you're thinking how in the hell is that tiny thing going to keep me safe. Well," Vive says and takes it out of my hand. "Don't you know big things come in small packages?" Vive holds it up and aims with her eyes on the target. *Me*.

I flinch.

"Oh honey, I'm not going to spray you. Hell, it'd hurt me this close." She hands the spray back to me because I know her nails won't be able to snap it back in the pouch.

"Thanks, but what's the difference between this and that?" I point to the larger can of spray. It only seems natural for quantity to be more important. "I want to keep spraying if I have to."

She laughs. "The difference is mace does last a little longer, but I hope you aren't going to be around to see." Vive adjusts her weight to the left side of her body and checks out her nails, "They both will make eyes and skin burn, plus make it hard to breathe." I swear I see laughter behind her eyes. "You like Bhut Jolokia?"

"Bhu..." I can't say it, much less like it.

Vive snorts again. I'm glad I'm amusing to her with my lack of knowledge. She continues, "The hottest pepper in the world. My momma loved to use a little in her spaghetti. You know, to give it a kick." She smacks her lips like she just had a bit of her momma's spaghetti. "Imagine *that* getting in your eyes. Stops you dead in your tracks. This here is stronger than that." She points to the smaller can.

The words run out of my mouth before I can stop them. "I'll take it." If I wasn't scared of the threats before, I'm scared now. And I can't wait to use my spray on the threatener.

"I told you." Vive takes a stab at the Joe Pesci lookalike guy, "She may not want to off anyone, but she wants to hurt someone *real* bad." She disappears behind a curtain, "I'll be right back with your protective spray."

I check my watch and realize I've been in here over forty-five minutes. My cell rings and I look at the screen.

"Good morning Bradley." I smile at the thought of how he is going to react when I tell him about my protective spray.

"Why haven't you called? I've been worried."

Crap! I forgot to call him when I got out of Macro Hard. I told him I would. "I'm sorry. I stopped to get a coffee and made a pit stop. Can we discuss it over coffee?"

"Yes and I'm alone today so I can really use your help."

Help? The last thing I want to do is work. I'm exhausted from cleaning all night. My silence makes him continue.

"Please? It's only for a couple hours, just to feed the dogs and take them out to potty."

I smile when I hear him say "potty." How can I resist that? My dumps will have to wait and the dumpers will have to put up with the dumpees one more day.

"Of course I will help you." Plus any alone time with Bradley is a bonus.

Vive comes around the curtain with a box in her hand. She begins to roll her nails on the glass countertop with her head cocked in the air.

I bend my head down so Vive won't hear me. "I've got to go, but I'll be there in a few."

"The who?" Bradley questions.

"No one. I'll see you in a minute." I push the *end* button and turn my attention back to Vive. She is taking the small can out and setting up an assortment of leather cases.

Her hands create a wand, like Vanna White waving across the letters on Wheel of Fortune. "As you can see, we have an assortment of colors to chose from."

There are pink cases, blue cases, purple cases, black, camo, you name it and Vive has it. I pick each one up and see how it looks in my hand. None of it looks natural, but I continue to repeat "death threats" over in my head.

Vive goes back behind the counter and brings out another box. She carefully opens it while looking around. By this time the store has five or so customers. She bends down close to my ear and whispers, "Come back here." She waves me around the counter.

I look around to see if anyone is staring like I'm on some spy mission, but they're too involved in looking for their own protective spray. I follow Vive behind the curtain to the back room. The metal shelves are filled with boxes stacked to the ceiling, all of which are housing her arsenal treasure trove.

I marvel at the warehouse. "I can't believe how much you have."

"Oh honey, you haven't seen anything. We are low on our inventory compared to last week." Vive climbs a ladder to get a very small box, no bigger than a pocketknife. "We get shipments every day. This stuff sells like hot cakes." She hands me the box and helps herself down.

She can't have any flavor left in her gum. I watch her chomp and move the ladder back to its original place. She takes the unmarked box and goes over to the desk.

She uses her nails as a knife and slices the piece of tape on the box and it pops open. "You seem like a nice girl." She takes out a tiny pink key case and holds it up. "I see you have several key chains so this won't be noticeable."

She hands me the small pepper spray can and I take it very carefully. I have no plans of spraying myself with my own protective spray. It fits perfectly in my hands.

Vive's eyes light up and her voice climbs, "Great! It will blend in with your everyday life. Just make sure you can get to it if you need to." She closes the empty pepper spray box and hands it to me. "I've been waiting to give this to the right person. Plus, part of the proceeds go the Breast Cancer Foundation. They only made a limited number." She pats the keys attached to her belt loop with one hand and her boobs with the other.

I smile. Even if I wasn't in the market for pepper spray, I'd still buy from Vive.

"We have a deal," I say, following Vive back out into the store to pay.

"If you need anything thing else, you let me know." Vive winks, "I mean *anything*."

I'm not for sure, but I believe Vive would track down the person making death threats toward me and get them herself.

"Thanks Vive."

"Let me know how it works out," she calls after me between chomps on her gum. "By the way, don't stand downwind when you're spraying it."

I turn around and Vive is leaning back on the counter the way she was when I came in over an hour ago with the same shitty grin.

Downwind?

How am I going to have time to determine downwind if someone is attacking me? I guess I'll figure it out. I secretly pray I won't have to find out.

Twenty-Two

"What's going on with you?" Bradley takes the extra coffee out of my hand. I'm careful to put my key chains in my pocket in fear the pepper spray will go off without me touching it, even though the instructions say it can't happen. I've come to realize that *anything* can happen.

I follow him into the kennel area. I look down the line of cages "I've had the worst night." The little black noses sticking out through the bars in anticipation of getting fed warm my heart.

Bradley takes the stack of silver bowls out of the cabinet. "What happened? More threats?" He lines the bowls up on the floor.

We fill up them and the howling begins. They know the ping of the pebble dog food hitting the inside of the metal bowls means food is on its way.

"It looks like I'm a suspect in the murders." I drop the measuring cup in the bag and turn to Bradley, "And if you don't like seeing me in an orange jumpsuit, we've got to figure this thing out."

"What?" Bradley's voice has disgust in it. He tries to dump a scoop of food in the bowl but loses most of it on the ground. I bend down to help him pick it up.

"Carl came by the house last night before work." I stand up and brush the food crumbs off on the front of my jeans. "He has a picture of me and Kent arguing at the kissing booth. Can you believe someone took a picture?" I look down at Bradley.

He stands up. "It only means one thing to me." He comes closer and brushes crumbs away from my cheek.

"Someone has been plotting to murder Kent and is completely setting you up."

I put the clues together. "It looks like we are fighting. He's dating my best friend and I killed him over jealousy or something. But why would I want to kill Dabi?"

Bradley and I walk down the kennels, sticking bowls in for the dogs to eat.

"Same thing. Jealousy is the number one reason for murder. Money is second." Bradley sounds exactly like Aunt Matilda.

Money is involved, I know it. Somehow, information about that is what I need to get my hands on at Macro Hard. Kent and Dabi had some kind of deal. But what? I recall Dabi's dad's conversation with the mystery man.

"There has to be a lead somewhere." I tell Bradley about the file and intruder at Macro Hard and my plans to snoop more tonight. Hopefully it will be my last night as a cleaning lady.

"Really, the only thing you have from the email threats is they are all sent from different locations." Why does he always have to be so logical?

"And the lipstick on the cup?" I remind him.

"Lipstick on a cup in a coffee shop means nothing. There are a lot of women who drink coffee with lipstick on."

He's right.

"But the threat came from one of those computers. It's strange the coffee was hot and the threat was just sent." Could it be a coincidence? I don't think so.

I'm so exhausted from no sleep, I can't even speak.

"I'll finish putting the bowls out. Why don't you go to the office and rest your eyes for a little bit?" He points down the hall.

It's awfully quiet here today. There doesn't seem to be anyone around.

I walk down the hall and ask, "Where is Bree again?"

"She called in sick." I watch him walk the opposite way with the empty bowls stacked up in his arms and his hair is flopping.

The coffee didn't do what it was supposed to and keep me awake. All I need to do is rest my eyes and I'll be like a new sleuth. . .er. . .woman.

"The light above the desk needs a good swift hit with the broom handle." Bradley yells in my direction.

The musky smelling office is one part of the building where Bradley hasn't used any of the fix-up fund. He says the animals don't use it and he can do paperwork in the kennels if he needs to. But it's a place to get away from the barking. I can rest my eyes, regroup, then go back and finish letting the dogs out. Then I can go home and get some real rest before my cleaning job.

When I switch the lights on, they flicker and buzz. I grab the broom that's leaning in the corner and jab the light like Bradley told me to do. It makes one big long buzz followed by a wave of light.

My body melts in the heavily padded black desk chair and I close my eyes. I recall all the dreams I have had so far concerning Dabi; the initials, the hand-written file, lipstick, and her break-up using Splitsville.com. Nothing is coming to me, only darkness.

I must have fallen asleep because I jump when a kennel door slams and the chains rattle. I open my eyes and gaze at the desk drawer. I pause. I don't want to think anymore. I close my eyes and visualize a drawer. A steel drawer and a black tube with faint writing. Writing that is almost rubbed off.

I open my eyes and hunt around for a piece of paper. My journal is at home and the visual of this drawer opening and closing with this black tube rolling around in it keeps playing in my mind. It must be important. I'll forget if I don't write it down.

Just like a kid, I open the old long metal drawer to Bradley's desk and sort through the junk to find a pen. I root through the usual items, stray paper clips, chewed pen tops with no pens attached, pencil with broken lead, a couple rubber bands, box of tissues, a tube of…

I pick up the black tube.

"Lipstick?" It has to belong to Bree. She's the only girl who works here. Most of the time she is so gloomy. I can't imagine her wearing lipstick especially as the shelter's in-house pooper-scooper. "Hmmm, does Bree have a girly side?" I laugh while taking the top off the tube.

I laugh picturing pale, meek Bree in red-hot lipstick, slowly pulling her hair out of her little pony tail holder as she begins to wave it around.

Streaks of pink line the shaft of the tube. "Ha." I roll the lipstick up revealing the full color. "I don't figure her for pink." I continue to talk to myself and swipe a little on my finger to apply to my lips.

I put the tube back in the drawer and continue to look around for something to write with. Of course there's nothing in here, but maybe the front desk will have something.

I grab a tissue from the box and rub the lipstick off. No matter how pretty pink is, it's never been my color. I fold the tissue and rub harder. The pink is staring me right in the face. The pink is…

I pause. Only one image comes to me. Coffee. Mug. As my eyebrows narrow, I purse my lips together. I fling

the drawer back open and the tube rolls up to the front of
the drawer, just like my dream. I grab it and rush down the
hall in the direction of Bradley's voice talking to the dogs.

"Bradley!" I scream and run faster. "Oh my god, who's
lipstick is this?" I plant my hands on my knees and bend
over to gain my breath. I really need to exercise, but right
now isn't the time to start. I guess that's one thing I can do
in jail-exercise.

All the dogs bounce around and wait for Bradley to
throw the balls. At least the rain has stopped.

He throws one ball and looks at the tube in my hand.
"Bree's. Why?" The dogs scatter after it. He takes the tube
from my fingers. He rolls it up then down. "You aren't a
pink girl, are you?"

I take it back. I straighten up. "No, but the person
sending the emails is." "That's the exact same color on the
coffee cup. The cup from the coffee shop where the email
threat was sent from! I'd know it anywhere. I need to see
her file." I jab the lipstick in his face. "Somehow Bree is
connected to all this."

Bradley throws the last ball and we hurry to the office.
He walks over to the old filing cabinet in the corner. While
he thumbs through the files, I continue to inspect the
lipstick and figure out how Bree is associated with
Splitsville.com. I've had hundreds of clients plus their
dumpees and I can't recall one named Bree.

I see the file in his hands. I can't wait to get my hands
on it.

Bradley sits at his desk and opens the file. He starts to
look through it. "Nothing unusual." He pauses as he reads.
"Good background check and her day job is at…" I watch
as his finger stops. He looks up with fear in his eyes,
"Macro Hard!"

I swing the file around on the desk to face me. I start from the beginning and read everything.

"Brittany." I point to the name at the top of the application. I shudder when her name leaves my lips.

"Okay?" Bradley doesn't put two and two together. "So her real name is Brittany."

Hello? Brittany. "Bree for short." I want to shake him, but I will take my time and explain all the ideas whirling around in my head.

"Kent, Terry Kent Goodwin, dumped Brittany, Bree, using Splitsville.com." I recall the poor meek OCD Brittany's picture. "She doesn't look the same. Similar, but she's let her hair grow and she's colored it. And her working here really throws me for a loop."

I clearly remember her short red-haired bob and she was neatly wrapped up in a cardigan.

"Really?" Bradley straightens himself up. "OCD? Isn't that the neat freak thing?"

My eyebrows lift and I nod. "Yes."

"And she picks up poop here?" He rubs his chin. "That sure doesn't add up."

"Only one way to find out." I grab the file and try to dart out the door.

Bradley steps in front of me. "No!" he says. "You're not going over there?"

I dare him to try and stop me. "Oh yes I am," I confirm. I may have uncovered my ticket to freedom and the murderer. "Me and my pepper spray." I tap the pink canister dangling from my keys and head for the Toyota.

***

According to my GPS, her apartment is only ten minutes from both the SPCA and Macro Hard. I imagine her in a board meeting sitting all prim next to Dabi. I picture the perfectly put together Brittany jumping up and strangling Dabi, but that would be too easy.

What did Brittany do at Macro Hard? Is that where she met Kent? I wonder if Brittany was the reason for his divorce.

Oh. My. God. Did Brittany pose as Kent to break-up with Erin? I need to check the email address and see. At a stop light, I reach over for my dream notebook and jot down my dream of the lipstick and add a note to look up the Erin dump from Kent. I need to see the email and find out where it came from. Kent might have been a snake, but maybe he didn't break-up with Erin after all.

The cloud cover remains low and rain drops slowly dot my windshield as I drive down the tree-lined residential area. Although I wish it hadn't started raining, it will create a distraction for any comings and goings on the street. People will definitely be running to their cars from their homes or paying more attention to the rain than to a spy.

As I make my way in front of Brittany's house, I notice the neighborhood-watch sign along the edge of the curb. I notice her car in the drive. The car I've seen her pull in and out of the SPCA in. A car that's too cheap to be executive material. As a matter of fact, knowing what I know about her, the Ford Thunderbird is the last thing I think Brittany would drive. Bree I can see driving it, but knowing Bree is Brittany, no way.

I don't recognize the BMW behind the Thunderbird, so I pull down the street and turn around in a driveway a few houses down from Brittany's and park. I have to strain to see through the rain to get a good view.

I look at my watch. I have a few hours to kill before work. I can sit here and wait. I have no idea what I want from sitting here, but I figure it will come to me. I turn the engine off. I formulate a new list. REASONS BREE IS THE MURDERER. I reach for all my files on the passenger seat. I want to read through them and see if anything jumps out at me.

When I open it, the perfect picture that Kent painted about her is almost unbelievable. She does a great job cleaning up after the dogs, but it's not a job I'd picture someone with OCD having.

I begin my comparison list.

1. Dyed hair—something a murderer would do. (Or at least they do in the movies.)

2. Longer hair—something a murderer would do.

3. She works at Macro Hard where she had to see Kent's ex-wife (Dabi) on a daily basis. A motive for murder. Jealousy.

4. Kent uses Splitsville.com to break-up with her and she's hurt, and angry. More motives for a murder.

5. She kills Dabi first and Kent figures it out. So now she has to kill him too. A reason for another murder.

6. I bet she used Splitsville.com to break-up with Erin so Erin can look like a possible suspect. Need to check on that.

7: She begins to threaten Splitsville.com because she's angry, but she doesn't know Jenn's true identity.

8. Is Brittany the girl that smacked Kent? Did Erin see her at the SPCA that day? Was Brittany the woman in the coffee shop?

I read slowly over my list a couple of times and make a couple of notes on each item, creating more and more reasons why Brittany could be the murderer. All evidence points to her. I know I can't confront her—yet. With one more night at Macro Hard, I may be able to dig deeper and find out what her job was there.

A car door slamming catches my attention. I look up to see Brittany in the baseball hat with a guy also in a baseball hat. I skew my vision, but the rain makes it too hard to read her aura. They are running to the car. They look like they are exchanging a few unpleasantries and the mystery guy stomps in a puddle.

I grab my camera and snap pictures of them.

I zoom in to get a better picture. I pull the camera back and look at the photo. "White. Puma. Shoes." If I were under oath, I'd swear those are the same shoes the intruder at Macro Hard had on last night.

9. The mystery guy with Brittany is the same guy who took the file at Macro Hard.

I jot down the last item on my list before the mystery guy pulls out and Brittany runs back into her house. I wait a second before I make a u-turn and follow the BMW onto Main Street. Unfortunately, with the rain, traffic is a mess and the BMW slips in and out making it hard for me to follow.

I take the next right and wind my way around the streets, straight for Erin's house. Erin might not want to see me, but she has no choice.

The complex looks completely different since the last time I was there. The cops have long since gone. The rain makes the building drabber than it really is, if that's possible. I dodge the puddles going up the steps by tip toeing over them. Icky drops of something are falling on top of my head from the stairs above. God knows what's dripping off them.

I knock.

I see the light from the peep hole disappear into black.

"Erin, I know you're looking at me." I jam the files back up under my sweatshirt so they won't get wet. "I need to talk to you."

"Go away." My happy-go-lucky friend is not going to open the door just because I say so.

I pull the files out from under my armpit and sweatshirt. "I don't have time for these high school games." Okay, so that most certainly won't entice her to open the door. I hold the file up next to my face so she can see it, "I think I know who did *it*."

I don't dare say who murdered Kent, because I am sure her nosy neighbors are listening.

My heart beats a little faster when I hear the click of the door lock and the slide of the chain. Erin is standing there in her Dartmouth sweatshirt and cut off sweats. I'm taken off guard. It's not an outfit you see Erin in too often. Me? Yes. I wear sweats daily. Erin, not so much.

She opens the door to let me in. I don't say a word or at least I don't tell her she looks like crap. I can't help but look at the big hole of carpet missing from the floor where a once dead Kent was found.

I'm concerned. I can't imagine her wanting to stay here. "Where have you been living?"

"In my car." Her voice is monotone like the color on her face. I try not to stare. Her aura is grey with a red overlay. The grey tells me she is sad or sick and the red overlay tells me she is trying to protect herself. Is she protecting herself from me or the police?

I can't believe I let her stay by herself. But with my news, I have high hopes her aura is about to change. I'm not such a good friend. "Oh, I'm sorry for fighting."

She lifts her head with the tiniest hint of a smile. "Me too," she says. We hug for a brief moment and she cuts to the chase. "So who did it?"

I take the camera strap off my shoulder and click through the pictures. I get to the ones of Brittany. "Is this the girl you saw fighting with Kent at the bar the night before his death?"

Erin takes the camera out of my hands and hits the zoom button to get a closer look. I peek over her shoulder to inspect Brittany up close.

Erin's face begins to shows some sign of color other than blah. "Yes. That's her." A little pink creeps into her cheeks.

"Is this the girl you saw at the SPCA?"

"Yes!" Her voice escalates, "And she's the girl I saw leaving the coffee shop the day you got the lead."

That's all I needed to hear. "She dated Kent and he used Splitsville.com to break-up with her." I hand Erin the file. She walks over to the couch and sits down. She begins to read the dump out loud.

"What?" Erin begins to pace. "Girlfriend? Splitsville.com?" She stops and shakes her head. "I can't believe I didn't know about her. I knew something was funny when I told Kent about your company. He turned white like he'd seen a ghost."

I take out Dabi's file and hand it to her. "Kent knew about Splitsville.com because Dabi used it. Actually Dabi and Kent are divorced."

The little bit of pink in Erin's cheek completely melts away. "I'm going to be sick." Erin runs down the hall to her bathroom. I go into the kitchen and retrieve a glass of water.

"Here." I hand the glass to her and she takes it. "I'm so sorry, but I have to tell you the details in order to exonerate you, me and Splitsville.com." I begin gently and tell her how I found out everything I know.

The sound of her laughter lifts my heart. "I can't believe *you* of all people is cleaning. And a building at that." She can hardly contain her composure. I laugh with her and it all turns out into a full outcry. We sob like babies.

"I'm so glad I have you." I hug her. "Let's get your stuff. Herbie misses you."

I gather all the files and wait for her to get some things together.

"I have to make a stop before we go home." We buckle our seat belts and drive off to Michael's to get a few of my questions answered.

I want to know if he knows Brittany and her capacity with the company.

Erin and I think of questions I can ask Harold during my night shift. I really need to find Brittany's file from Macro Hard. I want to know how long she's been there. If she knew Kent and Dabi when they were married. Everything, before I go to the police.

Michael and Belle are running across the street as if on cue. I smile because he looks so funny dragging a dog who obviously doesn't want to be in the rain. I beep the horn to grab his attention.

He runs back toward us and hops in the car.

"Michael, Erin," I make a quick introduction and gesture between the two. "Erin, Michael. We are all suspects in these messy murders I'm trying to solve." I check my watch to see how much time I've got left. If I hurry, I can make it home in time to rest my eyes for a couple hours before I have to put on my jumpsuit for another exciting night of scrubbing toilets and throwing out tampons.

Michael nods at Erin who nods back. "Hey, what's going on?" He turns his attention to me.

"I want to know if you know this girl." I take Brittany's picture out of her file and pull the digital camera photo up from today. I hand them to him to look over.

His eyes wander back and forth from the camera to the photo. There doesn't seem to an ounce of knowing who she is. He hands the picture back to me and the camera to Erin. "Who is she?"

"Her name is Brittany and she dated Kent." He takes the picture back out of my hand and takes another look.

"*This* is Brittany?" He holds the picture closer to his face. "I knew he dated a girl named Brittany because people gave him crap about her. She doesn't look so bad."

I pluck the picture from his fingers. "Well, she may be the answer to our prayers. I'll keep you posted."

Michael looks out the window to make sure no one is around. He picks up Belle and he bolts to his apartment building trying to dodge all the puddles in his...*white pumas*!

"Do you see his shoes?" I fling my body across the seat and plaster my hands on Erin's passenger window. "Freakin' white Pumas."

My stomach curls. Everything Michael and I had talked about, all the sneaking around Dabi's apartment, having keys to her office, me getting a job there- everything! What if he did do it? What if he's collecting evidence for the police to use against me?

"What?" Erin pushes me back in my seat. "You don't like Pumas?"

Ay, ay, ay. "Michael, you have some 'splainin' to do." I do my best Ricky Ricardo accent. On our way home, I tell Erin everything I know about white Pumas and how they have made my life a living hell.

Twenty-Three

I don't get any sleep before it's time to start my night shift at Macro Hard. I don't think I can sleep if I try. Thinking about Brittany—and now Michael—is a shot of adrenaline I don't need.

Aunt Matilda listens to every word I'm telling her about all the clues I have put together.

"You need to tell Carl." She holds the phone up for me to take.

I come to the conclusion that she's talking nonsense now. "I don't see how that's going to help. I won't know for sure until I check more out tonight." There is *no way* I'm telling Carl or Ian about anything I found out. "They spent all that money to go to college to be a cop. They should already know all of this stuff."

Aunt Matilda crosses the floor of my office as graceful as a ballerina. There is just something wonderful and soft about her. The way she moves like a butterfly is one trait I didn't get from her. "Carl may have Brittany linked somehow. He might be able to trace them all."

I know he'd be able to, but I'm leaving that up to Bradley.

Before she walks out the door, she tilts her head to the side, smiles and says, "Herbie and I are going to my house for a while." Her hand grips the crown molding on the door and she swings back around. "The old people at the retirement community love dogs."

I chuckle at the fact she's the same age as the residences.

"Have fun." I walk into the kitchen where Erin is propped up on one of the bar stools. She is wrapped up in Aunt Matilda's arms.

"Want to come?" Aunt Matilda asks Erin.

"Where?" Erin flings her bangs out of her eyes.

"Herbie and I are going to the home of the near dead." Her eyes twinkle.

Erin looks over at me with a cockeyed look. "Where?"

I laugh at Aunt Matilda's quirky humor. "Retirement community."

Erin hops off the stool and slips her flip flops on. "Sure."

"Let's go." Aunt Matilda winks and floats out of the house with Erin and Herbie in tow.

These dumps are never going to get done. I make my way back in the office to get at least one dump done before I go to Macro Hard. Splitsville.com has taken a back seat to this sleuthing junk and that's not what I promise as a business. Once I hear Aunt Matilda and company pull out of the driveway, I begin my calls.

"Hi, is this Linda?" I question the older voice on the other end of the phone. I'm already agitated. I specifically ask dumpers for a number that no one other than the dumpee will answer. I don't have time to go through parents or grandparents to get to the dumpee.

"This is Linda."

I jerk my head back and hit *click* so I can see Linda's photo. There she is, a middle-aged woman --- My first middle-aged woman.

I'm completely taken aback. "Ah, yeah." I think about Aunt Matilda and how she'd feel if someone she dated dumped her using Splitsville.com. I quickly put it out of my mind because Aunt Matilda hasn't dated, *ever*.

I get out of my chair and look in the oval mirror hanging on the wall. My eyes stare deep into my dark pupils. Get a grip.

"I'm Jenn from Splitsville.com and Justin hired me to break-up with you." I tap under my eyes. This night job is going to be the death of me. Oh, another plus about doing jail time, I can sleep all day.

"I'm on a business trip and I don't know what you are talking about." Linda is a bit older and wiser than most of my clients. "Did you hear me?"

"I do hear you Linda. But most importantly do you hear me?" Just being older doesn't give her the right to be a bitch. What is it with old people? When is it okay to say, "Screw it, I'm old and I can say whatever I want to whomever I please?" Well, not today!

"I should've dumped that lazy bum a long time ago." Linda's tone is sharp.

I look at her middle-age photo and see the sour-puss look on her face. No wonder he wants to dump her. I'm kind of mad at myself for feeling sorry for her when I first looked at her picture.

"He waits at home for you all week long while you're gone on these business trips with God knows who. . .er. . .it says here Daniel. Okay," I gather my senses. "You're gone all week with Daniel while Justin waits around for you."

"He needs to get off his lazy butt and get a job. Then I wouldn't have to go on these trips."

I lay my head on the desk. "So are you telling me that you and Daniel aren't an item?" All I can think about is getting this dump complete, getting on my fancy jumpsuit and questioning Harold.

"Whoa, whoa." Linda is definitely smarter than most and a bit more complicated. I'm tired and I'm not on my game right now. "Justin breaks up with me and now you want to know if I've cheated on him. Right. I don't have time for this."

"You don't have time for this?" I jump at the chance to scream at her, "I don't have time for this! Do you have death threats against you? Do you have to clear your name of murder? Do you? Do you Linda?! Do you understand Justin has dumped your middle aged cheating butt?" I scream in the phone waking up every little sleepy bone in my body. I've totally lost it.

"Yes. Now I can move on with Daniel." Linda got the last word before the line went dead.

I email a dump notice to Justin and leave it at that. I bend down and turn my computer off. In the kitchen I find my jumpsuit neatly ironed, by Aunt Matilda of course, on the barstool. I open the refrigerator and pack a few snacks. Maybe I can get to Harold's heart through food.

***

The rain has given way to a chilly spring night. The town is quiet. Every business has closed up for the evening. Aunt Matilda's truck is exactly where it should be. I stop at the red light and glance over at the retirement community. Through the window I see Erin, Aunt Matilda, and Herbie entertaining the group of residents gathered around them.

It's good to see Erin smile.

With no traffic, I pull into Macro Hard and feel happy to see there aren't any cars in the lot except one—Harold's. I grab the files sitting on my passenger seat, all the snacks I prepared to bribe Harold, and hand lotion. I made sure to bring my own lotion because my hands are starting to dry and crack from the cleaning chemicals. But the calluses are looking much better.

I wave at the security camera above the door before I swipe my entry card. I know Harold is watching.

"On time tonight, I see." Harold is already at his perch and ready to go. I stop when I see his yellow tone aura wrap around his security hat and through his soft grey wispy curls sticking out from under it.

People who have an undeveloped psychic intuition are surrounded by yellow tones.

"Do you think you're going to get some other work done?" He is referring to the files
under my arm.

"Good evening." His aura is telling me to be cautious, he could call my bluff. I have to get some information out of him. I plop the sack of goodies next to his sack of goodies. "I brought you some snacks since you let me eat some of yours last night."

"Hmm." Harold stands up and picks through the snacks. "Veggies, bagel chips, fruit. *Dip?*" His thin lips turn up in a smile of approval.

"I'm glad you like it." I look down the hallways on either side of the desk and it's dark and quiet.

His grin doesn't last long. "What's the catch?"

I play if off, but he knows something is up my sleeve. "No catch." I walk over to the closet to retrieve my cart and begin filling up the bottles. I look over at Harold with an empty bleach bottle on my hand. "Ya know, they really should invest in some hand friendly products."

I go about my business and begin pushing the cart down to the bathrooms. I can get a jump on them while Harold settles down with the sack of food. I hope it relaxes him a bit so I can snoop.

I look up and Harold is standing next to my cart.

"What's in this file?" I keep my files with me because I don't trust that he won't go through my things. After all, he is the security guard. "More investigating?"

I take the bleach spray off the cart and walk into the bathroom. "Mm hmm." I spray along the base of the toilets going from one stall to the next. "Put it back." I don't have to say anything else. I hear Harold shuffle out of the bathroom.

After finishing both the men's and the women's bathrooms, I'm ready to take a snack break and find what I'm looking for.

"Break already?" Harold looks up from the paper he's reading.

"I guess we can't all read all night and get paid for it." I smile getting a diet coke out of my cooler next to his chair.

"Actually you're doing much better tonight."

"That's because I want to finish early. I didn't get to nap today and I'm tired." I take a carrot from the sack and offer one to him. I take the file from the cart and pull out Brittany's picture.

I'm tired of waiting around for the right opportunity to ask him questions. Either he's going to tell me something or not. He can call the police, Mr. Stone or whomever he pleases on me. I won't be back after tonight, or I hope I won't be back.

"Do you know this girl?" I hand him the drab photo of meek Brittany.

"My goodness." Harold makes a few noises under his breath. "What do you want with Brittany? Is this why you're working here?"

"So you know her?" I walk around to his chair and look at the picture again. That innocent smile, that neatly

coifed hair and outfit to match are certainly not the images
you associate with a cold-blooded killer.

"Sure do. I've spent a lot of time with this girl." He
hands the picture back to me. "Little obsessive, but kind."

"How so?" I can't believe he's saying the same things
Kent did about her.

"For starters she always kept the closet tidy.
Everything has a place she'd say." He shakes his head and
points back to the picture. "That girl can tell if a rag is out
of place. I'm not kidding." He clicks the computer screen to
twelve images showing the outside of the building and the
parking lot. "And she always filled the bottles before she
left for the night. Plus I never had to get bleach for her."

"Why would she care about rags?" I find it strange that
Brittany cared about the cleaning of the building, but I
guess OCD people obsess about a lot of different things.

He continues to scan the videos making sure all is safe
at Macro Hard and doesn't look up. "Why wouldn't she?"

"Didn't she have to worry about her job?" I watch
Harold push several different buttons and zoom in on the
parking lot.

"She did." He zooms in on a car next to mine.
"Strange." He zooms the cameras in a little closer. "I don't
recall that car being parked next to yours."

I creep around to the monitor and take a closer look.
Funny, because I don't either. I distinctly remember only
two cars: mine and Harold's. I squint and make out the car.
I swear it's the BMW from Brittany's house.

"There wasn't a car." I run around the security desk
toward the glass front doors and grab my keys off the cart.
"Somebody is trying to get into my car." I hear Harold's
footsteps behind me and feel a little safer. I don't know
why; he doesn't carry a gun or anything.

Without looking, I get my pepper spray ready and leap over the perfectly manicured bushes, toward the back of the BMW speeding away. I turn to see if I can get the license plate, but it's going too fast. My car door is open.

"Damn!" I look in my car to find the contents of my glove box emptied out onto the floor. The list of motives why Brittany killed Dabi and Kent is stabbed into the dashboard with a Swiss army knife.

"Are you okay?" Harold questions, with the phone attached to his ear. "I'm calling the police."

I'm too scared to stop him. My heart is racing; my breaths are short and quick. This investigation has gotten a little bit bigger than me. Maybe it's time I tell the police everything.

Within ten minutes Carl is on the scene, shortly followed by Ian. Harold is back inside keeping a very close eye on the building through the safety of his cameras.

"Well, well." Carl walks around my car. "What do we have here?"

I roll my eyes. I don't want to focus too much because everyone's aura is colliding. Then Carl may question if I have the same "gift" as Aunt Matilda.

Carl hands the list of motives to Ian.

"Have you been doing a little investigating on your own, Ms. Davis?" Ian has a spark in his eyes. "Why don't you tell us everything you know?" He opens the door to his cop cruiser for me to sit and wait while Carl looks around my car for clues.

Strangers invading my car is where I draw the line. Obviously someone knows who I am, and with the death threats, I need to make sure I'm safe. My Blackberry goes off, signaling a dump. I look at my watch.

2 A.M.? Who is up doing a dump at 2 A.M.? I totally bet it's what I call a drunk dump. That's usually the late night dump when lovers fight and using Splitsville.com is a handy tool to get back at each other.

I thumb through it as Carl and Ian finish looking around. It's not a dump, it's another threat.

Look at you sleeping so sound in your bed. Are you scared? Soon your heart will be ripped like all the hearts you've ripped.

I gasp and put my hands to my mouth. "It's not the same person," I whisper as I reread the words.

If BMW man was here and knew I was here, the email had to be sent by someone else, someone who thinks I'm at home—Bree.

I put my head in my hands. I feel like the tears are going to come flooding out. Now I have two separate people to worry about.

Carl and Ian look over. I try not to give away what's going on in my head. Brittany can't be the one sending death threats. But the lipstick, Erin identifying her, the motives all add up. I'm so confused.

Carl leans onto the cop car. "You can start from the beginning. Or you can tell us who and why someone would break into your car?"

I get out of the car. "I've got to finish my job." I walk away and Carl puts his arm out to stop me. "What?"

"Who did this Olivia?" Carl starts to ask all sorts of questions. "What do you know about Brittany that we don't?"

"You ask a lot of questions for the professional one here." I jerk the note from his hands. "You know where to find me when you have a subpoena." I walk past Ian and stare him straight in the eyes.

I squeeze my eyes shut and open them. Ian's aura reminds me of sour apple jolly ranchers. I stumble forward and Carl catches my fall.

His eyebrows narrow. "Are you okay?"

I stand tall and brush my hands down my jumpsuit. I'm not okay, but I can't let them know that.

"I'm fine." I hold my head high and keep my eyes on the door. If I can just get myself inside and sit down, I'll be fine. I can't risk looking back at Ian.

Relief overcomes me once I get back into the safety of the building. Harold is still staring at the cameras.

"Thanks for nothing." I take the file off the cart and write down "sour apple." "You left me out there high and dry."

Harold hands me a sticky note with a bunch of numbers on it.

I read the numbers out loud. "What's this?"

"I rewound the security camera footage outside and zoomed in on the car. That's the license plate number." Harold is one sly cookie.

I slip the piece of paper in the file. I take Brittany's picture off the ledge of his desk and put it back in her file.

"Does Brittany have anything to do with what happened tonight?" Harold asks.

"I don't know. Can you tell me anything else about her?" I pull up the other chair next to Harold and sit down. I have to get my nerves straight before I can think about looking for more clues.

He shrugs. "Only that she was a great housekeeper."

"Housekeeping?" I try not to sound surprised. "I took her job?"

"She quit and they needed a replacement."

"Did you know about Kent?"

"Of course, everyone knew about her and Mr. Goodwin. Let me tell you, Mr. Stone was none too happy about Dabi not ripping up that prenuptial agreement where Mr. Goodwin gets alimony." Harold continues to spew like a volcano, "Now it's none of my business, but poor Brittany was left out of the big functions." Harold uses finger quotes around "big."

"What big functions?" I write down what Harold is telling me.

"You know, dinners, awards." He waves his hand in the air. "Mr. Stone said that the housekeeping staff wasn't welcome."

That explains why Brittany isn't in any of the event photos from Dabi's photo albums. But it doesn't explain why she would kill Kent. It completely explains why she'd kill Dabi. Maybe Kent had promised to marry her and she knew he'd get the alimony.

"Whoo-wee, I remember the night Mr. Goodwin came in here to see her and they had a big fight." Harold looks into the air like the event is playing in his head. "She accused him of going back to his old ways. Especially by accepting the new white shoes Ms. Stone had given all the employees." Harold takes a sack of grapes out of his brown bag and begins to unzip the baggie. "Dabi had given him a pair, but Brittany said he shouldn't accept them because it looks like he's gone back."

I put my hand in the air. "Stop!" Shoes? "What white shoes? Can you describe them?"

"Mr. Stone had made a big deal with that shoe company with the cat. . .a. . ."

I interrupt him, "Puma?"

"Yeah, that's the one, and Puma gave Mr. Stone shoes for his employees. Oh, Brittany hated it."

"Well, what do you mean when you say gone back?" I bet Brittany was talking about how Kent had taken Dabi for her money.

Harold pops a grape in his mouth. "That's where I draw the line of snooping." He pops a few more to make a mouth full.

"Do you have a list of employees?" I wonder if I will recognize any one from a list.

"Naw, I just watch the cameras." He smiles. "But I do know where Human Resources keeps a copy."

I wink at him. Harold is the eyes and ears of this place. He may have some psychic intuition that he definitely hasn't tapped into yet.

"Are they saying you had something to do with Ms. Stone's and Mr. Goodwin's death?" Harold begins to question my questions. I follow him down the hall to the Human Resources department. There is a list of employees hanging on a corkboard. I take it down. I glance through it and don't see any familiar names.

"Let's say I have had some type of contact with both of them. But I didn't do it."

Harold laughs, "I know. Because if you did, your finger prints would be everywhere because you sure can't clean worth a darn."

Twenty-Four

I'm happy with all the information Harold gave me about Brittany and her ties to Macro Hard. It might've answered a few questions, but not all of them. She knows I have to be snooping around or at least the mystery BMW man does.

My thoughts circle back to Michael. He has a white pair of shoes, Kent had a white pair of shoes, and both mystery men had a white pair of shoes. I know Kent didn't work for Macro Hard and Michael doesn't and they both own a pair. If I can only pin point the mystery man.

"Harold, thank you for all of your information and making me realize cleaning isn't my thing."

The yellow aura completely surrounds him. "I had a feeling you wouldn't last. It's a shame, I really like you, Olivia."

"I really like you too, Harold." I want to say something about his untapped psychic ability, but it gives me an excuse to come back and visit one late night.

I take my phone out of my pocket and dial Bradley.

"Did you scrub the floors?" Bradley is amused by his question.

"Funny." I drive out of Macro Hard's parking lot for the last time. "Can your brother-in-law run a license plate number for me?" I don't want to give any leads to Carl or Ian. Like I said before, they spent years in college to learn how to investigate. While I spent years in front of the TV watching Angela Lansbury.

"Sure. It may take a while to get the results."

That's good enough for me. I read the number off twice so he can write it down and check it.

Once I get home, I have no problem falling asleep on the couch. I'm confident that Brittany doesn't know I'm Jenn. I have a sneaky suspicion she's desperately trying to find out who Jenn is. She's seen me with Erin though and that gives her reason to not like me.

The sound of bells wakes me from my deep sleep. I shield my eyes from the light creeping through the once pulled curtains that are now hanging wide open. Aunt Matilda is standing over me with her trusty old notebook and Herbie is beside me licking my face.

"I thought you might be dead." Matilda continues to scribble. "Until you started talking about white shoes in Brittany's closet." She points to the page in her notebook where she's been taking notes on my dream. "Something about Carl and jolly ranchers."

My mind is full of cobwebs as I look at my watch and realize it's almost night again and I've slept the day away.

"Really? Did I say something about Carl?" It's inevitable that I talk to the police, but I have to figure out if a few of my hunches are right. I need time to put my clues in order, and in doing that I have one last thing to do— break into Brittany's apartment.

"It wasn't anything enlightening, but it's time to get up. We are having dinner company."

That explains the banging of the pots and pans in the kitchen. My house is so tidy I barely recognize it. And fresh-cut flowers in a vase on the table are a telltale sign this isn't just any dinner.

Herbie rushes to the door, barking like a mad dog at the sound of knocking. There's no time for Aunt Matilda to tell me that Carl and Ian are the guests when I open up to find them standing there in plain clothes.

"Good evening, Ms. Davis." Carl smiles with Ian standing behind him. If they spent as much time on the case as they had getting all cleaned up for a dinner, they might have the case solved by now.

"*Hello, Carl.*" I do my best Jerry Seinfeld impression when he says hello to his neighbor Newman. Sort of my smart-alec way of being annoyed because they're here.

Aunt Matilda glides her way in between me and the screen door allowing them into the house. I look at Aunt Matilda whose gaze is fixed on Carl.

I step back.

"Don't you think this is sort of weird having dinner with me when you have me as a suspect on a murder case?" I'm appalled to even think about sitting across from them let alone being able to break bread with them.

"We are off duty." Ian slides his way past me following Aunt Matilda and Carl into *my* kitchen.

Erin rounds the corner. She seems more annoyed than I am. "I told her this wasn't a good idea, but she insisted it was." Erin and I both know not to question Aunt Matilda, well…at least not to her face.

I schlep back to my room and take a quick shower before returning just in time to sit and eat. I can kiss spying on Brittany tonight goodbye.

Herbie is an altogether different story. His gentle spirit is turning slightly yellow. I watch as he goes from one door to the other in an uneasy trot. His black eyes fix on mine and he begins to let out a low growl.

Ian looks over at Herbie. "What does he want?" Herbie doesn't break his stare. He wants me to let him out.

I hesitate as his aura turns yellow. I jump up from my chair as Aunt Matilda gets up from the table and picks him up.

"Maybe he needs to go in your room until our guests leave." She hands him to me and follows me back down the hall. "What's going on?" She says in a low tone.

"I don't know." I use my fingers and make a circle around his body without telling her his aura is yellow. You can never trust a yellow aura animal. That means they are up to something and can go off any minute. I'm afraid to let him out. Animal's senses are greater than ours and maybe the killer is outside. Or maybe he doesn't like the vibe I get having cops in the house. Cops that think I killed not only one person, but two.

Aunt Matilda goes back to the table.

I put Herbie in the spot on my bed where he likes to lie. "Hey, buddy. It's okay." I assure him before I go back to dinner. I walk back down the hall into a room full of laughter and clinking glasses.

Carl is telling stories about Aunt Matilda and the crimes they use to solve. I watch as her eyes light up with excitement. I can see her hay days running in her head by the smile on her face.

"How did you do it?" Ian isn't following along with Aunt Matilda's gift.

"Oh, I guess I'm just intuitive." Aunt Matilda has always been cautious of telling new people about her stint with the Park City Police Department.

Carl laughs. "Yea, I'd say." He fills everyone's glasses.

Of course Erin is rolling her eyes because she never truly believed in Aunt Matilda's ability to help with the police, but she never questioned how the crimes got solved. She most certainly never wanted to hear what I had to say about people's auras. "It's not natural, Olivia. Don't you want to let life unfold?"

Yes, I want to let life unfold, but when it unfolds in front of your eyes without your permission, it's a little hard to control. As I've gotten older it's been easier and the dreams seem to be less frequent. But these two murders have turned into a nightmare.

"I'll tell you what. . ." Erin's sways her glass in the air, almost tipping out what Carl just put in. "I've never seen any. . ." Erin hiccups. "Anything." She brings the glass to her mouth.

"I think Erin's had enough." I signal Carl to put the wine bottle away before he begins to top Erin's glass off.

"I've not." She points her finger toward me. "I deserve to have a drink, seeing that my boyfriend who's been married, who used your service to break-up with his ex, who by the way…" she turns to Ian, "is sending threatening emails to. . ."

No. No. Erin, don't tell Ian. I know Carl knows, but Ian will not let this die. I open my mouth to stop her just before she plants her face down on the table.

My heart is pounding, fearing she is going to jump up any minute and tell everything she knows. I know I should tell them, I know I should give them the evidence I've collected, but I'm not ready to give all the pieces of the puzzle. Not yet.

Everyone laughs but Ian. He's stone faced. Nervously I chuckle to break any tension Ian may feel. I can tell he is very intent on solving his first murder case in Park City, let alone two.

"I guess she's had too much wine." Carl blurts out and Erin wiggles her little finger in the air keeping the rest of her upper body flat on the table.

I get up and help her out of her seat. Ian comes over and does most of the lifting.

"She can go back here." I nod toward the guest bedroom.

He picks her up and carries her down the hall behind me. Once he has her on the bed, I turn to go back out.

"Wait." His voice is demanding. "Ex what?"

I bite my lip and roll my eyes. My back is to him. "What?" I know I have to turn around and face him. Alone. The worst place to be when you read auras. I prepare myself and turn on my heels.

His Jolly Rancher sour apple aura is starting to yellow a little like mustard. My legs shake and I grab the door knob for support. I don't want him to question why I do this when we are alone.

"You know what?" he whispers and comes a little closer. I close my eyes. "Whose ex is who? Are you withholding evidence from the police, Olivia?"

"I have no clue what she's talking about." Another white lie to the police. If they don't get me for murder, I'm sure they can get me for tampering with evidence.

"You know I'll throw the book at you if you aren't telling the truth." He jabs a finger in my chest bone. "I'm not saying you did it, but I think you know more than you're letting on."

I'm not about to give in to Ian and his bullying. It only makes me want to figure this thing out on my own more, and let them figure it out on their own. "Am I under arrest?"

I push my way around Ian and walk back to find Aunt Matilda and Carl still reminiscing about old times.

I walk over to the front door. I open it and stare at Aunt Matilda. "I think it's time for them to leave."

I swear lightening shoots out of her eyes. She's always telling me to mind my manners, but I don't have to do it in my own house.

"Okay." Carl looks at Aunt Matilda, then Ian, then me. "Well, Matilda thank you for a lovely evening. It's been fun talking about old times." He taps Ian on the forearm and points for him to walk to the door. "Olivia."

I fake a smile. "Carl." I nod. "Ian." I slam the door behind them.

The nerve of him coming into my house and accusing me of…well, the truth. If I want him to know the truth, I'll tell him.

"What is it?" Aunt Matilda stands up and walks over, taking both my hands in hers. This is exactly what she used to do when I was a child and upset about a fight with Erin. "What's wrong? Did you see something?" Aunt Matilda has a funny way of asking questions indirectly to what she is thinking.

"I don't know." I'm so mad at Erin that I can't focus on anything Ian said. "I can't believe Erin was going to tell Ian about all the evidence I've collected. I can't go around accusing Brittany of emails she might not have sent, even though everything points to her." I'd hate to accuse someone falsely.

"Baby steps." Aunt Matilda saunters down the hall and let's Herbie out of my room. "Being a detective takes baby steps." She smiles at Herbie who was running around and sniffing every inch of where our guests had been.

Baby steps. The last time I heard her say that was when she described our getting to know each other when my momma left.

I'm happy to see Herbie's aura is back to normal and we can get on with our night. I check on Erin a couple more times before it's time for me to get back on my normal sleep schedule. It's been a long couple of days and I'm looking forward to snuggling with Herbie.

Twenty-Five

"Okay, wake up." Aunt Matilda is standing over me with her notebook and writing away. "I've let you sleep long enough." She jingles out of the room and Herbie jumps down to follow her.

I turn over. It can't be. Is it? The blue dots on the clock read 12:30 PM. I get out of bed and pull the blinds. It's definitely day-time. I guess working the night shift at Macro Hard did a number on me or maybe it was the cleaning. Either way I must've slept pretty good.

I check on Erin before I go see what Aunt Matilda is up to. She's sound asleep. Her arm is lying over her eyes. For years I've been telling her to get a night mask, but she claims this is the only way she falls asleep.

Quietly I shut the door and walk down the hall. I can see my blinking Blackberry on the counter.

"I can't believe I slept that long." I pick it up and check the new dumps deposited into my email. For a business that's under scrutiny, I've had a lot more clients. "I have to get some of these done, *today*," I tell myself.

I admit, I'd rather be spying on Brittany, but life does go on. Death threats or not.

"You continue to talk about lipstick and Bree in your sleep." Aunt Matilda follows me into the office. "I really think you need to check this out. These could be the clues you need."

Really, it's not a bad idea. It'll have to be a time when Bree's not home. Maybe I'll see if she's at the SPCA working. That way, I know she won't be home. I didn't get a great look at her place in the rain the other day, so another quick drive by, in the sunlight won't hurt.

I put the dumps in the back of my head. I won't be long. I'll drive by, see what I can and then come home to work.

I decide to make sure and call Bradley.

"Where have you been?" he asks. "Or do I want to know?" He talks a little louder over the dogs barking.

"How about dinner tonight?" I want to go over everything with him and see what he thinks I should do. Whether I should go to the police or wait and see if they come to me. The one thing I don't want to do is implicate myself any more than I already have.

"Sounds great. Bree…er…Brittany," he whispers, "is closing so I can leave on time."

"What time is she supposed to leave there?" I really do need to do some work today. It will be great if I can squeeze in a dump before doing my drive by.

"Not for a couple of hours." Bradley just made my day.

"I hope she doesn't know it's me you're talking too." I confess to Bradley. "I'm going to drive by her house again." If she is emailing me because of Splitsville.com, that is one thing, but threatening to kill me is another. This is what I need to find out before I go to the police.

"Why? What are you going to find out from driving by?" I can hear the disapproval in his voice.

"I don't know. Anything." I can tell Bradley isn't happy with this.

"Listen Olivia, why don't you go to the police? There's no reason for you to keep this a secret. Let them do their job."

"Hey, did you give your brother-in-law the license plate number?" I look up all my new clients on the computer. I don't have any time to spare. I tap my finger on one that looks pretty cut and dry. Zach is dumping a girl who he's been on one date with, but she refuses to leave him alone.

"Don't change the subject. See, the police have more resources than you and I. If you give them the number, they'll be able to trace it faster."

"Brittany might not know it's me behind Splitsville.com, but the mystery man from her house does. Call me if she happens to leave work early."

"She won't. She's the one closing at 5 P.M."

Before I hang up, Aunt Matilda is standing in the door frame with her notebook under her arm. "I'm going to do a drive by her house today." I point to the notebook because she knows I'm talking about Brittany. "She's working today so there's no reason to worry about me."

"I'm not worried. I want you to keep your eyes open, especially for the person who broke into your car at Macro Hard." Her words may say she's not worried, but her aura tells me she is.

God! Why can't Carl keep his mouth shut?

I stand up and walk over to her. I'd never do anything to put my family in danger. I wrap my arms around her and the space between our hearts becomes warm. I'll always be grateful for Aunt Matilda. Although I don't have a living mother, she's the closest thing to one.

"I will." Love radiates out of her eyes and I smile. "I promise."

She turns to walk out and I go sit back in front of the computer to break-up with Betty.

***

I use the mouse and scroll down the computer screen to read Zach's reasons for dumping her when she answers the phone. "Is Betty there?" I pray she's a quick dump. If I need to post bond, I need to do some dumps.

"Who's this?"

Zach has paid me extra money because he doesn't have a photo of her. He went on one date and she's stalking him. He says he felt if she was dumped from someone else, she might leave him alone.

"This is Jenn from Splitsville.com." I stop to wait for a reply. "How are you today?" I don't know where that came from. How do you think she's doing today, when she's about to get dumped.

"Who?" Betty begins at number one in "process."

"Jenn from Splitsville.com." Oh how I wish I had a picture of her. "Zach is not interested in you. He's done with you." How painful can this be? They went on one date, *one* date.

"This is none of your business." Oh Betty it is my business when someone is paying me and money is involved.

Betty is starting to get defensive. I don't get it. How could she really care after one date? I mean, if Bradley didn't want to see me after our first date, I'd be sad, but I'd move on. *I think.*

"It *is* my business. Zach made it my business because he hired Splitsville.com to let you know he's not interested. Hey, didn't you meet on a dating website?"

I smile, knowing I have good details about how they met. *Of course it's not going to work out sweetie*, I want to say but don't.

"Yes, but…" Betty, you better watch it, you're getting a little testy. I know I'm starting to really get to her.

I have to interrupt her before she makes a mockery of herself, "Listen, Betty. I hate to tell you this, but Brian and his friends made a bet to see how many dates they could get off the dating website. Of course he asked you out and you accepted. Now part of the bet is that he has to go out on a date. And *a* date means one, not two or three, but one." I hold my finger up in the air as if she can see it. "He's been on one date with you, and several other girls since you." *Wow! He's a jerk.* "Stop stalking him. You're creeping him out."

"I'm not stalking him!" I take the phone away from my ear as she continues to scream "no I'm not," without taking a breath.

I hold the receiver up to my mouth and scream back. "Yes you are! You've been out on one date." I look over at the time. Brittany is supposed to be at the SPCA in an hour. I have extra time to do this dump and get ready.

"Do you call him?" I go back to Betty and refocus on the dump. Zach is paying me double to get rid of her ass.

"Yes."

"A lot Betty. You call him a lot, and does he answer?" Zach says he doesn't answer her daily phone calls and is thinking about getting a new phone number, only he's had this one for a couple years and changing numbers really is a pain.

"No." Betty sniffles into the phone. I'm hoping that she's getting it.

"Okay, there you go. He doesn't answer because he's done with you." Now we're getting somewhere. I bend down and pick up Herbie's ball and throw it out the office door. I smile as he scampers after it.

"He can tell me himself." *Maybe* we aren't getting somewhere. I rest my head back on my chair and roll it to the side when I hear Herbie run into the room squeaking his

ball. I bend back down and grab it out of his mouth. He
jerks away and runs off like he won.

"No, he doesn't need to tell you because he hired me.
He doesn't want to talk to you." I totally hate to be rude,
but in some cases, you just have to be.

"I care about him." Betty whimpers in the background.

"I'm sorry. I can tell you care about him, but he's not
good for you. A good guy wouldn't use you as part of a bet.
How long has it been since you talked to him?" What is it
with these girls? They go on one date and fall, hook, line
and sinker.

"A few weeks ago."

"So you haven't physically talked to him since the day
after your one and only date?" I wish he'd put that on the
form. I'd really be driving that little tidbit in.

"Yes. But I'm not going to give back his sweatshirt."

I laugh. Does she really think he's worried about a
twenty-dollar sweatshirt? "Trust me, he doesn't want it
back."

"I care…"

I have to stop her. She spent one night with him and
hasn't talked to him since. How does she care about him?

"Stop! I know you care about him, but he's freaked
out. You call and leave plans for the two of you and he only
wants you to leave him alone." I pause for a second and go
back in for the kill, "Betty, do you understand that Zach has
hired me to break-up—well, you technically aren't even
dating. Regardless, he's hired me to tell you he will no
longer be asking you out on any more dates."

"But we made plans."

"I'm sorry I have to be the one to tell you, but your
calendar is now free. I hate to be rude, but it's over. He

only wanted to go on one date with you and other people on the dating website."

"We had great sex. He said so," she blubbers in the phone.

Whoa! I scan the form quickly and don't see anything about sex on there. "Sex? You slept with him on your first date? Obviously he didn't like it because he never called you again." No wonder she's so hung up on him.

"He said it was the best blow job he ever had." Betty sounds pretty proud of herself.

I roll my eyes and take a deep breath. I glance around the corner just to make sure Aunt Matilda isn't around because if she heard these next words out of my mouth, she'd fall dead of a heart attack.

"Blow job? You didn't even have sex! You know what you need is to go brush your teeth and move on." I don't want to know any more details about Betty's abilities or talents.

"Arrgh! Fine!" Betty slams down the phone.

Twenty-Six

I drive by Brittany's house twice to make sure no one's there, or—no unexpected guest. Even though Bradley said she's at work, you never know. She might have a killer melt-down and need to come home, or just plain leave.

I park a couple houses down, by the corner, so the neighbors won't know exactly which house the unfamiliar Toyota is visiting. I look out the window and stare at the "neighborhood watch" sign. I'm sure there's been a lot of good that has come out of this program, but hopefully not today.

I glance over at Brittany's immaculately manicured lawn. I've always wondered how they make grass look 3-D with all the lines going every which way and I can picture her edging it with a pair of scissors that she just took to a sharpening stone.

And. Those. Flowers! There isn't a single tulip that's wilted or the slightest bit drooping. I snicker as I realize she's planted the tulips in the order of the colors of the rainbow.

The other houses in the cookie cutter neighborhood aren't as tidy as Brittany's, I notice driving by.

I look in my rear view mirror and my side view mirrors to make sure no one is around. The coast is clear. I get out of my car and walk down the street toward Brittany's.

The house numbers are painted on the side of the curb. Who ever came up with modular homes is a genius. All the homes look the same. Maybe they have different colored shutters, or the garage is facing the side instead of the front, but the similarity is noticeable.

Brittany's garage is one facing the front, but the dead giveaway is the yard. I bet her neighbors hate how pristine it looks.

Not a life in sight. The neighbors don't seem to be home. Nothing is moving.

I walk through the grass up to the flower garden and lift up every lawn ornament that's sprinkled throughout her mulch. Surely there's a spare key somewhere. Doesn't everyone have a spot?

Walking around the house, I see a small shed is situated in the back right-hand corner of her yard. I bet Brittany keeps all her tools in there, spic and span. I've always heard you can tell a lot about a man by how well he keeps his tools. I bet the same goes for Brittany.

I glance at the windows above the patio and see one that's cracked—only it's about six feet off the ground. I run my finger along the teak bench directly under it and realize it's not going to be easy to climb into.

I look back at the shed, hoping something is in there I can use to climb on because there is no way I can hoist myself up to the window from the low bench. I slip through the cracked shed door. The slightest bit of sun shines on the most welcome sight. A step ladder.

"Perfect." I grin, wiping off the cobwebs. Obviously she hasn't used this in a while. *Of course she hasn't*, I think *She's been too busy murdering people.*

Quickly I carry it back to the porch and move the bench slightly to the left. I climb up the step-ladder to look in at the perfectly folded laundry on the dryer. "My luck." I shake my head. I don't know what I'd do if my laundry looked like that. It wouldn't be natural if I didn't have to search the basket for something remotely not stinky.

I hoist myself up, turn my body like I'm getting on a horse and slide down on my belly, feet first. So much for a quick drive by.

Never in a million years did I think sneaking in and out of Aunt Matilda's house when I was a teenager was preparing me for this.

"Shit!" I pull my foot out of a ceramic dog bowl and shake it in the air. Brittany has a dog? Bradley never mentioned a dog; maybe if he did, I might not have been so willing to break into her house.

I leave the tipped over dog bowl and decide to clean it up on my way out. Something Brittany would never do. She'd clean it up immediately.

I take a quick glance around to get my bearings and make sure a dog isn't going to attack me. I swear Good Housekeeping could come in here, right now and not have to stage a thing.

I look through the kitchen and down the hall to what I'm guessing is Brittany's room. Maybe she doesn't keep it as clean as the rest of the house. Everything matches. Everything! The comforter, pillows, shams, and curtains all have the same print.

I smile, knowing my thread-bare Scooby Doo pillow cases, up against my plaid comforter and Mickey Mouse sheets would send her into a tizzy.

I'm careful not to touch anything. I walk across her bedroom into her bathroom.

I look for anything that's not meticulously clean. A little dot of mold will make me feel good. I get the gloves out of my back pocket and put them on. The cabinet door under her sink whines as I open it. Glancing in, everything is in a glass container. I'm lucky to find a stray tampon in my junk drawer, much less keeping them all neat in a glass container under my sink.

I take my key-chain mini mag out and twist it on. I don't want to touch anything without seeing what it is. I reach in the back for one of the many black tubes. I select one like the black tube I've been carrying around for the past couple days and have grown very fond of. I turn it over to get a true name color because the one I took from the SPCA has been rubbed off.

"Passion Pink." Go figure. I could've come up with that name. I put the tube back in the container because when I tell the police all about my discovery, they will be able to compare the two or twenty she has under there.

I go back into the bedroom. I don't see any pictures, jewelry, or anything personal. I have to find something to tie her to Dabi and Kent. Something that will give her a reason for murder.

I walk down the hall and a ping of jealousy strikes me when I turn the corner to her office. If I had an ounce of OCD, maybe I could have a neat tidy office too.

The hard wood floors creak as I walk over to the small cabinet next to the leather chair. The leather groans when I sit and pull open the top drawer. I rub my fingers along the tabs of the dozen or so files all neatly color coordinated.

I hesitate. I watch my gloved fingers cross over the typed labels. "Yes!" I pump my fists into the air. I'd know those labels anywhere. It's the exact same label used on the file missing from Dabi's office. Nice and neat, just like someone who has OCD.

With a little luck and a lot more searching, I'm sure I'll find the missing file somewhere in this Martha Stewart house.

I sit down in the floral print high back chair in front of the computer and text Bradley a quick message.

"Still looking for some clues. Is she still there?" I hit the green send button.

"She's still here," he texts back.

"Let me know when she leaves," I quickly respond.

"Slap." Slap? I read Bradley's text again.

"Slap?" I have no clue what he's talking about. Brittany's computer is on and I type in "slap in text language." Goggle pulls up "sounds like a plan."

It is a plan.

I use the mouse to drag the arrow across the computer screen and search the pull-down menu in her history so I can delete what I just Googled. The last thing I want is for her to find out someone has been here and messing with her computer.

But what is a little snooping going to hurt?

I search through Brittany's history. There may be something she looked up that can lead to the murders. J Crew, Gap, Macro Hard products, Splitsville.com...

I gasp, "Splitsville." I look at the date and time she last viewed it. According to my calculations she was on it 20 minutes before I received an email threat sent from the internet café, which is almost ten minutes from her house.

I have definitely tied her to the emails. But I have to find the file in order to tie her to the murders.

My phone vibrates. I look down and see a text from Bradley in all capital letters. "GET OUT! She's coming home for lunch."

I look at the drawer where the files are. And for a split second I want to grab them, but I don't.

I text back, "Is she working tomorrow?"

With a second to spare he types back, "YES GET OUT!"

I click out of her computer and go back to the laundry room. Looking at the spill, I take the entire roll of paper towels and throw it on the mess without rolling them out.

I look around for a place to throw them away. If I leave them in the trash next to the dryer, she will know. So I open the dryer door and throw them in there. Hopefully by the time she finds them, I'll have this thing solved.

I look at the window and decide to use the door. I figure it'd take me longer to climb back out the window than taking the real way out of a house.

I run around the back of the house to get the ladder and stop when I feel my shoe squish something. I can smell it before I pick it up. "Eww!"

I rub my shoe into the grass to get off the large clumps of dog poop as I walk to the ladder.

I grab the ladder and run to the shed. The buzz of the garage door chain roars and I quickly shut the shed door and tiptoe run to the side of the house.

I plant my body up against the warm brick house with my palms flat to the heat. As if my hands have suction cups, I make my way along the side of the house and peek around the corner.

"Crap." I roll my eyes and whisper. I'm on the wrong side of the house. I can't just go back around or she'll see me out her windows and if I cross in front, she'll see me there too.

I look over at the neighbor's house and bolt across their lawn. If I cross to the other side of the street, I can keep my head turned away from Brittany's house in case she does see me.

I nod at a young couple walking their infant in one of those strollers with the net. What are those parents worried about? A bird swooping down to get their young or the sun giving them a good dose of vitamin D?

"No!" The mom screams.

Startled, I look up to apologize for being in her space. "I'm sorry." I plead to the crazy looking woman.

"Not you." She points. "Him!" The cute little family takes off down the street.

Tramp, Kent's dog he got from the SPCA fund raiser, is galloping full speed ahead right toward me. I take off in the opposite direction of the parents, toward my car. I don't think I've ever run before. Or I can't recall a time when I needed to.

Brittany is running out her front door screaming.

She sounds desperate. "Stop!" I look back and see Tramp closing in on me. Brittany is not far behind him flailing her arms in the air. "He won't hurt you!"

My mind yells RUN and my legs continue to follow.

"Stop! If you don't I can't catch him!" I hear Brittany scream as she stops. "Hey, Hey! Olivia?"

If I don't take her advice, I may have a heart attack. Tramp smells my shoes. He is surrounded by his silver aura indicating he understands why I am there. I bend down to catch my breath and stroke his furry coat.

With one hand planted on her hip and her other hand pointing at me, Brittany states, "You are Olivia." Her eyes cross examine me, "Do you live near here?"

For a split second I thought she knew I was in her house only seconds ago, but by the expression on her face I can tell she doesn't.

She takes Tramp by his collar. "Well? Do you?" Her eyebrows turn slightly in.

I smile, relief flowing through me. She doesn't know I'm Jenn from Splitsville.com. "No." I pick up the community newspaper in the front yard we are standing in. "I deliver these." I hold it out to her.

Her face becomes distorted and she cocks her head to the side. "Really? Bradley said you work in the dot com world."

My smile broadens. "Extra cash with the economy and all." I change the subject, "Your dog?" I have to know how she got Tramp.

I really can't believe Erin didn't know where Tramp went and Bradley didn't tell me Brittany had a dog.

"No, er, yes. Um…no." She looks confused.

I question, "Which is it?" If she's not confused, I sure am. "Yes or no."

She strokes Tramps head. "My ex-boyfriend's dog." Her face scans mine. "Tramp showed up at the SPCA one day and I took him. I didn't tell Bradley so if you can keep it between the two of us that'd be great."

"Sure." Sure I won't! "Well, I've got to go to another neighborhood now." I walk away.

"Funny." She turns back to face me as I continue to walk. "I've always seen them thrown from cars." She throws the paper back in her neighbor's yard.

I keep my eye on the prize. My Toyota. I can't get to it fast enough. I have my man…er…woman and I know it.

Twenty-Seven

"Now what happened again?" Bradley questions me over another glass of wine about my debut burglary.

To avoid his stare, I look out the window realizing it's the time of the year where the night's darkness comes earlier. "I got out of her house just in time."

Erin comes out with a lighter to light the torches I have planted around the patio. She looks a lot better than she did this afternoon when I checked on her. She has color in her cheeks, and she's smiling. Well, maybe smiling is a little strong, but she's not crying, so she's good.

I continue with my story. "I completely went around the wrong side of the house to get in my car, so I had to cross the street like I was a walker, only Tramp ran out of her house and started toward me."

Erin stops shy of lighting the last torch and asks, "*My Kent's Tramp?*"

I jump around in my seat, "Yes!" I motion for her to sit in the empty chair next to me. Since I am certain Brittany is the killer but doesn't know exactly who I am, I feel a lot safer sitting outside. "She said the police brought him into the SPCA and she took him home without Bradley knowing."

"I wondered where he went." Erin is caught off guard. "I asked the police, but they said there was no dog." I can see the relief on Erin's face, the worry she'd been holding in about Kent's missing dog. "I thought the killer took him."

"He's alive and well living with crazy-boots Brittany."

"She told me the dog was a gift, and I let her bring him to work." Bradley gets up and paces back and forth. "I can't believe I didn't know that was Tramp. He sure cleans up good."

A red flag shoots up in my head. I put my hand up in the air. "Wait, Kent adopted Tramp at the fund-raiser, but Brittany said she got him from the SPCA and then told you she got him as a gift. Something isn't adding up."

Bradley's eyes squint the way they do when he's in deep thought. "Hmm." He rubs his hands through his hair and locks them behind his head. "No, he didn't come back to the SPCA or I would've seen the paperwork."

I bite the corner of my lip. Brittany's words creep back into my head and send a chill up my spine. "Between you and me," she'd said. Just another one of her secrets?

Did Tramp really show up at the SPCA after Kent's death or did she take Tramp after she "offed" Kent?

Bradley continues to squint and he confirms. "Nope, the only paperwork I got on his adoption was from the fund raiser at the park."

I recall the day I went around the kissing booth to pet Tramp. "That's when Kent started hitting on me for a kiss and I told him the booth was closed." I slap my hand over my mouth and look over at Erin.

"What?" Erin cries out, "What are you saying?" She jumps to her feet and stands over me like she's ready to clobber me with the torch lighter. I've blown it. That's what I get by not thinking before I speak.

"Erin, I wasn't going to tell you since Kent is dead. It wouldn't do any good and it was before..."

"Before what? You're my best friend!"

I stand up and grab her by the shoulders. "That's right. I'm your best friend. And I know Kent cared about you. We were at a *kissing* booth. He tried to kiss me. And now someone is going to great lengths to pin me to his murder."

She stares at me, finally blinking. "Who would do that?" she whispers. She and Bradley pace back and forth. Her aura shifts from red to crystal so I know she's not really mad. Thank God. I don't know what I'd do without Erin.

"Someone went as far as taking a picture of Kent and me arguing," I said to Erin with her back to me.

She stops and looks at me while a viridian green creeps around her. She's confused. No! I want her aura to stay crystal. She has to know I'd never willingly hurt her. And I want her to believe that Kent really did care about her. I truly think he did.

It hits me. Michael pops into my head. I know exactly what I have to do. I have to go to Michael's. I need to see him in a baseball cap. The mystery man had a baseball cap at Brittany's and at Macro Hard. Michael knows Brittany and he knows I took the job at Macro Hard.

Even though his aura tells me he couldn't commit murder, his white Pumas that Erin and I saw may prove otherwise. I get my keys.

"I have to go. I have to talk to Michael." I head to the door, but stop for a second to root through a pile of clothes.

"What?" Bradley stands in the light, causing a shadow to cast on the clothes.

I shove him to the side, and frantically start flinging the clothes out of the basket. "I need to find my baseball hat. I have to see if Michael resembles the mystery man." I grab the hat and leave the house.

"I'll stay here with Herbie." Erin plops on the couch next to the dog.

"You're not going without me." Bradley follows me to my car. He plants himself in the front seat.

I don't want Bradley in danger, but I'm thrilled he wants to be with me. I only hesitate for a second. "What if Michael set this up the whole time and took the picture of me? He has those same white Pumas." If my "gift" is off and if my reading of Michael is off, my aura reading days might be over. I glance at Bradley and hope that's not true. I don't think I'll ever get tired of looking at the shimmering blue that outlines his body.

The traffic down his street is heavier today than I've seen it. With the break from the rain, I'm sure people are taking advantage of the park. There is a line of cars trying to get through but I can't wait any longer. Patience may be a virtue, but it's one virtue I'm willing to live without.

I park. "I'll be right back." I instruct Bradley to stay put. This is as far as I want him to go.

He grabs my hand on the parking brake. "I'm through letting you do this on your own." His eyes are deep and full of concern. "You're nuts if you think I'm going to let you confront him on your own."

I could argue. I could throw a fit and insist he stay. But the fact that he is willing to come with me. . .to be by my side. . .fills me with warmth and a comfort I haven't felt since before my parents left. I nod and we get out of the car and walk to Michael's apartment. I don't know exactly what I'm going to say, but I have to get him to try on a baseball hat with his white Pumas. It's the only way to know if he's the mystery man or not.

I jump. "Ian?" The cop is standing in front of Michael's building.

"What are you doing here?"

"I. . .er. . . I." I don't know what to say.

He coolly looks Bradley and me over, and at that same moment I realize that the line of cars isn't because people are trying to get to the park. They're rubberneckers. Is Michael dead? Oh God, am I too late? Worse, am I wrong? Then I see him. Absolutely not dead. Carl has him in handcuffs and is dragging him to his cop car.

I leave Bradley to deal with Ian and run over to him. "Michael?"

He doesn't look at me. His head is hung down and his shoulders slump. The handcuffs jingle as he walks to the police car.

"Michael?" I want to get an aura reading, but it's all foggy.

"Please get Belle. Take her home with you. She knows you." Michael pleads with me. "I didn't do it Olivia, I swear." He starts to cry and turns to Carl. "You have to believe me. I didn't do it!"

"Let me guess, your brother?" Carl turns away and looks me dead in the face. "I'm ashamed of you. You know he's the killer?"

"No Carl." I look down at my feet. I don't know who the killer is. I don't know if it's Michael, Brittany or both.

"I'm going to need a statement from you." Carl lowers Michael into the back of his cruiser. Bradley holds me back. Carl slams the door with Michael pleading his innocence.

Bradley stands with Ian, who's keeping the traffic moving. He flashes Ian his SPCA badge.

"Since I'm with the SPCA, can I take the dog?" Bradley asks Ian. Dang, he's good. No wonder I'm falling for him.

Ian goes upstairs to retrieve Belle while Bradley and I wait without a word between us.

***

Our drive back is silent except for little Belle's whimpering. Bradley strokes her and whispers that it's going to be all right, and all I can think about it seeing Michael in a baseball cap.

Once home, we let Belle and Herbie romp around in the yard. We let them romp too long. Carl pulls up and we're still outside.

"Good evening folks." Carl takes his hat off and walks over to the back porch. "Can I have a word with you, Olivia?"

"Do you have a subpoena?" I love how Bradley stands up between Carl and me, like he's my knight in shining armor.

"No, I just want to talk with her." Carl looks past Bradley and into my eyes. "Off the record."

For some reason I trust Carl. I put my hand on Bradley's shoulder, "It's fine." Bradley turns to me questioning my response and I smile. Carl has history with my aunt. That has to count for something. Carl and I wait until Bradley and Erin completely shut the door.

Carl is as serious as a heart attack. "Listen, I know you didn't kill anyone." His eyebrows form a platform over his eyes casting a shadow that makes me shudder. "I believe you are just like your Aunt Matilda. You *know* something." He puts a lot of emphasis on the word *know*.

I don't know what to do with this. What does he know about Matilda? What does he think I can do? Will he blow my cover? I have to stall. "So what if I do, why would I tell you?"

"We need to bring these murders to a close. The FBI is breathing down my neck. They want to know everything I know about Splitsville.com."

My stomach sinks to my toes when I hear
Splitsville.com and FBI in the same sentence. So he's
leveraging his information. I'm not so sure I can trust him
after all.

He pulls out a baggie. "Why was this stuck in your
dash?" He holds it up next to my face so I can see it's the
list I made about Brittany's motives and the Swiss Army
knife. "We've combed all the security tapes from Macro
Hard and it seems there isn't any footage of the car you
describe leaving the parking lot. Do you have any clue who
broke into your car and what this list of motives is about?"

I do the only thing I can. I whisper, "Give me five
minutes alone with Michael Schultz. Then I'll answer a few
of your questions." I search his face for his reaction, but
he's good. He doesn't flinch or give an ounce. "He didn't
do it, Carl."

"You know I can get you for withholding evidence."

"I don't have evidence and you know it. I'm like
Matilda, remember? Threats will get you nowhere." I walk
away, because if he's not going to give, I'm not going to
give. "Good night, Carl."

"You're *exactly* like Matilda," he blurts out. I keep
walking, and he finally adds, "Okay. Five minutes."

A slow grin creeps across my mouth. I know I have
Carl exactly where I want him. I only need a minute to get
the cap on Michael—just to make sure.

"I get numbers one through six, but eight. . ." He
points to the list of motives I made for Brittany. "It says
here that she begins to threaten Splitsville.com because
she's angry, but she doesn't know Jenn's true identity." He
takes his readers off his face. "What do you mean
threatens? How did she threaten you?"

"Emails." I don't play stupid because I know Aunt Matilda told him.

He looked at me for a good long while. "Do you have copies of the emails?"

I cut to the chase. "Yes, but they aren't traceable to any one person, only places." Herbie is scratching at the door. I walk over and let him and Belle out. "She's sending them from public places in Park City or hasn't Aunt Matilda given you that tidbit of information?"

I'm happy to see Herbie's aura is back to normal. He runs around sniffing every inch of the yard with Belle following along after him.

"You've already accused her. Why?"

I tell him about the lipstick on the coffee cup and the lipstick I found at the SPCA. "But I don't want you to let Michael go."

"I think you need to leave that up to the police."

"I think you forget who you're dealing with. If I am like my Aunt Matilda, which I'm not claiming to be, but if I am, I do know more than what I've told you." I have to play my cards right or I may never save Splitsville.com.

"Excuse me?" Carl obviously doesn't like to be threatened. Red aura is not his color.

"I'm asking you to keep Michael in jail and not use anything I say about Brittany for a couple of days. I have a theory, and I might be way off base, but I need a day or two."

Carl knows I'm not going to budge, "So if I give you the couple days, you'll help me like your Aunt Matilda did years ago?"

"Yes." I worry I might've just made a deal with the devil, but it's giving me time to save the lid from being blown off Splitsville.com.

***

The jail isn't located at the police department. It's on the outskirts of town by the old mill. I guess they put it there because no one ever goes to that side of town. The prisoners are just your local drunks or shoplifters. Never had any murderers in there. They are usually shipped to the state's bigger facilities.

I pull into the lot and park under the one spot light next to the door. This is probably the safest place to be in town, but whoever has the BMW is still out there somewhere. I glance around on the way in.

"I'm here to see Michael Schultz." I tell the lady behind the bars, who sits right inside the double doors. I hand her my driver's license.

She takes it and makes a copy of it. She pulls a list out from under the phone and drags her finger down it.

"Mm, hum." She hands my ID back to me and smiles. "Through the doors."

I hear the click as the doors unlock. I pull it open and walk in. I wait for the woman to walk around and unlock the door with bars in front of me.

"I have to check under your baseball cap." Her eyes wander around the rest of my body. I made sure I left everything in the car. I have no desire to be searched.

I pull the baseball cap off my head to show her there's no weapons, food or even a hairstyle under it.

"You can sit here." She locks the door behind me and shows me the chair in the corner.

I wait for a couple of minutes with my knees together and hands in my lap. I stand up as soon as Michael rounds the corner.

Michael rushes over once he sees me. "Olivia, how's Belle?" he questions.

"Belle? You're in jail charged with murder and all you can think about is Dabi's dog?" I can't believe him. If I was in jail, Herbie would be the last one I'd think about. I hand him the baseball cap. "We have five minutes. Tops. Put this on."

"Why?" He inspects it like it's a joke. "How's Belle?"

"She's great. She and Herbie are running around the yard. Put. It. On." I grab it out of his hands and stick it on his head. "Stand still."

I take a few steps back. A still calmness comes over my body. I close my eyes and inhale. I allow my lungs to fill up. In a sick way, I secretly wish Michael is the killer, but I know he isn't. He doesn't resemble the mystery man at all.

Now I'm going to have to keep one eye open. Whoever broke into my car knows who I am, and it's *not* Brittany. Nor has the mystery man told Brittany who I am.

I don't walk out until Michael is safe and sound in his cell. He is probably the only hardened criminal in here. Hell, he's probably the *only* inmate they have. Nothing *ever* happens in Park City. Well, not before all of this.

" Did you get what you're looking for?" A voice booms out from the darkness.

I jump and point my protective spray at Carl who is sitting on the bench outside the door, waiting for me to come out.

"Jeez, Carl you scared me." I drop my arm to my side. "You almost got sprayed." I ignore him and walk over to my car. "I asked for a couple days." I need to get home and into bed. I've got to be well rested if I'm going to figure this out within forty-eight hours.

Carl throws his hands up in the air. "Sorry. Do you want to explain any more about who might've broken into your car? And what's up with the pepper spray."

"No, I'm just a single girl." I slam my car door and pull out of the lot with one eye on the road and the other eye in the rear view mirror.

Twenty-Eight

I toss and turn all night. Herbie can feel my anxiety and begins to stir. I still haven't brought myself to take him back to the SPCA. I vowed I'd never get a pet, much less a dog, and now I can't think of my life without him. He stops circling and looks me straight in the eyes.

"Thanks for keeping me company." I pat the bed next to me for him to come lie close. It's like he's always been a part of me and my life; like he fills a void that I didn't even know had been there. "I don't care how much you miss your doggie friends. You aren't going anywhere." He tilts his head up like he understands what I'm saying. He begins to lick my face.

I've always heard dogs can read what you're feeling inside. Maybe he has a gift like me and that's why we found each other. He's there when I need him to give me those reassuring kisses and I want to make sure I am there for him too.

We lie there until 9 AM. I have about an hour until Brittany has to go to the SPCA and work all day with Bradley while I go and snoop more through her immaculate house. Bradley swears he's going to keep a close eye on her and call me if she leaves for any reason whatsoever.

Finally, I fall out of bed and schlep down the hall to let Herbie out.

Aunt Matilda and Erin are already having a cup of coffee and watching the news.

"Still no leads on Dabi's murder or Kent's?" Aunt Matilda hands me a cup.

"According to your friend, Carl, Michael did it."

She knows as well as I know that he didn't do it.
"You'll figure it out." Aunt Matilda sweeps my hair behind
my shoulders. "You always do."

I shake my head. Hopefully after today, that will
change. Because I'm going to find the answers, and then
the police will leave Erin and Michael out of it.

Aunt Matilda walks over to the door letting Herbie
back in. "What are you doing today?"

Herbie comes over and jumps on me. I take a couple of
pink dog treats from the counter and give him a couple.

I don't want her to worry. "Ah, a little of this and a
little of that." I shrug and take my coffee back to my room
and begin to plot for the second break-in.

This time I have a plan A. I will only look for the file
that's missing. I also have plan B. If I can't find something
with real meat, I'll take Aunt Matilda's advice and go to the
police with all the information I have.

I take my usual route around Brittany's street and pull
into my usual spot in front of the neighborhood watch sign.
There's no sign of life on the street. I'm beginning to
wonder if anyone lives in these houses.

I hurry toward Brittany's house.

Relief sweeps over me at the sight of the same window
that's still cracked. I go back to the shed to retrieve the
ladder and trace the same steps as yesterday. Only this time
I look for poop mines.

A few minutes later, I'm lowering myself into the
laundry room and make sure not to step into the bowl.

Everything looks the same as it did yesterday. Not a
crumb of food on the counter. Not a speck of dirt on the
floor.

I look around in amazement. How does she do it with a
dog? I shake my head. I couldn't even do it without a dog,

but now Herbie drags in all sorts of grass on his paws and when he eats, crumbs are all over the floor.

I stop in sheer fear when I hear the rattle of the garage door chains. Oh my God! She's back? My hand trembles as I take my phone out of my pocket and notice two missed calls.

Bradley.

I creep around the family room in search of a good spot to hide but the only place is the closet. With my hand on the knob and my teeth gritted together, I slowly open the door as I hear a voice come through the laundry room.

The coat closet is as tidy as the rest of the house, which gives me plenty of room to squat. I put my hands up to my pounding heart. I can feel the blood rushing in and out of my veins. I steady myself, praying I don't fall over.

I put my ear closer to the door. At first it's just Brittany frantically talking and her muted cry. I lean in more to see if I can make out what she's saying.

Through the crack, I see she's speaking in her cell with it pinned between her ear and shoulder.

My phone rings. My heart pounds in my throat. I grab the phone and jam it down in the carpet. It's Bradley. I press *end.* I turn the ringer to *silent,* hoping Brittany's sobs covered up the ring.

Of all the stupid things. This is why I'm not a spy. I throw my hand over my mouth and make sure the squeal of panic I feel isn't going to come out. I peek through the closet door crack. There's no way she heard my phone ring, right?

My heart feels like it's about to pound right out of my chest. I press my lips together in fear I may cry out or she might hear my chattering teeth.

I look back out the crack, I see Tramp making his way over to my not-so-good hiding spot. I can't stand to watch him scratch at the door. He's going to give me away! "No!" I say with a hiss but he keeps scratching.

"Is your bone in there, buddy?" Brittany is suddenly there beside him. She jerks opens the door and looks in and her eyes lock on mine. "Ahhh!" She screams just as Tramp begins to bark. She flees through the laundry room.

"No!" I gasp and run after her. The last thing I need is a breaking-and-entering charge along with the murder charge. "Brittany! Stop!" I scream.

She stops shy of the garage door and turns around. The surprise on her face tells me that she didn't know it was me in the closet. I don't blame her. Anybody crouching in a closet would be scary.

"Olivia?" She narrows her eyebrows and searches my face for an answer. "Why are you in my house?"

Slowly I walk backward as she starts to walk fast toward me.

"I...I..." I don't have any time to spare. "I need to know why you are threatening me." I stand tall and hold my own, even though blood is pulsing in my head.

Of course! She doesn't know Splitsville.com and Olivia Davis are one and the same. She puts her hands up to her chest.

"Me? Threatening you?" Her voice escalates. "Are you crazy?"

"Are you or are you not sending emails to Splitsville.com from the Internet cafe?" I'm not about to let her get away with this. I *have* the lipstick. I pull the tube from the SPCA out of my pocket and jab it in her face as if it's a weapon.

She grabs the tube from my hands. "How do you know about that?"

"Because, Brittany," I say, channeling my Splitsville.com persona. No prisoners. No sympathy. Just straight to the jugular. I had no idea that being Jenn would actually help me. I'm Jenn."

"You?" She steps back. "You are Jenn from Splitsville.com? You're the one who broke up with me on the internet?"

"Um, yeah," I mutter under my breath. I'm back to being Olivia and suddenly feeling bad.

I'm taken off guard when she starts to cry. I've seen her go from scared, to mad to sad all within a few minutes.

She puts her hands up over her eyes to shield them from me. But her shaking shoulders and silent whimper let me know she's really upset.

I walk a little closer to her and rub my hand along her arm for a little comfort. "Listen, it's a job." For a moment I forget that she might be the killer.

"I know it is, but it's my heart." She starts to sob. "I loved him and he didn't have the decency to break-up with me in person." She shakes her head and starts blabbering.

"No! No! I didn't want to hurt Jenn, you—whoever, but Mac said to get Kent back by breaking him and Erin up. I didn't even know who Jenn was. They were empty threats!" She screams louder. "I swear!"

"Mac?" I step back and catch myself up against Brittany's car. Why is his name having an effect on me?

"Kent's best friend." Brittany put her head in her hands as her tears start to flow. "He couldn't believe Kent broke up with me."

We both look up to see Carl's cop car pulling into her driveway. Carl gets out with his hand on his gun like he's ready to draw it at any moment.

Brittany wipes the tears off her face with her hands. "Great. I guess you called the police."

Carl walks closer. "Ms. Davis." He nods his head toward me, then faces Brittany. "Are you Ms. Brittany Darlington?"

I ignore his arrogant light purple aura, which is taking over all the space in the air.

Brittany nods and I keep my mouth shut for once. "Yes, I'm Brittany."

Carl takes the cuffs off his belt. He cuffs her hands in front of her. "I think you have some explaining to do as to why you are illegally using the internet to make threats against Ms. Davis and her company. I have obtained records from The Coffee Bean computer and traced the threatening emails to you."

"I'm sorry," Brittany says in a hushed whisper. "I never meant to hurt her."

I'm glad to see a greener glow around her instead of the red aura from a few minutes ago. Her spirit has begun the healing process of forgiveness and peace.

I watch Brittany walk silently to the cop car with her head down. The neighbors have gathered in their front yards.

After Carl puts her in the back of the police car, he comes walking back to me.

"Listen, I wasn't planning on confronting her." I explain why I'm there.

Carl puts his fingers up to my mouth to make me shut up. "The day I saw you at the coffee shop, I was serving a subpoena for their computer. Your aunt told me some of the threats were coming from there and I knew it needed to be checked out. Stop implicating yourself." He turns to go back to his cruiser. "Can you take her dog with you? She said she'd get him back from you later."

I just nod. What do I look like, the dog whisperer?

"We will talk about this later." Carl wags his finger between the house and me.

I'm sure we will, I think, but dare not say it aloud.

Twenty-Nine

My Toyota can't get me home fast enough. I replay Brittany's confession in my mind. My gut tells me she didn't kill Dabi or Kent.

I have to take a hard right turn into my driveway. The street is lined with cars for the annual neighborhood yard sale. They are bumper to bumper.

She is sitting on the bar stool at the kitchen counter looking through Dabi's photo album when I walk in with Tramp.

Her mouth flings open and she shouts, "Tramp! Come here boy."

I smile seeing the joy on her face. It's the first time I've seen her really smile since Kent's death. I laugh as Tramp showers her with big wet kisses. Erin's going to be okay.

Erin looks up at me. "How did you get Tramp?"

"You won't believe it." I throw my keys onto the pile of clothes on the couch.

"Try me." Her eyes are curious.

I walk over to the coffee pot and pour two mugs of coffee. "Of course I had to find out if Brittany was blind threatening me or if she killed Dabi and Kent."

Erin put her hands in the air. "And?"

"I really think she only threatened me because of the service."

"How do you know that?"

"I asked her point blank. Granted, now she knows I'm Jenn, which isn't good, but..." I look back at the sound of the door opening in the bathroom. I'm sure Aunt Matilda is going to love this story. She's going to tell me that I should've left it up to Park City's finest. "But she is sorry for it." I don't tell Erin about Brittany's aura.

I run the spoon in circles to stir cream in my coffee. "So if Brittany didn't do it, who did?"

Erin sighs. "Let's go over it one more time."

I know the next words out of my mouth aren't going to sit well with her, but something about Kent doesn't add up. I really think these murders are related to him and I also think Dabi was an innocent victim.

"Suppose Dabi wasn't the first woman Kent took to the cleaners." I watch Erin shift around on the bar stool. I put my hand up in the air. "Hear me out. What if he's done it before? Maybe *that* woman hired someone to kill him."

She shakes her head. "That doesn't explain Dabi's murder."

We both pause to take a sip of coffee and ideas splash around my head.

Erin perks up. "What if Dabi was going to rat someone out? But who? It wouldn't have been Kent though, because he did make it right with her. He paid back all her money." Erin takes another sip and sets the cup down. The color suddenly drains from her face and her voice drops to a whisper. "He told me there were other women, but never mentioned their names."

I look out the window and watch a few excited garage salers boasting about their finds. I turn back around and pace alongside the counter.

"I just don't get it." I tap my fingers on the stack of mail on the counter. A Central People's Trust envelope is on top. It's our local bank. "I'm missing something. I feel it."

Wait. I don't bank at Central People's Trust. But Dabi Stone does, I literally *feel* the answer. I look more closely at the envelope. It's her name on the label.

"What?" Erin looks at the envelope. "What is it?"

I look at all the other mail on the counter. I had forgotten I'd taken it from her apartment. "Dabi Stone's bank statement." Before I can talk to myself about the legal implications of opening someone else's mail, I use my index finger to lift the seal.

Erin looks over my shoulder and gasps.

"What?" I look down at the cancelled checks lying on the counter that fell out.

"Why would she give Timmerman five-hundred-thousand dollars?" Erin's hand is up to her mouth.

"Who?" I question.

"Umm…" Erin looks down the hall. "Mac Timmerman, Kent's best friend."

I squint down the hall to see what Erin is so leery about. Someone is walking down the hall and it's definitely not Aunt Matilda.

Erin nervously stands up. "Oh, Olivia this is Kent's best friend, Mac—he, um, came by to give his condolences." I can hear the tremble in her voice, but she's trying to keep it calm.

Mac nods. There's no smile or sparkle in his dark eyes. His goatee is hard to forget. He's the same guy with Kent the day at the kissing booth.

Everything seems to come to a halt. Mac…Mac…Mac. His name takes over my mind.

"Nice to meet you." I smile while shaking his hand. I quickly pull away at the sudden jolt to my stomach. A black cloud starts creeping along his thinning black hair and down his arms.

He smiles, but his aura grays his teeth.

"I'll let you catch up while I go get something from my office." I walk away, trying not to lose my balance.

Oh my God, I keep repeating in my head. I know his voice and I know that name. I pull up the files on my computer and search. Mac Timmerman, the same Mac that was dumped by Carla, is smiling that same crooked smile that he was just smiling in my family room.

I put my ear closer to the door where he and Erin are standing. I hear Erin's voice amplify. "No, Mac!" She sounds frustrated. "He didn't say anything about money or deals. He stopped hustling."

Mac's words are muffled, but they sound angry.

I gather myself together and rush back into the room. "Um...did I miss something?" I can feel the tension. Erin doesn't take her eyes off Mac and Mac isn't smiling and showing those crooked teeth.

He looks at me. He plants his feet firmly with his stocky arms crossed. "No, this is between me and her." His eyes squint.

I get chills as he looks me up and down. I walk over to the window and privately pray to see Aunt Matilda coming toward the house. Or anyone for that matter. All I see is a BMW parked on the street. My heart sinks. It's the same BMW that I saw at Brittany's and Macro Hard. Mac.

I jerk around when I hear the lock click at the back door. Mac is standing in front of it. Still no smile. "And you too, now." He sounds so sinister. The black aura has taken over his entire frame.

He takes his baseball cap out of back pocket and puts it on.

My lips are grim in a straight line. I don't like what I'm seeing or hearing.

Erin looks between the two of us. "What are you talking about Mac?"

He reaches behind his back and pulls out a gun out of his jean waistband. "You two." He shakes his gun between us and the couch. "Sit down."

"What are you doing?" Erin puts her hands up.

Mac waves his gun. "Get on the couch!" he yells and we scuttle over.

"Listen Mac," I say, trying to calm him down. "We won't tell anyone about your and Kent's business. You can just leave." Slowly I exhale out every particle of air left in my lungs. My voice sounds like many of the people I dump and I feel like I'm going through the steps. Disbelief. Hurt. Shock.

"You couldn't just let it go." He grabs my arm and drags me across the living room into the kitchen and pushes me up against the counter. "I couldn't figure out how I know you, but it just clicked." Mac snaps his fingers in the air. If looks could burn holes, I'd be a geyser. "Splitsville.com. Did you get pleasure in breaking up with me for Carla?"

Everything, all the clues, roll in my mind like a slot machine.

"Olivia?" Erin asks, panic rising in her voice. "What is going on?"

I keep a close eye on Mac as he paces back and forth in a state of anger. He throws his baseball cap against the wall and lets out a small groan. He thrusts the gun toward me. "I had this all planned out, but you have to be nosey don't you?"

I jump.

His black turbulent aura is starting to scare me. His white Puma shoes scare me more. "I came here to see if Erin knows anything, but she doesn't."

"What's going on Mac?" Erin begins to shake. I reach over to calm her.

"She's Jenn from Splitsville.com." He tells her. He closes his eyes and shakes his head.

"So." Her voice is flat, sad and scared.

"You're so dumb. Rich and dumb." Mac's crooked teeth are more jacked up in person. "I told Kent to let you be the last score, not Dabi. But, *no,* he had to go and fall in love with you." He jabs his gun in Erin's chest. She bursts out in tears.

I stand up.

"Sit back down!" He screams through his clenched teeth. "I have no problem killing you."

"What?" Erin presses her hands against the sides of her face. She's in a state of shock. "What are you talking about?"

"Shut up!" Mac bellows. Erin and I cower together as he pulls the window blind closed. "I had it all planned out. All the clues pointing to you." He looks to me like it's no big deal that he's pinning a couple of murders on me.

I do give him an award for being creative and manipulative. My mind is boggled because I never suspected anyone other than Brittany. Officer Ian isn't here, and I'm not wired, but I want to get him talking anyway. I need time to figure out how to get us out of this alive. "What happened, Mac? Did Kent turn on you?"

He scoffs. "It was great. Kent and I had a deal." He turns the faucet on the kitchen sink and bends down to get a drink.

Now's my chance. I reach over and ever so slowly, taking my keys off the pile of clothes next to me, and slip them into my pocket.

He whirls around, water dripping down his chin, and flails his gun at Erin. My hand freezes. "He got a conscience when he met you. Dabi was our ticket, along with Carla." He isn't in control of his words. "Dabi gave him everything. Even these stupid shoes." He points down at the white Pumas. "But then he goes and confesses that he only married her for the money and she forgave him." Mac laughs out like a mad man.

Erin looks over at me with cautious eyes. Her head shakes back and forth, telling me not to make a sound with my keys.

"Only Dabi didn't forgive me. She was going to go to the police so I strangled her." The words roll off his tongue like it's no big deal. "It would all come back to Kent as the killer, but he was going to rat me out with all my women, just like he did with Carla. That's when she used Splitsville.com to dump me."

Erin and I watch Mac. I calculate my next move, but my mind is blank. I can only pray that help is on the way. Help being in the form of one Brittany picking up her dog, but it seems too much to hope for.

"I took the picture at the kissing booth." An evil grin crosses Mac's lips up to his ears and a sparkle comes from his eyes. "Originally I thought Erin would be the one Brittany threatened, but when Splitsville.com popped up on the radar and associated dear Dabi with Kent, I couldn't resist."

"You!" Erin jumps up. Tears pour out of her eyes and down her cheek.

"Ah ah ah." His finger wiggles back and forth and Erin eases herself back onto the couch.

She turns her body toward me. "He killed Kent!"

"Shut up!" Mac fidgets more. "I've got to think."

"Mac." I know how to talk people off a ledge. I do it every day with Splitsville.com. This is going to be a test of how good I really am. "What about Brittany?"

"She's just another person with a motive." He seems pretty pleased with himself. "That's where you came in. See, I had her use Splitsville.com to get back at Kent and then threaten you, so if you didn't pan out as the murderer, she would."

He laughs hard. "And Tramp. That was classic." He slaps his hands together beaming with pride. "After I killed Kent, I left the door open to make it look like the dog ran away. But I brought him to Brittany and the police don't even know Kent had a dog."

"You. . ."Erin gets back up, her hand flying full force at his face.

He grabs it and pushes her back down. Tramp runs down the hall to Erin's side and begins to lick her teary face.

"I have a couple of questions." I want to understand everything before he kills me. Thank God I know my Blackberry frontwards and backwards and it's in my back pocket. I pressed the record button when Mac turned and then put it on the pile of clothes next to me.

"*What?*" He turns on his heels toward me with an annoying infliction in his voice. "Does it matter? Because now I have to kill *you.*"

Damn! I put my hands up to my heart to keep it from pounding out of my chest. I pinch my hands together hoping not to feel any pain and praying this is a nightmare or vision. "Ouch," I mutter. Nope, not a vision. I'd give anything for Aunt Matilda to be standing over me.

"I don't have time for this." He holds the gun up to me.

"Wait!" I want to know why. I put my hands on my legs and press down. I can't keep them from shaking. My body is cold. I already feel dead.

"You ask *why*? Because of the money. We had a great thing going. Kent and I bagged the rich women. We got everything we could out of them. We were living large." He starts to pace again, but this time his steps are harder, angrier. He throws his fists in the air. "Erin was a big score for us. She doesn't have a family member to stand in our way." He stops and walks to the window. He opens one slate of the blind and peeks out. "Too bad his heart got in the way."

I can't tell if he's shaking out of fear, anger or sadness. I'm completely shaking out of terror. "Now I have to kill you." He clenches his crooked teeth together.

With my keys in my hand and my finger on the pepper spray, I swing my hand around. With a hope and prayer that my finger is on the trigger. I press as soon as it's in front of me.

A stream of spray goes right into his eyes. "Aaaaaa!" Mac screams out holding his eyes and falling to the ground along with his gun.

Before I can get the gun, the front door crashes to the floor. Carl rushes in, gun drawn, and pointed straight at Mac—Ian is right behind him.

"Don't move!" Carl screams at Mac. Mac continues to roll around on the ground.

I throw my hands up in the air and stand still. My mouth opens and nothing comes out.

Ian grabs Mac's hands and plants his knees in Mac's back as he cuffs him, while Carl gets Mac's gun.

Bradley runs over to me with panic in his eyes. "You're all right." He wraps his arms around me and my feet come flying off the ground as my heart sinks back into place. I can clear my throat now that the lump is gone.

Erin slumps back on the couch, resting her hand on her head.

I glance over my shoulder and Aunt Matilda rushes into the house. Immediately she makes sure Erin is okay.

"We got here just in time." Carl watches Ian roll Mac on his back and read him his rights.

Shocked, I ask, "How did you know?" I look back and forth between Bradley, Carl and now Aunt Matilda. My heroes all lined up in front of me. Even Carl and Ian.

Ian lifts Mac up to standing. Mac's eyes are swollen, red and still shut.

He jerks around and tries to get out of the cuffs. Ian takes him out of the house.

Carl says, "If it wasn't for Bradley's brother-in-law's handy work, we would've never have traced the license plate back to Mac."

Confused, I look at Bradley. "What?"

"As soon as my brother-in-law let me know that Mac Timmerman owned the BMW, I left the SPCA to get the information to Carl." He turns to Carl.

"Well, Brittany did confess everything to Ian during her interrogation." Carl is modest giving Ian most of the credit. "As a matter of fact, she told them that Mac was looking for Erin because he knew Kent had confessed to Erin that he and Mac were a grifting team." Carl nods toward Bradley. "Bradley came just in time with the news on the BMW. Brittany confirmed it's Mac's car."

Bradley takes me back in his arms. "I was worried about you because you weren't answering your phone."

I slip out of his arms and grab my phone off the pile of clothes. "Oh, I almost forgot." I hand my phone to Carl. "Everything you need to know is on here." I might not be so bad at this sleuthing thing after all.

I look over at Erin who's curled up in the fetal position on the couch, with Tramp by her neck.

She looks up. "Mac was going to kill us right here." She sobs. She falls back on the couch and Tramp licks her face.

I walk over and sit by Erin since everything seems to be under control. Her sobbing has subsided to a dull whimper.

"You know I wasn't going to let that happen." I pat her leg for reassurance but I'm totally lying through my teeth because I thought we were goners *for sure*!

She smiles and says, "Of course you can say that since he's in handcuffs."

"Tramp!"

We turn to see Brittany coming in through the smashed doorway.

"Thank you for taking him." She rushes over to the couch.

It's interesting how Tramp doesn't get up or wag his tail when he sees her.

"Tramp?"

I can see the hurt in her eyes and hear it in her voice as Tramp buries his face into Erin's lap. I watch Tramp's aura turn a nice crystal like Erin's.

Brittany pats the top of his head. "I guess he does technically belong to you."

"Yes, he does." Erin isn't about to let Tramp go.

Carl walks over and stands between Brittany and me. "We have cleared Ms. Darlington of any murder charges, but we do have the matter of the threatening emails."

Brittany turns and begins to plead with me. "I told you they were just out of anger. I wasn't going to do anything I promise."

Carl puts his hand up and Brittany buttons up her lip. "Do you want to bring charges against Ms. Darlington?" he asks.

I look at Brittany. I take a quick step back as the gold band begins to surround her.

"Let's just put it behind us." I smile. I'm not about to mess with a gold aura or the guardian angels that come with it. "On one condition."

"Anything," Brittany quickly agrees without knowing what I'm going to say.

"You have to continue to work at the SPCA." I smile.

Aunt Matilda walks over and puts her arm around me. Her sweet face lets me know everything is going to be all right.

Thirty

"What do you say, kid?" Officer Carl looks at me like he has something more important to say.

"What?" I curiously look at him and Bradley.

"Since you're so good at this aura business." He glances at Aunt Matilda, and hands me a file that reads "unsolved". "I'm moving up to the FBI division and I'd like you to help me figure out a few things."

"Ouch!" I grab my shoulder from Aunt Matilda's body nudge. I turn my head and raise my eyebrows. "What was that for?"

Aunt Matilda smiles. "You're behind on your bills and your dumps because you have spent so much time on this case. You could use the money." Aunt Matilda has always wanted me to embrace "the gift" and this is the perfect opportunity.

Bradley steps up behind Aunt Matilda and shakes his head. "No." His face is stern. "This can be dangerous."

I look into his eyes. "I've never been able to have a good job with my "gift."" I walk around Aunt Matilda and rub my hands down Bradley's arms, resting them in his hands, "This is my chance to embrace the person I really am and use my gift for a good cause."

Carl smiles with gratitude.

We all watch the police cruiser take Mac off to Park City Police Department where the FBI is waiting for him.

I turn back to Bradley and Aunt Matilda. "See," I point to Ian's cruiser rounding the corner, "I did something good. I didn't break anyone's heart and it feels good."

Carl chimes in, "So can I assume it's a yes?"

The excitement builds at the thought of using my gift to help people and to have a real job. But I also don't want to hurt Bradley or disappoint Aunt Matilda.

I face Carl, Aunt Matilda and Bradley. I hold the unsolved crime file in front of me. "Let me look at it and give me a couple days to think about it."

This way I will be able to talk with Aunt Matilda and Bradley.

"A couple of days." Carl walks over to Aunt Matilda. "What about that date we talked about?"

Erin and I look at each other and giggle like two little girls.

Aunt Matilda blushes.

"I guess I can take you back to your rightful owner." Carl picks up Belle. "I'm assuming you don't mind if I let Michael go?"

"No, I don't mind." I pat Belle on the head.

"I'll call you." Carl winks at Aunt Matilda.

I smile and watch Carl walk away, his amber aura floating around him. I have to believe I have something to do with it.

About The Author

Tonya is an International bestselling author. She writes humorous cozy mystery and women's fiction that involves quirky characters in quirky situations.

Splitsville.com, the first novel in the Olivia Davis Mystery Series, is a double finalist in the Next Generation Indie Book Awards in the Mystery and Humorous Categories.

Carpe Bead 'em is a finalist in Amazon's eFestival of Words in the Women's Fiction Category.

She travel to various writer's groups giving workshops on marketing and promoting no matter where you are in your career, and a self publishing.

Become a member of Tonya's STREET TEAM! It's a gathering place of readers who love Tonya Kappes novels and Tonya gives away monthly prizes! To sign up for Tonya's STREET TEAM, newsletter, view book trailer, and upcoming news, check out Tonya's website, Tonyakappes.blogspot.com.

CPSIA information can be obtained
at www.ICGtesting.com
Printed in the USA
FFOW04n1312260816
27185FF